READY TO TAKE FLIGHT?

Use your game cards to send
your own dragons into battle!

◆

Turn to the back of this book to
receive your orders . . .

RISE OF THE DRAGONS

THE LOST LANDS

RISE OF THE DRAGONS

BOOK 2

THE LOST LANDS

JESSICA KHOURY

- SCHOLASTIC INC. -

Library of Congress Cataloging-in-Publication Data available
ISBN 978-1-338-26362-6
10 9 8 7 6 5 4 3 2 1   20 21 22 23 24

Book design by Abby Dening

First edition, March 2020

Printed in China   62

Scholastic US: 557 Broadway · New York, NY 10012
Scholastic Canada: 604 King Street West · Toronto, ON M5V 1E1
Scholastic New Zealand Limited: Private Bag 94407 · Greenmount, Manukau 2141
Scholastic UK Ltd.: Euston House · 24 Eversholt Street · London NW1 1DB

1

Island of the Blue Dragons

Sirin sat on a sandy beach, watching a dozen Blue dragon hatchlings dip and dive in the turquoise waters of a hidden lagoon.

The Blues seemed as comfortable in water as they were on land, and their slim, agile bodies undulated in the waves, reminding her of the old sea serpents she'd sometimes seen on antique maps. The hatchlings seemed to take particular joy in flicking the water with their tails, throwing glittering sprays of water onto Sirin. She shrieked and covered her head, and suddenly a small Green dragon lunged in front of her, snarling at the swimming Blues and ready to defend Sirin tooth and claw.

Want me to bite them? the little Green's eager voice echoed in Sirin's thoughts. *I will bite off their tails if you want me to!* She wagged her tail like a puppy eager to please her master.

"Easy!" Sirin said with a laugh. "They're only playing, Sammi."

Sammi. Her Lock. Whose heart and soul and mind were now bound together with Sirin's.

Covered in sand from nose to tail tip, the little Green huffed indignantly and shook herself.

Slimy water lovers, all of them! she huffed, her high voice echoing in Sirin's thoughts.

Sirin had come to love Sammi-the-dragon as much as she'd loved Sammi-the-cat back in her old life, but sometimes it still shocked her when she heard her new Sammi's voice in her own mind. It tickled the inside of her head, like a chill running over her scalp.

Want to go for a swim? she sent back, her own inner voice sounding wobbly, as she was still getting the hang of sending mental messages to her Lock.

Water, eugh! The little Green lifted her nose imperiously and resumed her sunbathing. *Let's fly!*

Sirin shook her head, her stomach tightening with fear as she looked up. "Joss and Allie said the sky isn't safe," she reminded Sammi. "We're in hiding, remember? There are terrible dragons looking for them. For *us* too, I suppose."

There was so much to remember about this world, but that was the point her new friends the Morans had emphasized most. *They're hunting us, and when they know you're with us, they'll hunt you too.* The Lennixes, a powerful family allied with the Raptors—evil dragons who'd happily make lunch of Sirin. These Raptors wanted to conquer *her* world, Earth, and they needed Joss's Lock, the fierce Silver Lysander, to do it. From what Joss had told her, if they ever got hold of Lysander, they'd use him to lay waste to Earth and devour, enslave, or otherwise destroy the people living there, just as they had done to *this* world.

"And you're *sure* you wanna hang out with us?" Joss asked her with a nervous laugh.

She hadn't seen the Raptors yet, but she'd only been in this world for three days.

The night she'd seen Lysander the Silver swooping over

London, with two human riders on his back, Sirin had known at once that her life was about to transform. After all, you didn't see a *real live dragon* and then go on your way as if everything was normal.

And Sirin had done so much more than just *see* a dragon.

Seated on Lysander's shining, scaled back, she'd held her breath in disbelief as the great Silver had angled for the sky, wings pumping. The next thing Sirin had known, the sky had flashed white and her skin had shivered with static electricity as they passed through a hidden portal. Then, wide-eyed, she'd stared down at a whole other world.

A world of dragons.

Now, three days later, she and her strange rescuers were hiding out in the middle of a vast ocean, on an archipelago of mossy green islands that looked, from the sky, like an emerald necklace dropped on the blue water. The islands were home to the great clan of the Blue dragons.

Sirin was in a new world.

She was Locked with a dragon.

She was an orphan.

That last thought sent a splinter of panic through her. She sucked down a sharp breath, squeezed her eyes shut, and drew her knees to her chest. Her heartbeat pounded in her ears. Against her collarbone, the dragonstone pendant suddenly felt as cold as ice. She'd been keeping it under her shirt, out of sight. It hurt too much to look at it, almost as much as it hurt to picture her mother's face.

Sensing Sirin's sudden turn of mood, Sammi was at her side in a flash, pushing her scaled muzzle into Sirin's lap.

Want a fish? Sammi asked. *Fish makes me feel better. I will catch the quickest, brightest fish for you!*

Sirin only hugged Sammi tight and waited for the wave of grief to pass. She refused to cry. She refused to think of her mother. She refused to feel anything at all.

That was the only way she would survive.

A low growl rolled over the lagoon, and Sirin looked up to the high rocky bluff across the water, where two enormous dragons had been conversing all morning. One, a faded Green that was larger than any dragon Allie had yet seen, she knew to be Bellacrux, the Lock of Allie Moran. Sirin was more than a bit terrified of the great Green, who seemed docile enough but with a dangerous glint in her eye that told of a fierce and ancient past. The other dragon, the Blue Grand and leader of these islands, was called Ash. He and Bellacrux seemed to have some history together, and Sirin had seen hints of affection between them. But other times they argued in their strangely beautiful dragon language called dragonsong, and when that happened, every dragon on the islands tensed up.

They were arguing now, and Sirin looked away, not wanting to be caught spying. She couldn't understand what they were saying anyway. Sirin had picked up only a few simple words of dragonsong in the last three days, and those still felt strange on her tongue.

"They're *still* going at it?" asked a voice.

She turned around and saw Joss Moran standing behind her. "Since dawn," she said. "What are they saying?"

Joss glanced up at the two large, angry dragons and winced. "The same thing they've been arguing about since we got here.

Bellacrux thinks Ash knows of some ancient dragon weapon that can take down the Lennixes and the Raptors, but he won't tell her what it is. If Ash doesn't come around, Allie says we'll have to leave. It's only a matter of time before the Raptors find this place."

Sirin nodded fiercely. "Absolutely. No way am I going back to . . . well, I don't even know where I'd go back *to*."

What did her social worker think had happened to her? Had she told everyone Sirin had been snatched up by a dragon? Likely not. Who'd believe that? Maybe they all thought she was dead. Sirin was surprised to find she liked that idea, because then she could believe it too—metaphorically, anyway. The *old* Sirin was gone, as was every boring, tedious, or annoying part of her life, like math exams and weird foster families and dodging back-alley pubescent bullies and . . .

And, of course, there was the *other* thing . . . the big, impossible, terrible thing she couldn't even let herself think about. The moment the image of pink hospital walls popped into her head, she shoved it out again.

"Lysander?" Joss tilted his head as his Silver dragon came loping toward them, his gaze unfocusing for a moment, which Sirin knew meant he was getting a message from his Lock. She wondered if she got the same look when Sammi was talking to her.

Sirin was still awestruck by the sight of Lysander, whose scales shone so brightly they seemed to glow. He moved with liquid grace, not so much running to Joss's side as flowing there. Though he was still very young for a dragon, he held his elegant head with dignity.

But right now, he looked worried, his eyes meeting Joss's. Sirin waited for them to communicate, and her heart skipped a beat when the blood drained from Joss's face.

"What's wrong?" she asked.

"Maybe nothing," he replied, but he looked queasy. "It's just . . . Lysander said he caught a scent on the wind. *Raptor* scent."

Sirin gasped, covering her mouth. "They're *here*?"

"Maybe, maybe not. But Lysander and I should go scout around, just in case."

"I'm coming too." Sirin stood and dusted sand from her jeans. She hadn't exactly come to the world of the dragons prepared for a beach day, and every part of her itched from getting sand stuck in her clothes. "Three pairs of eyes are better than four."

Hey! squeaked Sammi indignantly.

"Er . . . make that *four* pairs of eyes. Sorry, Sam."

Sammi had only just learned how to fly, and she was always eager for a chance to show off this new skill.

Joss nodded. "Let's go, then. Before Lysander loses the scent."

"Shouldn't we tell Allie first?"

Joss waved a hand dismissively. "It's not like she's the boss. Besides, she's on the other side of the island, collecting oysters for dinner, and it'd take half an hour just to find her. We'll just take a quick look around and be back before she ever knows we were gone."

They climbed onto Lysander's back, Joss seated in front of Allie. The Silver spread his wings and launched into the sky, and Sirin looked down to see his shadow shrink away as they rose higher and higher. Sammi flitted all around.

"What if it's Raptors?" she said into Joss's ear.

He shrugged. "Probably just a false alarm."

But Sirin heard the tremble in his voice.

Lysander glided on a warm breeze, the membrane of his wings

fluttering like sails. Sirin's breath caught in her throat. She felt a moment of queasy fear when she glanced at the sea far, far below, and she gripped Joss's shoulders tighter. The sun glinted off Lysandar's silver scales, which shone so brightly Sirin could see her own distorted reflection in them. He really was a magnificent creature.

The shiny one is old and slow! Sammi chortled in her mind. *Bet he can't keep up with me!*

Sammi darted ahead, and Lysander accepted the hatchling's challenging growl with a roar of his own. The Silver shot forward with a powerful thrust of his wings, forcing Sirin and Joss to hold on with all their strength. The breeze turned to a gale that pulled at Sirin's hair.

Careful, Sammi! she warned. *There might be Raptors up here!*

Let them come! Sammi snarled back. *I am Sammi the Fierce, and I fear no one and nothing!*

Sirin sighed and shook her head. There was no reasoning with hatchlings, she'd learned, especially ones as headstrong and ferocious as Sammi.

They flew farther and farther until the Blue islands were a scatter of green pebbles on the ocean, ringed by white beaches and reefs. The water sparkled in the sun, turquoise shallows fading into dark cerulean depths.

The sight was beautiful. But Sirin pulled her gaze from the world below to instead scan the sky, her stomach knotting as she wondered if she was about to meet, for the first time, the terrible Raptors—or the merciless humans who rode them.

2

The Scent of Raptors

The salty sea wind and the draft from Lysander's wings washed over Joss as they flew. Sammi, her initial burst of energy spent, bobbed in the Silver's wake, her wings tenaciously flapping as she fought to keep up.

Smell anything? Joss asked his Lock.

The wind has shifted. The scent is lost.

Joss chose his words carefully, not wanting to offend the Silver. *Are you* sure *you smelled—*

I know their scent, Joss, Lysander cut in testily. *Like charred bone and old blood.*

All right, all right, I believe you. I just don't want *to.*

That makes two of us, my Lock.

They flew in a widening loop around the islands, but it was the eastern sky they watched the most. That was the direction of the mainland, though they couldn't see it from here. The horizon curved in a brilliant blue line of ocean, making their island refuge seem cut off from the whole rest of the world. But Joss knew the coast was less than a day's flight away, and Fortress Lennix was not far beyond that.

They searched for fifteen minutes, flying ever eastward until the Blue islands had vanished behind them, but they saw no sign of suspicious dragons, Raptor or otherwise. The more empty sky they crossed, the more Joss began to relax.

Perhaps . . . I was mistaken, Lysander finally admitted, disgruntled.

Joss patted his Lock's neck. *You were right to be wary. Better to be on the safe side.*

He told Sirin they would do one more sweep from north to south before turning back to the islands. She nodded and shut her eyes, probably relaying the message to Sammi, who flew a short distance away.

Sirin fascinated him. She told the most amazing stories of the Lost Lands—or *Earth*, as she called her world. She didn't seem at all afraid of dragons, despite having not known they existed until three days ago. And she never complained when Lysander looped or spiraled, testing Joss's and Sirin's grip strength until they were clinging by their nails to his silver back. Sirin was tough, and she wanted to learn *everything* about dragons.

Joss was pretty certain now there were no Raptors closing in on the islands, but he didn't stop scanning the sky. If there was one thing he'd learned about Lennixes, it was that they were full of sly tricks.

"I still can't believe I'm riding on a *dragon*!" Sirin said in his ear.

He grinned. "Pretty great, huh?"

"So, are unicorns real too?" Sirin asked.

"Uni-*whats*?"

"You know! Horses with horns, sparkly, possibly poop rainbows?"

Joss gasped. "They sound terrifying! Are these unicorgs a big problem in the Lost Lands?"

Sirin laughed. "Forget it. What about wizards?"

"Wizards?"

"Oh, c'mon! Magic wands, pointy hats, long white beards? Solemn, grumpy types, like to keep owls and newts about?"

Joss looked at her over his shoulder. "Are all Lost Lands girls as odd as you are?"

"I suppose you mean *nerdy*." Sirin sighed. "Unfortunately, no. A lot of them are total bores. At least, the ones in my class were. They couldn't tell a dragon from a troll, but if you tried to explain it to them, you'd be socially crucified."

"Ah," he said, beginning to understand. "Yeah, humans here can be that way too. Some are all right, some are real sheep turds." He thought very specifically of Kaan Lennix.

"How many humans live in the Dragonlands?" Sirin asked.

"The Dragonlands?"

Sirin swept her arm, indicating the spread of water below. "That's what I've been calling your world, in my head. What do *you* call it?"

"I never thought of it before," he replied. "Just *the world*, I guess. But I like the Dragonlands better."

"So how many people live here?"

"Dunno. Thousands, I suppose."

"Thousands?" she echoed strangely.

"Why? How many are in the Lost—I mean, Earth?"

"*Billions.*"

Joss blinked. He couldn't even *think* of such a number. But maybe there would be billions of people here too, if there weren't Raptors gobbling them up all the time.

JOSS!

Joss immediately stiffened as the mental shout from Lysander resounded through his mind. *What's wrong?*

There. See it?

Feeling his Lock's mind guide his eyes to the right place, Joss peered into sky—and there it was. A small, dark speck against the pale sky, the silhouette of its wings and tail unmistakable. He heard Sirin inhale behind him. She had seen it too.

Lysander dived, Sammi trailing him, until they were gliding just over the ocean's wrinkling surface. The Silver was well camouflaged against the glinting water.

Raptor? asked Joss.

Lysander's nostrils flared as he sniffed the air. *Yes. One alone. Probably a scout.*

A shiver of fear made Joss sit up straighter. *Has it seen us?*

I don't think so.

"What do we do?" asked Sirin.

"We have to go back. If they're scouting this area, they might find the island even sooner than we feared. We have to warn Ash that the Blue clan is in danger. Maybe now he will finally listen."

Lysander wheeled, and Sirin's arms clamped so tightly around Joss he couldn't draw a breath, but he hung on doggedly until the dragon's flight evened out again and Sirin let go. Joss felt Lysander's muscles ripple from effort beneath his shining scales, and in his mind he felt Lysander's worry mirroring his own.

3

Kaan the Keen

Zereth the Red wanted nothing more than a warm bed and a hot dinner, but instead here he was, on the far outskirts of Raptor territory, hovering in a cold sky with an empty belly. Meanwhile, his rider crowed, pumping his fists in the air.

"Fly, you boneheads!" Kaan Lennix yelled at the Silver dot shrinking in the distance. "That's right, sheep boy! We're coming for you—*ahhhhhh!*" His shout turned to a scream as beneath him, Zereth went into a dive. The Red couldn't take it anymore. He was *hungry*, and there was a glimmering patch on the water below that signaled a school of fish. Talons outstretched, the dragon grabbed two bunches of fluttering, flopping fish and tossed them high, then spun to snap them up in his jaws.

Clinging to his mount's crest with all his strength, Kaan dug his spurs into the dragon's sensitive skin. He was hanging completely upside down and losing his grip, with the dark ocean far below.

"Stop that!" he screamed. "Turn over *right now!*"

Zereth growled in response, righting himself in the air. Angry twin streams of smoke curled from his nostrils. Zereth was the newest member of the First Flight, having been promoted to fill the space left by the deserter coward Timoleon, and he'd thought it an honor to be given a Lennix son as a rider—until he'd actually *flown* with Kaan. The youngest Lennix had been free with his sharp spurs and his sharper insults, until Zereth had thought it would have been better to not be promoted at all than have to endure this human pustule on his back. Now he had half a mind to roll again just to see if he could shake the screaming brat right off. It was what Valkea would do, and Zereth was a great admirer of Valkea. *She* wouldn't suffer Kaan's indignities. In fact, she'd somehow managed to shake the boy altogether, and now she flew with Tamra Lennix, who was as crafty as she was cruel. Zereth wished he had a rider like that, or else no rider at all.

But in the end, he submitted to Kaan's orders and turned back toward land and the distant Fortress Lennix, regretfully leaving behind all those tasty, tasty fish. As satisfying as dumping Kaan into the ocean would be, it wouldn't be worth the wrath he'd suffer at D'Mara Lennix's hands. He remembered the words Valkea had whispered to him just last week, in the secrecy of her chamber in the Raptor Roost. It had been him and two other dragons, Valkea's most trusted.

We must bide our time, she had said. *The Lennixes are weakening. The heir Declan has deserted them. Krane is getting older and slower. And they don't have Bellacrux anymore to enforce their rules. All we have to do is wait, and soon enough, the other Raptors will be begging for new leadership. Then, my friends, we will be ready. Then, my fearsome ones, we will strike!*

He hoped they would strike soon. *Something* had to change. Hunting was poorer and poorer every day. The craving for food in Zereth's belly was a sharp, constant pain, and he fended off a sudden urge to flip over and gobble up Kaan. The Raptors needed to find the Silver, needed to return to the Lost Lands, where, according to the rumors flying thicker than gnats, they would feast to their stomachs' content. But so far, the Lennixes had done nothing but bungle every attempt to harness the Silver.

Like Valkea—and a growing number of Raptors—Zereth was ready for a change in regime. Humans should serve dragons, as far as Zereth was concerned, not the other way around. Dragons were bigger, deadlier, longer-lived—the apex predators of every world they inhabited. The Lennixes had disrespected the food chain long enough.

Clearly, it would take a dragon's leadership to bring them to the Lost Lands.

But until their numbers grew large enough to overwhelm those Raptors still loyal to the Lennixes, Valkea, Zereth, and the others who thought like them would have to bide their time.

And . . . endure certain humiliations.

Clenching his jaw, Zereth flew at a steady pace, the pain from Kaan's jabbing spurs still lancing down his sides and into his wings.

"Just wait till Ma hears this," Kaan gloated in his ear, his voice cracking. It had been doing that a lot lately, jumping from high to low, splintering in mid-sentence. "It was me—not Tamra or Mirra or Pa or Decimus—but *me*, Kaan Lennix, who found them: that mudbrained sheep boy *and* his stuck-up Silver. Oh, I can't *wait* to see the look on Ma's face when I tell her!"

For once, Zereth agreed with the youngest Lennix spawn. Lysander was the key to the Lost Lands, the most coveted dragon in the world, and the Raptors' number one enemy. It had been Kaan who had ridden Lysander through a portal and returned to tell Zereth and the others about the Lost Lands—a world of glittering towers and green hills and *so many fat sheep*, enough to sate even the hungriest of Raptors. It was everything this world was not, and it could all belong to the Raptors, if they could just get their claws on that Silver.

"And," Kaan added, still gloating, "wherever Joss and Lysander are hiding, we'll also find his sheep girl sister and that traitor Bellacrux! This is the best day of my *life*!" He dissolved into snorting laughter.

Below him, Zereth bared his fangs in a gruesome version of a smile. He too was pleased and eager to share their delicious news. He was sure Valkea would reward him for it, before leading him and the rest of the Raptors to capture and crush Lysander, Bellacrux, and their human Locks.

4

A Flight United

Allie sat, arms crossed over her chest, upon the great Green dragon who had once been known as the Lennix Grand. Bellacrux hovered on a warm thermal, high above the largest of the Blue islands, her calm mind battered by Allie's tempestuous thoughts.

I'm going to put a leash on Joss's neck—if the Raptors haven't already snapped it! I'm going to tie him to a tree and Lysander with him! I'm going to—

Be still, little warrior, sighed Bellacrux for the hundredth time. *They are impetuous, as all young ones are.*

I'm young, but I'm not impetuous!

Indeed you are not, my Lock. But your circumstances have forced you to grow up quickly.

Allie didn't feel very grown-up. She couldn't imagine any grown-up could feel as terrified as she felt just then. Her eyes scanned every inch of the horizon, and the sweat running down her neck wasn't just from the hot sun.

Joss had been gone for over an hour without a word as to where he was going or why, leaving Allie to hope against all hope that they hadn't been seized by the Raptors. She'd dragged Bellacrux from her argument with Ash to search, but without knowing what direction Joss and Lysander had gone, they were stuck waiting over the islands, helpless.

He took Sirin with him, Allie told her Lock.

Allie wasn't sure what to think of Sirin. Joss had befriended her instantly, but Allie was worried the girl might be too soft to survive in a world of dragons. She seemed nice enough, but *nice* didn't do you much good against a horde of ravenous Raptors. Allie still had bruises and aches from their last encounter, and now she rubbed the singed ends of her hair where a blast of dragonfire had nearly roasted her just days ago. She watched every cloud that drifted overhead, worried Raptors might come pouring out of it, snarling and snapping.

Any progress with Ash today? she asked, trying to distract herself.

Bellacrux snapped her teeth, a puff of smoke curling from her lips. *He is as unmoving as a mountain! He could help us turn the tide against our enemies, if he would only admit what he knows of the weapon.*

What did *he tell you about it?*

Only that when he was a hatchling, the Blue elders whispered of a lost weapon, a great power, that they would use to end the Raptor threat. It was the very weapon once used to defeat the Raptors back in the Lost Lands, but it was left behind when my kind were exiled from that world, and the Blues could not hope to find it without a Silver to lead them back. When they died, they took all knowledge of the weapon to their graves. Only Ash is old enough to remember what it was, and the rock-brained fool refuses to tell me.

Allie sighed. She had been thrilled when Bellacrux had first told her of her plan to find the mysterious weapon, the day after they'd escaped from the Lennixes—and scooped up Sirin in the Lost Lands. But her hope had begun to fizzle out with every passing day that Ash refused to talk. She knew what worried Ash and stilled his tongue. Any weapon that could help them could also help the Lennixes, if they got to it first. He thought it safer that it be lost forever. But to Allie, that seemed like a risk worth taking.

There! Bellacrux shifted in the air with a great flap of her wings, turning toward the east. In the distance, Allie saw what looked like a refraction of silver light off the ocean's surface, until the glimmer pulled away and turned to a dark fleck in the sky. Only one dragon shone like that. Allie's body unclenched with relief, then hardened again with fury.

She nourished the flame of her anger through the fifteen minutes it took Lysander and Sammi to reach the islands, with Joss and Sirin on the Silver's back.

She started yelling even before all the dragons had landed on the beach.

"Stupid!" she shouted. "Stupid, stupid, *stupid*! You knuckle-headed, mush-brained dingbat!"

Joss gave her a weary look as he slid off Lysander. Sirin dropped down beside him, pale and not meeting Allie's gaze. Bellacrux glared at Lysander until the Silver's wings dropped and his head dipped in submission.

"What is this about?" Allie demanded. "Do you *miss* being a Lennix, is that it? You want to go back to them?"

"Wh-what?" spluttered Joss.

"Missing their fancy clothes, your shiny watch? Missing getting to storm around giving people orders?"

Joss scowled. "Lysander smelled something strange on the wind, Allie. We had to check it out before he lost the scent. There was no time to tell you."

Allie's stomach clenched, and she reflexively looked to the sky. "So you just charged off on your own? Joss!"

"He wasn't on his own," Sirin pointed out. "*I* was with him."

"No offense, Sirin," Allie said, "but you don't know anything about this place or us or the Lennixes. You both could have been killed."

"Hey!" Joss protested. "Enough! We don't need your permission for everything. You're not our mum, Allie."

"Yeah," said Sirin in a hard voice. "You're not my mum."

Maybe she wasn't anyone's mum, but Allie had one job and one job only: keeping Joss safe. It was what their ma and pa would have wanted her to do, and she wouldn't let them down. Not again. She'd held her tongue before, when Joss had trusted the mysterious stranger who'd turned out to be D'Mara Lennix. But she couldn't afford to make a mistake like that again.

"Well, what did you find?" Allie asked.

"One Raptor, a scout," he said. "And before you ask, no, it didn't see us."

But Allie's skin went cold. "How do you know that? If you could see it, it could have seen you! Every Raptor in the Roost could be winging straight for us as we speak!"

Joss was starting to look afraid. "Well . . . we're a whole day's flight from Fortress Lennix. Even if it did see us, that scout won't be even halfway there by now."

This is bad, very bad, Bellacrux sent to Allie. She snuffed the air, nodding to the west, where black clouds had begun to swell. *It will storm tonight. They cannot cross open water in that squall, and neither can we.*

Allie relayed Bellacrux's words to the others, then added, "So we will leave the moment the storm passes. This is our last night on the Blue islands, and thanks to us, the whole clan could be in terrible danger."

Joss nodded, looking dazed and a little ashamed.

"*Never* fly off like that again," Allie said to her brother, in a low and terrible voice. She didn't know it, but she sounded a bit like Bellacrux herself when the Grand was at her most dangerous. "Please, Joss. Promise me."

"I promise," he said miserably. "I didn't mean to put anyone in danger. But I'm sure it didn't see us."

"Well, we have to act as if it did." Allie knew she sounded harsh, but she had to make Joss understand how much danger they were in. Didn't he remember that great battle they'd fought? Didn't he see the dragon Herlenna fall from the sky, and the turncoat Raptor Timoleon catch fire? When Allie slept, she still dreamed of that awful night and woke feeling the heat of Raptor fire all over her body.

"What do we do?" Joss asked, looking thoroughly cowed now, his head dropping just like a hatchling's after an older dragon had scolded it.

"I . . ." Allie didn't know. Where else could they hide? Not even Bellacrux knew where the Red dragons hid away, deep in their mountain caverns. The Yellows were far, far away in their sandy deserts and unlikely to take them in when they had Raptors on their scent.

"The Lost Lands?" Allie wondered aloud. "We have Lysander,

after all. What's stopping us from just *going*? We could hide there forever and unless they found another Silver, the Raptors could never follow. We could be safe."

They all looked at Sirin, who shrugged. "I mean, there are a lot of places on Earth where you could hide three dragons. It wouldn't be easy, but it would be possible."

Joss and Lysander exchanged looks, then Joss said, "Well . . . yeah. But that would mean . . ."

He didn't have to finish the sentence for Allie to know what he meant.

It would mean abandoning all the other good and true dragons in *this* world. Ash, the free clans, the hatchlings swimming in the bay, not to mention the humans who lived here . . . they would be left to the Raptors.

"We could save ourselves," whispered Allie. "We could go right now, this minute."

A silence followed, and she could see the others thinking it over. It was tempting, the idea of true safety. But she also saw how Joss winced, how Lysander sighed, how even Sirin, who still knew so little about all of it, looked uneasy.

Bellacrux looked steadily at Allie, silent. Waiting for her to make up her mind.

Allie stared back at her Lock. "Seems we have to make a choice. Run and save ourselves . . ."

"Or stay and try to save everyone," finished Joss. "The good dragons and the people of this world. They don't deserve to burn in Raptor fire, Allie. Maybe we could run away and hide forever and survive. But I don't think we could *live* with ourselves. Do you?"

Lysander snorted in agreement, clearly on Joss's side.

Allie glanced at Bellacrux as her Lock sent, *For once, the boy speaks with wisdom.*

"Sirin?" Joss asked. "What do you think?"

Sirin blinked, as if surprised she got a vote. "I don't want to leave any other hatchlings like Sammi to get hurt. I'm in."

"In *what*, exactly?" asked Allie, who was apparently the only one still undecided. It was really, *really* hard to say no to the idea of holing away in the Lost Lands, never having to fear the heat of Raptor fire again. "What's our plan? What can we possibly do against the strength of the Raptors? I mean, let's be practical. We could start leading the other dragons back to the Lost Lands and safety, but it would take months to find them all, and the Lennixes would definitely track us down before it was done. So how do we stop them first?"

There is only one way, sounded Bellacrux in Allie's thoughts. She looked at her Lock inquiringly and found the Grand gazing intently back at her. *The reason we came to the Blue islands in the first place.*

Ash made it pretty clear he won't talk, Allie reminded her Lock. *Whatever he knows about his lost weapon, he isn't going to tell us.*

That was before Lennix scouts were spotted an hour's flight from his island. Whether they spotted Lysander or not, it means the Raptors are closing in on the Blues' hideout.

Allie again rubbed the singed ends of her hair. *You think that will change his mind?*

I think it's worth one last shot, Bellacrux said.

Chewing her lip, Allie considered. *And this weapon. You're sure it exists? And that it can stop the Raptors?*

I know if it did not exist, Ash would not be so loath to speak of it. If it really had the power to protect the Lost Lands and banish the Raptors once, it can do it again, here.

While Allie relayed her private conversation with Bellacrux to the others, the great Green gazed into the infinite blue of the sky above; on the eastern horizon, the clouds spread like a stain, dark and angry. The squall she had predicted was on its way.

We must all be in accordance, Bellacrux told Allie. *A flight divided soon starves, but a flight united hunts with success.*

Allie laid her hand on her Lock's shoulder. "So that's it, then. We have to make our choice as a team. We either flee to the Lost Lands and never return, or we convince Ash to tell us how to find the weapon that will stop the Raptors for good, and that will save this world the way it once saved the Lost Lands."

She let them mull it over for a long moment.

"Everyone in favor of going to the Lost Lands, raise a hand. Or, er, claw."

No one moved. A low wind rippled over the beach, raising swirls of white sand all around them. In the bay, the hatchlings splashed and chirped, oblivious to the storm brewing in the distance.

Allie let out a long breath. "All right, then. Everyone in favor of finding this mysterious long-lost weapon and giving the Raptors a dose of their own dragonfire?"

Joss raised a hand. Lysander snorted. Sammi and Sirin looked at each other, then Sirin popped a thumbs-up. Finally, Allie nodded.

So be it, said Bellacrux. *The time for hiding is no more. Now is the time to fight.*

5

The Tale of the Skyspinner

The Blue clan's home was a vast network of caves that ran beneath the islands and even under the sea itself. They were filled with many glimmering pools that cast shifting reflections on the rocky ceilings, and clusters of bioluminescent coral and algae clung to their edges, providing soft pink, blue, and yellow light.

Allie walked through these tunnels by Bellacrux's shoulder, apprehension knotting her stomach. Lysander, Joss, Sirin, and Sammi followed close behind. The sound of dripping, rippling, flowing water echoed all around them, punctuated by dragon snarls. The place was beautiful, but it also gave Allie goose bumps. She couldn't help but feel she was back in Fortress Lennix, stumbling through narrow corridors while Raptors watched her hungrily and licked their teeth. The Blues didn't attack humans, of course; that didn't mean she felt totally at ease in their stone labyrinth. There were no humans here, and the Blues seemed as wary of the three kids as they were of the Blues.

After following the maze of tunnels, the band entered the largest chamber through an arched stone doorway decorated with multicolored clamshells, whale bones, and spiky conchs. Usually dragons came and went through the watery tunnels that opened into the large pools in the chamber floor, leaping up out of the water like seals. But all fell still when Bellacrux entered and let out a roar.

"ASH!" she called out, then continued in dragonsong, "We must speak."

The scaly heads of a few young ones lurked in the pools like waiting crocodiles, their wide, anxious gazes traveling from Bellacrux to Ash.

The Blue Grand stood upon a high shelf of rock halfway up the great cavern wall, where he often reclined to watch the clan's hatchlings gambol and tussle below. The hatchlings were gone now, hiding behind rocks and in the pools, not wanting to get caught up in the argument about to break loose between the two oldest dragons on the islands. In one far nook, several dragons curled protectively around the sacred clutch of eggs.

"Bellacrux, leave me be. I have given you my final answer on the matter," said Ash in dragonsong. Allie was understanding more of the language every day, and her fluency had improved by leaps and bounds. Behind her, she heard Joss quietly translating for Sirin.

"And I told you," continued Ash, "I would banish you all if you asked again. So choose your words carefully, Bellacrux the Green."

"Old friend, we don't have much time," Bellacrux said. "Tell us what we need to know before it's too late."

"*KATA!*" roared Ash, and Allie recognized the dragonsong word for *no*. The Blue Grand's voice thundered through the damp, dimly lit caverns. All the dragons in the cave—as well as the three young humans—cowered at the Grand's fury. All but Bellacrux. She glared back at the old Blue leader, unruffled.

Ash stared back, his nostrils flaring, but when he saw Bellacrux would not be cowed, he let out a huff of smoke and shook his great head. "I had second thoughts about granting you and your little band asylum, Bellacrux, but you saved my life more than once in the old days, and I owed you. But as I have told you a thousand times since you arrived, I will *not* share the secrets I vowed to keep. I can't help you with your Raptor problems."

"Our problems are soon to be *your* problems," pressed Bellacrux. "The Lennixes will come for your clan, Ash, sooner or later. Then they'll defeat the Yellows and Reds and none will be left to oppose them. None will be left who are True to the Wing. Our survival is at stake."

"So is our *freedom*." Ash's talons curled over the stone ledge, sending a rain of rock dust trickling down. "The weapon you seek is dangerous. It attacks not flesh, not bone, but the very *soul* of a dragon. Even those with the best intentions are tempted by its power. And imagine if the Raptors found it first! No, it is too risky. We must lie low. There are rumors of dissent in the Raptor ranks, dragons growing weary of Lennix rule. If we wait, they will tear themselves apart. No need to go on wild hunts for old myths."

"The Raptors are on their way here *now*," Bellacrux said.

All the dragons in the cavern released surprised snorts and murmurs, while Ash went stone-still.

"How could you know this?" he asked.

"Because our Silver spotted one of their scouts this morning, not an hour's flight from here. They're getting close, Ash. It could be a matter of hours before they land on your beaches."

Ash stretched to his full height and spread his wings as his furious roar shook the cavern. He was nearly as large as Bellacrux, his dark blue scales rippling with his movements. In the gloomy light, he looked as black as obsidian, but his eyes were vibrant blue flames. Allie's heart leapt into her mouth at the sight, and she was forced to clap her hands over her ears until Ash quieted.

"You have betrayed us!" he snarled. "The Raptors would not even be scouting this area if they weren't looking for *you*! And now your Silver has practically invited them to our cavern door!"

Bellacrux bowed her head. "You know this day was coming. Tell us what you know of this lost weapon, this thing that can help us defeat the Raptors for good. No more delaying, no more excuses. Just *tell us*."

Spitting a jet of flame into the air, Ash turned to the older Blues clustered near his ledge. They listened raptly as he delivered a stream of orders, then they disbanded to prepare for the coming battle. As the cavern erupted into activity, dragons rushing every which way, Ash turned back to Bellacrux. He stared at her a moment, and it almost seemed he would keep shouting, or even challenge her to a fight.

But then he shook his head, his wings folded with weary resignation.

"Very well." He sighed. "Come, and I will tell you the tale of the Skyspinner, and the Banishing of the dragons."

Ash's private cavern was a spectacular sight. Its stone walls had been carved by centuries of talons, depicting detailed scenes of bygone battles and Blue Grands of the past. From the ceiling hung great, glittering stalactites and jutting white crystals. A waterfall splashed down one wall, into a clear pool glowing with luminous algae. On the floor were spread mats of palm fronds but little else;

the Blues seemed to disdain the type of cushiony comfort Allie had seen in the Raptor Roost.

Ash lay on the ground and waited for Bellacrux and Lysander to settle, while Sammi tumbled in the corner, ignoring Sirin's shushes.

"Tell us, Ash," said Bellacrux. "Who is this Skyspinner?"

The Blue Grand inclined his head. "She was the last of the great dragon queens who once ruled our kind."

Bellacrux gave a grunt. "I've heard of the old queens. They were of no clan, neither Red nor Yellow, Green nor Blue. They were hatched from stars and were the mothers of all dragonkind, as ancient as the world itself."

"Their scales were as black as the night," added Ash. "And each one was endowed with a special, unique power. One could sing new islands out of the sea, another could quell the mightiest of storms with a lash of her tail. But one by one, they vanished, moving on to other worlds, never to return. Until only one remained: the Skyspinner. She pledged her protection over the Lost Lands, and for centuries was the highest authority among our kind. Those days were the great golden age, and we lived alongside humanity in peace and prosperity. We built great civilizations together, explored new islands and continents, and it seemed nothing would limit us so long as we worked together, human and dragon, Locked through the centuries."

Allie closed her eyes and imagined a dragon as black as night, older than the mountains. The Skyspinner. A queen of dragons, mightier even than her beloved Bellacrux. She felt her Lock imagining along with her, picturing the golden days of the Lost Lands, of a world prosperous and peaceful.

I never quite believed in the dragon queens, Bellacrux told Allie. *But perhaps I was wrong.*

"But those days were not to last." Ash sighed. "For humans are ever greedy. Wars broke out, and kings rode dragons into battle, twisting their Locks to their own dark ambitions and turning them into weapons of death and slaughter. On dragonback, humans raided other lands, destroyed their neighbors' cities, and spurred their Locks to feast on their enemies. Once the dragons tasted human blood, it poisoned their minds and they were driven to taste it again and again."

The beautiful images in Allie's mind melted in a torrent of Raptor fire, and she could smell the smoke from the cities they had razed, see the flames leaping higher as they dived, roaring, onto their human prey. Shivering, she pulled closer to a grim-faced Bellacrux.

"The Skyspinner knew the time had come to intervene. She led the true dragons and their human Locks in a great, final battle against the Raptors. But when she realized they would not be stopped, the Skyspinner conceived a last, most desperate plan. She concluded the two species must be separated, for each drew out the worst in the other. Therefore the Skyspinner drew upon her own special power: the ability to command her children, even those who had turned against her. She took control of their minds and—"

"She could control their *minds*. That's—" Joss stopped himself, clapped his hands over his mouth, and whispered, "*Sorry!*"

"Yes," snarled Ash. "She could control their minds. And with this power she exiled the dragons and their human Locks with them, to this realm we now call home."

"Their Locks?" whispered Allie. "You mean . . ."

Ash looked at her. "Indeed. Your ancestors were humans who chose banishment with their dragons. And after the Skyspinner exiled them all, she plummeted to her death."

"Wait a minute," said Allie. "How can this dragon queen help us if she's dead?"

Ash curled his lip, as if she were being stupid on purpose. "Her *heart*, of course, her dragonheart forged in a distant star. Now it lies somewhere in the Lost Lands. For when a dragon dies, unless they are consumed by fire, their flesh turns to stone—and their hearts turn to jewels. And whoever holds the heart of a dragon queen also wields her power . . . and whoever holds the Skyspinner's Heart may command all of dragonkind."

Allie jumped to her feet. "We have to find it. We really could stop the Raptors! We could order them to never harm a human ever again!"

This was the answer to the impossible question she'd been asking: How could she protect the ones she loved *and* save the rest of the world from the Raptors? Well, *this* was how. By becoming so powerful no Raptor could ever touch either.

"Where is it?" asked Allie. "Where in the Lost Lands will we find it?"

"That," replied Ash, "I cannot tell you."

"Well, what good is any of this if we can't even find the Heart?" Joss said.

"We will find it," said Allie. "Whatever it takes. Surely there must be some record of that battle, and where the Skyspinner fell. Sirin?"

Sirin stared at her blankly. "Don't look at me. It's not like we've got some monument back on Earth that says, *Here lies the Skyspinner.*"

Ash sighed deeply. "I can already see how you covet this power. It tempted me too, when I was young and foolish and did not understand its danger. You would be wise to beware. For great power comes at a great price. It is a terrible thing to turn dragons into puppets, even ones as foul as Raptors. And if the Heart should fall into the Lennixes' hands, *you* six will be responsible for the ruin that follows. With the knowledge you now carry, the fates of this world and the Lost Lands both rest on your shoulders." Ash considered them with a look of unmasked doubt, then heaved a mighty sigh. "May the stars keep you fools from dooming us all."

6

Big News, Big Plans

D'Mara Lennix was having a very bad day.

First, she'd awoken to the sound of an argument in the Roost and had found Valkea at the heart of it. The ferocious young Red had been unsatisfied with the small, skinny sheep provided for her breakfast and had let the entire fortress hear her fury. Now she was demanding she be given the shepherd to snack on instead.

D'Mara knew their food situation was getting worse. The fortress was already on a skeleton staff. But search as they might, there simply was not enough good stock left in this world. They were teetering on the brink of a crisis, and every day D'Mara had to scramble harder to keep the Raptors happy.

After settling things in the Roost—or at least, by delegating the problem into Edward's hands—D'Mara had returned to her tower to think. On the way, she'd stepped in dragon dung right up to her ankles. When she'd yelled for help, that shifty girl Carli had come sauntering over and D'Mara could swear she'd been laughing under her breath. D'Mara had simply stepped out of her boots altogether and proceeded to her tower in her stockings, humiliated and furious. She would send down orders later to have Carli punished for her insolence. It cheered D'Mara a little to contemplate what that punishment would be, whether a lashing or a finger cut off or the girl's thick red hair shaved to her scalp. Maybe all three. Yes, all three would do nicely. And D'Mara would be sure to stop by later, to give a nasty chuckle of her own in return.

But the anticipation of punishing Carli didn't lift her spirit for long.

As she gazed down at the landing yard, where Edward was still trying to smooth things over with Valkea, even bringing Decimus into the mix, D'Mara thought about which Raptor she ought to promote to Grand. Bellacrux's old chamber had been sitting empty for too long.

Usually, dragons elected their own Grand, and almost always they chose the oldest and largest of them for the job. But D'Mara wasn't sure she could trust her Raptors, or at least not enough of them. If they voted for Valkea, D'Mara had no doubt the Red's first order of business would be to roast every Lennix and feast on them through the night. No, Valkea would not do at all. It would have to be a dragon she trusted, one who would do *D'Mara's* bidding without question. Krane would be ideal, but his scale fever was a sure disqualification. She considered Decimus but worried promoting him might make it look as though Edward were the new head of the Lennix clan. And that might feel even worse than being torched and devoured by Valkea.

D'Mara was still brooding when a Red dragon came hurtling out of the mountains, straining for breath and flying clumsily with fatigue. She leapt up just as the Raptor crashed onto the landing yard and his rider jumped down.

Kaan was back.

He'd been on a routine scouting trip, nothing special. So normally D'Mara would barely have noticed the return of her younger son—*only* son, she reminded herself as she rushed down the steps of her tower in a new, clean pair of boots.

The loss of Declan, for all his meekness and cowardice, was an open wound in D'Mara's soul. He had betrayed her and flown off on that foolish Blue, Ramon, without a single look back at the life he was abandoning. Now there was a gaping, ugly hole at the dinner table each night and at muster every morning. Worse, she knew the Raptors were whispering about it, and Valkea and her followers were *laughing* behind her back just like that brat Carli. Everywhere D'Mara went these days, she heard low, mocking laughter in the shadows.

She was a little worried that she might be going mad.

Angry at letting her mind be distracted by Declan yet again, D'Mara resolved—for the hundredth time—that she would never think of him again.

He's dead, she decided. *He died in battle, serving the clan. We mourned him and he is gone.*

Some lies were easier to swallow than truth.

Now it was her remaining son who demanded attention. Literally. He furiously waved his red sash in the air, the signal for *big news*, which was why she'd run down from her tower rather than waited for him to come to her. D'Mara marched through the loggia, masking her anticipation with an annoyed expression.

"Yes, we all see you," she snapped as she stepped into the landing yard. "Put that thing down. You look like a fool."

Kaan lowered his sash, grinning. He was breathing hard, just like his mount, the newly promoted Zereth. The Raptor was so winded he could barely stand. A crowd was beginning to gather. Valkea and a few other Raptors had stuck their heads out of the loggia, and Tamra crept in on cat's feet, her sharp eyes intent on her brother.

"I hope you have a very good reason for pushing Zereth so hard," D'Mara said.

"I saw the Silver!" Kaan blurted. "It was off the south coast, near that old burned-up village. It took off to the southeast, so there must be something out there—islands, maybe."

"The Blues?" asked Edward, who'd approached from the left.

They'd sent a raid to an island on the western coast three nights ago, thinking it was the Blue clan stronghold. It had been the same night the Lennixes had chased down Bellacrux and Lysander, and lost Declan. The next day, Raid Flight Blue had returned with bad news: The island had been home to only a few vagrant Blues, and no Grand or eggs at all. They'd then launched scouts in all directions, hoping to locate the real Blue hideout. Honestly, D'Mara hadn't expected to get lucky so soon.

"Did you give chase?" she asked Kaan.

He shook his head. "I didn't want to spook them, and if it *is* the Blue clan they're staying with, I knew I wouldn't get close without them attacking me in greater numbers."

D'Mara blinked. This was a surprisingly acute move on her son's part. Perhaps Kaan was not the dunderhead she'd always thought him to be.

But then he proved her wrong again by sticking his tongue out at Tamra, gloating for his sister's benefit. Tamra rolled her eyes.

"Enough, both of you," said D'Mara. "Whether the Blues are there or not, it's the Silver who is the real prize. Raptors, assemble! We'll take the First, Second, *and* Third Flights."

Edward stared at her. "D'Mara . . . that's nearly all of them.

And there's a storm brewing in the south. That's no weather to fly in."

"That's exactly what *they* will be thinking."

Edward swallowed and nodded.

"We let the Silver slip through our hands three times already," she went on. She pulled her black leather gloves from her pockets and tugged them on; they sealed to her wrists with loud snaps. "This time, there will be no mistakes. No more bargains."

For the first time in weeks, D'Mara was feeling *good*.

She looked around at all the dragons who had gathered and said in a loud, clear voice, "This time, when we take the Silver, we take him alone. As for his friends—and especially that brat he's Locked with . . ." She gave a thin, tight smile. "Well, let's just say no Raptor will go hungry tonight."

7

Wings in the Storm

Allie couldn't sleep that night. She tossed and turned on her bed of woven palm fronds. They'd been sleeping in the great main cavern with the majority of the Blue clan. All around them, dragons were piled over one another, talons and tails sprawled across the stone floor, their snores and chuffs and smacking lips echoing endlessly through the dark. The storm raged outside, the thunder so loud it could be heard even through the cave's stone walls.

Every time Allie shut her eyes, she saw a dark sky bristling with Raptors, felt the heat of their fire blistering her skin, smelled the burnt-metal scent of melting dragon scales. Opening her eyes again, she stared into the darkness and felt sweat running down her neck.

She hoped that the search for the Skyspinner's heart would take a good long while so they wouldn't have to face the Raptors again so soon. Then she felt guilty for hoping that, thinking of all the lives the Lennixes and their dragons could destroy the longer it took Allie and her band to stop them.

Hearing a non-dragon sniffle, Allie sat up and peered around, her vision sharpening gradually in the dark. There was just enough pink light from the coral pools to illuminate Sirin, who sat on her own pallet, knees drawn up to her chest, her face buried in her crossed arms. Allie wasn't the only one having trouble sleeping.

She crept over to Sirin, taking care not to wake Joss. Boy and dragon breathed in unison, synchronized even in sleep. Sometimes Allie suspected the bond between her brother and his Lock was even stronger than the one she shared with Bellacrux. The Green Grand was snoring a few feet away.

"Sirin?"

"Huh?" Sirin looked up. Sammi—snoozing beside her— curled her tail reflexively around the girl's waist, as if Sirin were a doll she was reluctant to let go of even in sleep. "Oh. Hi, Allie."

"What's wrong?" Allie asked. "Are you crying?"

Sirin rubbed her eyes. "No."

"You don't have to do this, you know. You could go home to your family. No one would blame you." If Allie was being *really* honest, she would have added that she didn't see how Sirin could help much anyway.

"No! I'm not going back!" Sirin said fiercely. "Please, don't make me! I swear I can help you. You have to go to Earth soon, right, since that's where the Skyspinner's Heart might be? You'll need someone who knows her way around!"

"Whoa, easy! No one's making you do anything. Just letting you know there are options. Sheesh."

Sirin watched her warily, as if she suspected Allie might toss her back to the Lost Lands then and there. "I never thought I'd go on an actual *quest*, you know? The sort I always loved to read about. Of course, it's a lot more terrifying when you're *in* the story, not just reading about it in real life. But that's what I really want right now. Something so different that it's like . . . like time has stopped, the way it feels when you're reading a really good book. As long as you keep reading, nothing bad can happen. Nothing will change around you. You're safe in a book."

"Sirin . . . this isn't a book. You're *not* safe here. What we mean to do is as far from safe as you can get." She looked closer at the strange girl. "What happened to you back in the Lost Lands, that *this* place feels safer?"

Sirin gave a bitter laugh, then changed the subject. "Why does it have to be you two, anyway? When did *saving dragonkind* become your responsibility?"

"The day Joss found that Silver egg, I guess." Allie could still remember her shock the day she'd walked into Joss's shepherd's hut and found him with the newly hatched Lysander. "If Lysander had been any other kind of dragon, then we wouldn't be here now. But a Silver changes everything. And if he's the only way we can get the Heart . . . It's not like Joss would let Lysander go without him. And I can't abandon Joss. We're family. He's my real, most important responsibility. I'd do anything to protect him."

"I know what you mean," whispered Sirin. "You're a good sister. He's lucky to have you."

Allie wasn't so sure of that. A good sister would have voted to keep her brother safe even if it meant running away and hiding and leaving the rest of the world to deal with their own problems. But even if Allie had been willing to do that, she knew Joss and Lysander never would have.

"Better get some sleep," she said. "Tomorrow—"

Allie was interrupted by a thunderous roar that rattled the stone walls and vibrated in her ribs.

Every Blue in the cave jolted awake.

"RISE, CLAN!" thundered Ash, who stood in the cavern's great entrance, the storm lashing his scales. In the hot white flashes of lightning, he looked mighty and terrible, his fiery blue eyes aglow. *We are under attack!*

The sky teemed with lightning and dragons. Raptors struck out of shadow and vanished again, as if a part of the storm itself. It had taken Allie, Bellacrux, and the others only minutes to evacuate the caves and take to the skies, but now the Blues, disoriented and panicked, scattered in all directions. Despite the orders issued by Ash and the other seniors, the clan was struggling to regroup and defend the islands. Some fled entirely, while others—confused by the thunder and lightning and darkness—mistook their own broodmates for the enemy and clashed awkwardly in the air.

Allie rode upon Bellacrux, circling the mountainous crest of the island. They'd gotten separated from Joss and Lysander, who had Sirin and Sammi with them. It was useless to call out; the storm drowned out even the dragons' roars. Allie's heart pounded, and she struggled to stay seated on Bellacrux's wet, slippery scales. When a streak of lightning flashed nearby, every hair on her arms and scalp stood on end.

Do you see them? she asked her Lock.

I see trouble, Bellacrux replied grimly.

Hurtling toward them, out of the belly of a great black thundercloud, came an enormous dragon. It was impossible to identify him or her in the darkness.

Lock, hold fast! warned Bellacrux as she pumped her wings mightily and tilted sideways, perpendicular to the ground below. Allie clenched her teeth and held on with all her strength, her fingers gripping Bellacrux's spiny crest. She felt the dragon beneath her swell and heat with flame, preparing to unleash a torrent of fire upon their attacker.

Then lightning flashed again, illuminating the approaching dragon, and Allie yelled, "STOP!"

It was Ash, and he wasn't alone. Lysander flew just behind him, with two figures silhouetted on his back.

"Falana te'ma!" roared Ash. His voice was just barely audible between rolls of thunder. *Fly away now!*

Bellacrux growled, tossing her head in the direction of the western sky, where a dozen or so dragons—Raptors and Blues— were battling. Flashes of dragonfire competed with the lightning, every blast illuminating the terrible scene for a few seconds. Allie glimpsed outstretched talons; gaping, fanged jaws; scorch marks over scales. With a shudder, she pushed her wet hair behind her ears and sent a mental query to Bellacrux: *Should we help?*

Bellacrux clearly thought they should, but Ash screeched and blocked the Green's path, forcing her to hover in place. Lysander bobbed to the left, waiting.

In dragonsong, Ash said, "We cannot risk the Silver, old friend. Take your flight far from here!"

All across the skies, dragons screamed in pain and fury. Most of the ones falling from the sky were Blue, and Raptor victory cries pierced the night. Allie thought, for a moment, she glimpsed Tamra Lennix astride the Red Valkea, the girl's eyes and teeth glowing white in a flash of lightning, delighting in the carnage.

"We still don't know *where* find the Skyspinner's Heart!" Bellacrux protested. "Isn't there anything else you can tell us—"

"Go!" Ash ordered. "NOW!"

Then Ash pinned his wings to his sides and fell into a clean dive, before swooping up and grabbing hold of a Raptor in his talons. Allie gasped as the great Blue Grand hurled the enemy dragon into the sea, then cried out as five more Raptors descended on Ash, shrieking and spitting flame.

The last she saw of the magnificent Blue, he was plummeting toward the sea, crawling with biting, snarling Raptors.

"Allie!" Joss yelled. She could barely hear him over the storm and snarls. "What do we do?"

"We fly! Stay ahead of Bell and me." If any Raptors followed them, she would be between them and Joss.

She hated running away, hated that they were abandoning the Blues. But Ash was right. They had to keep Lysander out of the Lennix's grasp at all costs, and besides, the best way they could help the Blues now was to find the Skyspinner's Heart and use it to stop the Raptors for good.

"Let's go!" Allie called out. "As fast as we can. And whatever happens behind you, don't turn around, don't slow down. We've got your back."

She saw Joss nod in assent, felt Bellacrux's mental agreement.

Fly, my Lock! she urged the Green. *Fly faster than you ever have before!*

Bellacrux and Lysander shot into the darkness, their small flight vanishing into the storm.

8

Red Lightning

In a blinding flash of lightning, Tamra Lennix saw the brief outline of two dragons fleeing the terrible battle—one enormous Green and one sleek Silver. There was no mistaking their identities.

"Oh, no you don't," she said through her teeth. "You're not escaping again."

Valkea! Fly!

Her Lock responded at once, wheeling away from the fight and swooping after Bellacrux and Lysander and their riders. There was no time to alert D'Mara or any of the other Lennixes. If Tamra didn't give chase at once, they'd lose the Silver in the clouds.

Loosen your grip, whelp, and stop yelling at me! Valkea thundered in Tamra's thoughts. *I know my way and I require no assistance.*

Biting back a mental reply, Tamra forced her fingers to relax a little on Valkea's crest. She blinked as rain stung her face, her breath sharpening when Valkea put on a burst of speed. The sudden change of pace nearly unseated the girl altogether.

Clumsy idiot, Valkea spat.

Being Locked was nothing like Tamra had imagined it would be.

Declan had often spoken of his bond with Timoleon, and how close they were—closer than he'd ever been to any of his family members. Tamra saw how even her father and Decimus respected and loved each other, and there was no mistaking the fact that D'Mara cared for her Krane more than her own children.

But with Valkea, Tamra had experienced none of the trust or affection she'd expected—even *hoped* for, if she was honest. After sharing Trixtan with her moody sister for so many years, Tamra had dreamed of not only having her own dragon, but her own Lock. Someone who would be to her what even Mirra, her own twin, could not be.

A confidant. A *friend*.

But if anything, Valkea was like another D'Mara: always giving orders, always criticizing, always sneering at Tamra's best efforts to please her.

Now, as Valkea tore through the sky with Tamra, trying her best not to annoy her Lock, while also staying seated, a hot spike of anger ran through the girl. She was a *Lennix*! She shouldn't have to live in fear of her own dragon. So she gripped Valkea's crest even harder than she'd been holding it before.

Can you go no faster? she taunted the Red. *Will we lose the Silver again because you couldn't keep up with him? Will you be known as Valkea the Slow?*

Valkea's reply wasn't so much worded as it was a blast of fury that scorched Tamra's thoughts, nearly blinding her. For a moment, she thought they'd been struck by an actual thunderbolt.

Redoubling her pace, Valkea flew like a bolt of red lightning, flames sparking on her tongue. And Tamra clung to her like a wildcat, howling with glee.

They were closing in on Lysander.

The Silver didn't seem aware of them on his tail, nor were the two riders on his back looking over their shoulders. The idiots probably thought they'd gotten away. Tamra recognized the dark curly head of her ex-brother Joshua. Blood and bones, but wouldn't she like to give *him* a shove—right off his dragon's back and into the ocean far below. The second rider, a girl whose black hair streamed behind her, Tamra didn't recognize. She was probably some equally worthless brat. A sheep girl to go with the sheep boy. Tamra would make them both bleat.

But just as Valkea came within snapping distance of the Silver's tail, a small, scaly head popped up from over the girl's shoulder. It was a hatchling, its little fangs shining white as its jaw fell open in surprise. It spotted Tamra and Valkea at once.

Now! Tamra bellowed to her Red.

Don't give me orders! Valkea snapped back.

With a desperate lunge, Valkea threw herself at Lysander just as he banked sharply in an evasive maneuver. Carrying her momentum forward, Valkea went into a dive, Tamra rising out of the dip and hanging on only by her nails. They were streaking straight toward the sea, though all Tamra could see was a mat of black cloud below.

What are you doing? Tamra asked.

Valkea didn't even deign to reply. She pierced the black cloud and Tamra was lost in its mist, unable to see even the snout of her dragon.

Valkea!

Still her Lock ignored her.

Then the Red whipped up so suddenly that Tamra's teeth clacked and bit into her tongue; she tasted blood in her mouth.

Valkea shot out of the cloud, right in front of Lysander, startling him. The Silver reared back, wings flapping frantically as he struggled to maintain balance without throwing off his riders. For a fraction of a moment, his soft underbelly was exposed, and Valkea took full advantage of the chance.

Her claws tore into the Silver, and Lysander shrieked. The two dragons collided hard in midair, the screams of all three human riders mingling in a clap of thunder.

Stop! Tamra cried. *He must be taken alive!*

Her Lock seemed senseless with rage and bloodlust. But Tamra's urgent cry must have penetrated her mind at last, because Valkea didn't go in for the kill, even though Lysander was floundering. Blood ran from his scales, the metallic smell of it mixing with the burnt-match smell of the lightning storm. Tamra put her hand to her cheek and found a spray of hot dragon blood on her skin. And wedged into the scales on Valkea's shoulder was a single, shining silver scale.

What have you done? she asked, aghast. *Valkea!*

Then, out of nowhere, came Bellacrux, with Allie Moran seated on her back, her eyes blazing. Her gaze met Tamra's for a split second.

"DON'T. TOUCH. MY. *BROTHER!*" Allie yelled.

With a roar to drown out the storm itself, the Grand spat a cascade of flame at Tamra and Valkea. The Red reared back, stumbling just clear of the deadly fire. Tamra was forced to shut her eyes and curl over to avoid having her face melted.

When she opened her eyes again, Bellacrux, Lysander, and their riders were gone.

And Valkea was plummeting, unconscious, toward the sea.

WAKE UP! Tamra screamed. "VALKEAAAAAA!"

The Red blinked, shook her head, then let out a harsh cry as she realized they were falling to their deaths. *Hold fast, Lock!*

Valkea threw her wings wide, pulling up just in time, her talons raking the choppy waves—

—and lightning struck.

All Tamra saw in that moment was a blinding white tunnel of light. All she felt was a prickling jolt that ran the full length of her spine.

It seemed to last an eternity.

But then the sky cleared—no clouds, no storm, no wind—and Tamra gasped as she found herself gazing into a placid-blue sky, above a glittering, massive city of silver and white.

Valkea too was so astonished she couldn't even throw out one of her usual insults. Instead, Raptor and Lennix coasted on a gentle breeze for a long minute, gaping at the strange land below. Beyond the city, the land was green and peaceful, and the air smelled fresher than anything Tamra had breathed before. And there were *people*—hundreds, thousands of them walking on the streets below.

Then Tamra felt the crackling energy again, saw the tunnel of white, and a moment later, they were back in the storm, buffeted by wind and thunder. It might all have been a dream, a shared hallucination.

No, Valkea said, and for once, there was no undercurrent of anger in her thoughts as she touched minds with Tamra. *It was real. It was the Lost Lands.*

But . . . how? That's impossible!

Then Tamra looked down at the Silver scale still stuck to

Valkea, and with an effort, she managed to pull it loose. It glinted like a coin in her hand, hard and smooth and still crackling with energy. Lights like tiny lightning bolts seemed to run beneath the surface, though they faded as Tamra watched.

It was this, she sent. *This took us through a portal. To the Lost Lands.*

Valkea flew higher and higher, to where the air was more still and the storm's fury raged beneath them. There she glided, her mind thoughtful. Neither one of them suggested giving chase to their quarries; the magnitude of what they'd just seen was too important, and they needed to regroup and rethink their strategy. For the first time since she'd Locked with the ferocious Red, Tamra felt they were synchronized, their minds running the same course.

Reaching the same impossible, wonderful, earth-shattering conclusion.

Tamra clenched her hand around the scale.

Valkea, she sent, *what if we don't need the Silver at all?*

9

A Gift from the Deep

Joss could barely breathe for the pain.

Doubled over beside Lysander, he blinked away tears and gripped his Lock's neck, trying to be strong for him. It was ridiculous to feel this way when he wasn't even the injured one. It was Lysander bleeding all over the place, not him. There wasn't a scratch on Joss.

But the Silver's pain was bleeding into Joss's thoughts, until it felt it *was* his own belly that had been torn apart. Valkea's claws had gone deep, through the unscaled skin over Lysander's stomach. Lysander had managed to fly only a few minutes more before he was forced to land.

He, Allie, Sirin, and the three dragons were in the worst place possible, a lifeless heap of rock in the middle of the ocean. There was nothing here but wet stone beneath a gray sky, and no other land in sight. The place couldn't even be properly called an island. It was only just large enough for three dragons and their Locks. They huddled there like bedraggled wet rats. Sammi was curled against Sirin, shivering and frightened. Bellacrux clung to the highest point of rock, keeping watch for any Raptor scouts who might be tracking them.

They'd been here all night, waiting for the storm to subside. When it had, Lysander was not strong enough to fly again. So they waited, Joss sharing his Lock's agony while Allie and Sirin argued about what to do. They'd been at it since dawn, and it was grating on Joss's ears.

"We have to stitch him up," said Sirin, who was remarkably the calmest of them all.

"We can't waste time!" Allie said. "Valkea must know she wounded Lysander badly. They'll anticipate we landed nearby. It's just a matter of time before they find us."

"He can't fly like this!" Joss snapped, still clutching his own stomach. *Lysander, Lysander! Stay with me!* "Can't you see he's dying?"

"The Silver will not die," said a tired voice in dragonsong. "And this will help."

They turned to see a scaled head sticking out of the water, resting on the rock. Bellacrux snarled, as if angry she hadn't noticed the newcomer swim up.

But it was no Raptor; it was Ash. The rest of his body was beneath the water, rocked by the splashing waves. The Blue Grand looked bone-weary as he laid a mouthful of wet seaweed on the stone. At once a pungent odor washed over them, reeking like rotten eggs mixed with fresh dragon dung.

Allie gagged. "What is that stuff?"

"*Athelantis*," Ash said. "From the deepest chasm beneath the Blue islands. We were gathering it for our own, when I smelled Silver blood in the water and followed it here. The plant will accelerate Lysander's healing, though it will be a few days until he is back to normal."

"Fetero, mel elon," rumbled Bellacrux. *Thank you, old friend.*

Joss held tight to Lysander as Allie and Sirin gathered the athelantis. The large, papery leaves were the color of blood, and the horrible smell made the girls' eyes water. They held their breaths so that they breathed it in as little as possible. Following Ash's instructions, they then used stones to grind the leaves to pulp, then carefully applied that to the gashes on Lysander's belly.

Despite the stomach-wrenching stink of the plant, it worked like a miracle. At once Joss felt relief, like cool water running over a burn. Lysander sighed, and Joss felt his Lock's mind relax at last. He pulled the Silver's head onto his lap and stroked his nose, the way he'd done when Lysander had first hatched.

Joss?

Lysander! I'm here!

Oh, it hurt, Joss. It hurt so badly.

Squeezing his eyes shut, Joss leaned over and rested his forehead against his dragon's. *I know. I felt your pain, my friend. Is it better now?*

Yes . . . but is it really worth smelling like a human latrine? Lysander stuck out his tongue in disgust at the stench.

Joss laughed aloud, wiping a tear from his eye. Lysander would be all right.

"What of the battle?" Bellacrux asked Ash in dragonsong. "Is it over?"

"The Blues have fallen," Ash replied grimly. "We lost . . . many. And the Raptors claimed our hatchlings. All is in ruin, old friend. I should have listened to you sooner."

As Ash talked, Joss realized that the old Blue was covered in burns and gashes even worse than Lysander's. His wings were tattered and broken. The ocean water around him was turning red with blood. How had Ash managed to swim this far in such a state?

"You're hurt!" Allie said, as if she'd noticed Ash's injuries the same moment as Joss. "Climb up on the rock, and I'll put athelantis on you too."

"Save it for the Silver," said Ash. He seemed unable to even lift his head without great effort.

"Will you be able to fly home?" asked Allie.

Ash said nothing. Joss glanced at Bellacrux and saw the answer in the Green's pained eyes: Ash would not fly again.

The Blue Grand was dying.

Bellacrux must have communicated this thought to Allie too, because all at once her eyes widened and she covered her mouth with her hands.

Why did he come all this way for me? Lysander wondered, still too weak to voice the words himself. So Joss asked Ash the question for him.

"Your clan must need you," he added. "And you need healing yourself."

"I came because I realize now that Bellacrux was right," Ash said. "The Raptors are corrupted to their bones. They must be stopped, at any cost. Even if it means drawing on the darkest powers."

"The Skyspinner's Heart," said Bellacrux gently. "Is there anything else you know that might help us find it?"

"I know only that it must lie in the Lost Lands. And . . . I know where you might find out more." Ash lifted his head and looked back, in the direction of the continent. "But it will mean venturing deep into Raptor territory, to the very heart of their scorched lands."

Joss's hand involuntarily tightened on Lysander's left horn. He didn't like the sound of that. Not at all.

"Wait a minute," said Bellacrux. "You mean . . ."

Ash nodded. "I mean you must go to Tashiva Lhaa."

Joss paused as he translated for Sirin. "Does . . . that mean what I think it means?"

"What does it mean?" asked Sirin. "What's he saying?"

"Tashiva Lhaa," Joss repeated. "In dragonsong, it means *killer library.*"

"Killer library!" Sirin gave a short, bewildered laugh. "It's probably not meant literally."

"Oh," said Allie, sharing a look with her Lock. "Bellacrux says it's definitely meant literally."

"A library that wants to kill us?" Joss shook his head. "I don't like this."

Bellacrux explained: "Tashiva Lhaa is the oldest place in this world. It contains records of ancient dragon history, but the ones who built it designed it to . . . discourage visitors. They didn't want the information within to fall into Raptor claws, so at the slightest sign of trouble, it's said the library destroys anyone inside. Few have entered and returned again. I thought the Raptors had destroyed it centuries ago, angry they couldn't seem to get past the library's defenses."

"What defenses?" asked Sirin, after Joss translated for her.

Bellacrux gave the dragon equivalent of a shrug.

"Ash, do you know—" Joss stopped. He stared at the rock where Ash's head had been. But there was no sign of the Blue Grand. No sign at all, but a last swirl of dark red blood on the water.

Ash was gone.

Truly gone.

Above Joss, perched on her high rock, Bellacrux raised her head and released a keening, mournful roar.

10

A Raptor or a Sheep?

D'Mara flung herself from Krane's back in a fury, her metal-tipped boots clacking as they hit the stone floor of the Fortress Lennix landing yard.

Foiled *again*!

Sure, they'd found the Blue hideout, decimated the clan, stolen the eggs and youngest hatchlings. Sure, by any other standard, the raid would be counted a massive success.

But they had lost the Silver.

Again.

All the eggs in the world wouldn't make up for that. How was she supposed to feed these new Raptors anyway? They might as well have dumped the eggs into the sea, and the hatchlings too. Without the Silver to open the way to the Lost Lands, they would all starve. And with every passing day that she failed to deliver on her promise, her control over the Raptors weakened further. Valkea made sure of that.

There were some days when D'Mara felt like there was a giant clock ticking over her head, counting down until the day she became some Raptor's dinner.

"Edward!" She grabbed her husband by his collar as he walked past her. "Where are you going?"

He scowled. "We flew all night, dearest. I'm tired. I'm going to bed."

"Bed! Dragon's teeth, I am surrounded by fools and sluggards!" With unnecessary harshness fueled by her fury, she grabbed his pointy goatee and gave it a sharp tug. "Prepare the Fifth Flight for a supply run. We need provisions and we need them *now*. I want sheep, goats, pigs—I don't care. If it walks, they are to pick it up and bring it back. Alive, preferably."

Raptors liked their meat as fresh as possible.

Edward hurried away to comply, and D'Mara headed into the Roost. She snapped at Kaan to fetch servants for the after-raid cleansing. The Raptors were perfectly capable of licking the dried blood and gore from their own claws and scales, but some liked to bask in the sun while humans did the work for them. Kaan groaned but obeyed.

"Nothing but disrespect and rolling eyes around here," D'Mara muttered under her breath.

She felt a feathery touch from Krane's mind; no words, only a soothing pat. Usually it was enough to calm her, but today she was more irritable than usual. She brushed her Lock's touch away.

Keep an eye on that Zereth and his cohorts. I don't trust him. He's Valkea's creature.

I am always watching, Dee.

D'Mara paused on the upper loggia of the Roost, her hands on the balustrade as she gazed out over the mountains. They'd been flying the entire day, and now the sun had begun to set. It burned like a golden coin, melting behind the peaks. It was a lovely sight, and it filled her soul with wistful aching.

What if we just left? she sent to Krane. *Followed the sunset and never looked back. Forget them all.*

Dee? That's not like you.

She sighed. It wasn't like her, neither the daydreaming nor the thoughts of running away. But the idea *was* tempting.

What's the point? she asked Krane. *My own family doesn't respect me anymore. The Raptors are turning against me. The Silver continues to elude capture. Why bother with the lot of them at all?*

Her Lock's reply came smoothly. *You know why. Or have you forgotten?*

No. She had not forgotten.

When D'Mara had been a girl, everything had been simpler. Her mother, Felda Lennix, had run the fortress and overseen the Raptors. When D'Mara was ten years old, Felda had locked her in a maze of stone chambers with a starved, infuriated Raptor.

"There are only two kinds of people in the world: Raptors and sheep. Time to decide which one you are," she'd said to her daughter, then she'd shut the door.

D'Mara had dodged, scurried, and wept as the hungry dragon had pursued her through the chambers, sure that she would die. Then, in the very last room, she'd found a servant man scrubbing the floor. Her Lennix instincts sharpened at the sight of him, and she lured him into the next room, where the dragon was lurking. In exchange for the Raptor's mercy, she offered the servant as a snack. When the Raptor's agreement had come, it had been like a thought in her own mind, a strange whisper curling through her skull.

That had been the day she'd Locked with Krane. He'd always told her that that old servant had been the best meal he'd ever had.

This was why D'Mara couldn't fly off into the sunset and leave her disrespectful, ungrateful clan behind.

Because her mother had shown her that in this world or any other, the only law that mattered was this: Either you take control and be a Raptor too, or you get eaten with the other sheep.

Raptors would always be Raptors. You could either join them, or be crushed beneath their talons. D'Mara knew which she'd rather choose, because she already *had* chosen—the day she'd fed that servant man to Krane. The day she'd betrayed her own species in order to save herself. She didn't just lead the Raptors.

She *was* a Raptor.

D'Mara straightened and turned away from the sunset. She had work to do.

She had a Silver to capture.

11

The Scale of a Silver

Tamra put her hand into her pocket and wrapped her fingers around the Silver scale. It was cold now, and no longer sparking with lightning-white energy, but it still filled Tamra with buzzing energy. She hadn't had a chance to tell anyone about what had happened to her and Valkea yet. Mirra had sensed something was up, but Tamra wouldn't spill a word. She couldn't risk anyone else telling D'Mara about the scale before she did. This was *her* secret, and it was a powerful secret indeed.

It was a secret that could change everything for the Lennixes. It would solve their food shortage, their endless search for the Silver, the discontent among the ranks, their resentment of D'Mara and thus all the Lennixes. And it would be *Tamra* who delivered all of this into her mother's hands.

But first, Tamra had to find D'Mara and tell her the news. She searched the crèche, where the newly procured Blue eggs were being installed on beds of hay by terrified human servants. The servants cringed when Tamra came in, ducking behind hay bales or dropping to their knees, trembling. Normally Tamra would delight in such a reception, and might have found time to torment them further by walking around as if deciding who to feed to

Valkea, but not today. Today she was on a mission, perhaps the most important mission she'd ever had.

D'Mara wasn't in the crèche. She wasn't in the hatchlings' rooms either, where Kaan was lecturing the petrified littlest Blues about the Raptor way of life. Later that day, Tamra knew, a human servant would be chosen as a sacrifice, to give the hatchlings their first taste of human blood—an important and crucial step in a young dragon's first steps toward becoming a Raptor. It was always one of Tamra's favorite moments, and normally she'd demand to be in charge of the First Blood ceremony.

But not today.

Finally, coming to a halt in the dining hall—another dead end—Tamra threw back her head and yelled, "Where in the blazes IS that old—"

"Hello, Tamra," said D'Mara icily.

Tamra spun, and there her mother stood in the doorway, a dangerous look in her eyes.

"Ma, I have to talk to you. In *private*." She glared at Mirra, whom she now glimpsed hovering in the hall outside, trying to eavesdrop.

"I don't have time for you right now," D'Mara said, sounding more like herself. "I've got to choose a sacrifice for the First Blood ceremony, and figure out how to feed everyone tomorrow since those stupid Raptors are devouring all—"

"I've been to the Lost Lands."

D'Mara stared at her, then slowly her face began to contort into disgust. "I will not tolerate—"

"I'm not lying!" Tamra shouted. Then, lowering her voice once more, she added, "It happened during the Blue raid—one minute, Valkea and I were flying through the storm. The next, we were in a clear blue sky over a silver city, just like the one Kaan described when the Silver took him through the portal. All thanks to *this*." She took the Silver scale from her pocket and held it up.

She could tell her mother was deciding whether or not to believe her.

"I can prove it," said Tamra, a little desperately. "Meet me tonight atop your tower with Krane. We'll fly up and I'll show you. Ma, don't you see? If I'm right—and I am—then this changes everything!"

"All right, then." D'Mara looked like she wanted to believe Tamra, but still couldn't quite manage it. "Prove it."

They flew in silence for several minutes, Krane and Valkea gliding on the rough winds that buffeted the peaks of the Black Mountains. Fortress Lennix vanished behind them, the glow of its lamps and braziers soon swallowed up by the shadowy summits. The air was freezing cold this high up, and flakes of snow stuck to Tamra's eyelashes and the fur fringe of her cloak. Behind a thick layer of cloud, the moon was a watery, pale smudge.

Her mother led the way, and once they were out of sight of the fortress, she and Krane halted. The Raptor hovered on powerful wingbeats as Tamra took the scale from her pocket. She let out a long breath that misted white in front of her.

Are you ready? she asked Valkea.

Let's do this.

Tamra clung tight to the scale as her Lock pulled away from Krane. Valkea began to fly in a widening circle, looping outward to cover every inch of sky in the vicinity. Portals, it seemed, were plentiful enough, though invisible. It hadn't taken Kaan long to find one atop the Silver, and Tamra and Valkea had fallen right into one during the raid. So she hoped they would get lucky again here, tonight.

"C'mon," she whispered to the scale. "Don't let me down."

She felt D'Mara's eyes on her, her mother's gaze hard with doubt and scorn. But that was nothing new. That was just how her mother was, how she'd always been. Judgmental, cruel, cold. Nothing Tamra ever did was good enough. When her mother noticed her at all, it was always to criticize or scold.

Tamra hated her.

But Tamra also longed, desperately, to win her approval.

And this was how she would do it: by delivering to D'Mara the one thing she desired most. Tamra would give her the key to the Lost Lands, an even better key than the Silver himself, because the scale did not need persuasion or threats to work. The scale wouldn't attempt to run away. And the scale didn't come with a bratty, ungrateful sheep boy Locked to it. It was the perfect chance to finally show her mother that she, Tamra Lennix, was the best of her children.

All she had to do was make the scale work again.

But it would not.

For an hour they searched the sky, Valkea roaming all around the peaks, Tamra clutching the scale, and they saw no sign of a portal to the Lost Lands. The scale never so much as tingled in her hands. Desperation and panic knotted up in her throat until she wanted to scream. Valkea too was growing frantic, flying faster and farther, snarling when Tamra told her to search some other area. She tried letting Valkea hold the scale, first in her talons, then her teeth.

It's no use, Valkea sent.

It has to work! You know what we saw—you know it worked before!

Perhaps the scale can only be used once. Perhaps we are missing some crucial step.

"Enough!"

Tamra turned to see her mother and Krane drawing abreast of Valkea. D'Mara's expression was difficult to make out in the dark, but her anger was clear in her voice.

"This is foolishness! I won't waste another minute up here!"

"Ma—"

"I should never have let you talk me into this insanity. That scale is worthless, just like *you*."

Tamra bit her tongue as her mother's Raptor wheeled away and swooped off in the direction of Fortress Lennix. The cold mountain winds burrowed deeper into her, until her very bones felt limned with frost.

Much later that night, when Tamra finally made her way to bed, she found Mirra awake, waiting for her.

The twins still shared a room, despite many pleas to be given separate chambers. Their beds were set against one wall, with a little space between them, and on the other wall was set a small hearth. There, by a crackling fire, sat Mirra, wrapped in a blanket.

"Where have you been?" she demanded.

Tamra was in no mood to answer questions. She'd anticipated

being a hero in her mother's eyes. Now she was less than dirt to D'Mara. She was a waste of time. A *failure*.

But that didn't mean Tamra was giving up. She still believed in the scale's power. She just had to find out *how* to make it work.

Then Mirra said, "What secret mission has she got you on?"

"Secret mission?" Tamra echoed.

"You're her favorite, so of course she'd choose you for whatever it is."

"Yes," Tamra said, thoughtful. She sat across from her sister. "Yes, I am on a secret mission."

"Well?" Mirra watched her, jealousy plain in her gaze. She had no idea about the scale, its power, or Tamra's spectacular failure tonight.

If Tamra was now disgraced in her mother's eyes, would that mean *Mirra* would be the new favorite? She wanted to vomit at the thought. She and her twin shared a great deal—a bedroom, their clothes, their birthday, even their dragon up until three weeks ago. But everyone knew Tamra was the better twin. She was smarter, tougher, and two minutes older. She couldn't *bear* to be seen as inferior to Mirra.

So she'd just have to drag Mirra down with her.

For a plan was forming in Tamra's mind. It was a weak one, but it was all she had. If she was lucky, it might give her the information she needed to activate the Silver scale again. And if it *was* to end in failure, then why not let Mirra share that too? They had to share everything else. Let their mother be furious at the both of them.

"Do you remember that old place Declan used to run off to?" she asked. "Some ruin he liked to go visit, to read *books*." She said it as though it were a shameful secret her brother had kept.

"I think so," replied Mirra.

"He tried to tell Ma about it once, but she wasn't interested," Tamra recalled.

Her twin snorted. "You know Ma—if it doesn't breathe fire, she's not interested."

"Well, now she is. There's something she needs me to research, something to do with Silvers and portals. And I think Declan's ruin might hold the answers. He did always say there was a bunch of old books and scrolls in there, with all sorts of dragony information in them."

"All right, I'm in!" said Mirra, without even a hint of suspicion as to *why* her sister would invite her into her secret, all-important mission. Blood and bones, Mirra really was the stupidest of girls.

"Good," said Tamra. "Then get dressed. It's time we took a little trip to the library."

12

Raptor Lands

Allie kept an anxious eye on Lysander over the next two days, as they sneaked through the heart of Raptor territory toward the library. The Silver never complained, but it was clear his injuries were slowing him down. They flew only by night, keeping low to the ground even though it meant navigating choppier air. To spare Lysander any further strain, Sirin rode behind Allie, while Sammi flitted beneath Bellacrux's wings like a sparrow shadowing an eagle.

When they rested, Allie and Joss exchanged nervous looks about Lysander's condition, communicating with their silent sibling connection that wasn't all that different from a dragon's Lock.

"When we said we'd take the fight to the Raptors," Joss whispered on the second morning, "I didn't think it would mean *literally* strolling into their backyard. If we keep going in this direction, we'll go right by Fortress Lennix."

"We'll be fine," Allie said. She tried to hide her own worry from him. "We just have to be smart."

"What part of *killer* library don't you get?" Joss asked. "As in, *the library wants to murder us?*"

"When Americans say *killer*, they sometimes mean *awesome*," interjected Sirin.

"Yeah, sure," said Joss. "I wonder if it'll eat us? Or maybe crush us to bits? Or perhaps it'll open up its floor and we'll fall forever into eternal darkness? *So cool.*"

Sirin looked thoughtful. "You know, in the real world, *killer* can be just another way of saying *awesome*. Maybe it's the awesome library!" But her voice was just a bit too high and a bit too trembly to hide the fact that she too was jittery with nerves.

Honestly, what was wrong with Sirin, treating all of this like a story? They weren't going to prance over a rainbow and meet a grumpy troll with some amusing riddle to be solved. No, they were venturing into the most dangerous region in the world, where they were more likely to meet a Raptor and find themselves promptly incinerated and devoured.

This was not a world that treated heroes well. It didn't reward courage with gold or pluckiness with victory.

Worse, as the hours passed and the morning faded into a scorchingly hot afternoon, the landscape started to seem more and more familiar. They flew in silence, no one having spoken a word since breakfast, all of them watching the world below with increasing nervousness. Allie realized she now recognized the mountains in the distance and shuddered. They were getting nearer to Fortress Lennix.

We will not come within sight of that place, Bellacrux reassured her. *And I am giving it an extra-wide berth, just to be safe.*

"What happened here?" asked Sirin.

Allie startled a little; the girl hadn't uttered a word in hours, and she'd almost forgotten she was there. She looked around at the landscape they were flying over. Great cracks crisscrossed dry, baked ground, and nothing grew, though a few gray, dead trees hinted that this was not always so.

"Raptors," she said. "This was probably a forest once, or farm-land. They'd have razed it so many times everything—and everyone—who lived here finally gave up."

"Where did they go?"

Allie gave a sour laugh. "They didn't *go* anywhere."

"Oh," Sirin said softly, and she must have finally understood what Allie meant. A little while later, they swooped over a few bleached skeletons—cows, sheep, one human—and the point was driven further home.

"They'll do this to Earth," said Sirin. "If they get through, they'll burn everything."

"And everyone."

"We have to stop them." Her voice was quiet but as hard and resolute as stone.

"Yes," said Allie. "And to do that, we have to find the Skyspinner's Heart."

Over the cracked, faded land raced the shadows of the three dragons. Allie cast another anxious look at Lysander, whose wings were starting to beat unevenly. The Silver looked exhausted. He needed rest. They all did, but there was nowhere safe left to go. Allie thought again about simply running, fleeing through a por-tal to Earth.

She must have imagined it too loudly, because Bellacrux picked up the thread of her thoughts.

We cannot abandon the others, my Lock. Running away would mean condemning all the innocent dragons still True to the Wing.

Allie thought of the Blue hatchlings dipping in the lagoon, of the eggs that would soon hatch not in their clan's warm dens, but in the cold halls of Fortress Lennix. She knew that no matter how far she ran, she would never escape the guilt of leaving them all behind.

Of course, she sent back. *Anyway, it's only a matter of time before another Silver is born. The Raptors will find their way to the Lost Lands eventually.*

The Heart really was their only option. If they could find it, they could not only stop the Raptors, they could *change* them—order them to be True to the Wing, as Bellacrux called it.

Let's focus on one step at a time, Bellacrux counseled. *First, we must discover where the Heart is.*

Before that, we have to reach the library.

Ah. A rumble sounded in Bellacrux's throat. *But we already have.*

Allie sucked in a breath as her Lock swooped low, diving into a canyon that crooked along the blasted landscape. She felt Sirin's arms lock around her middle and didn't even snap at her to let go, because she too felt a flutter of terror. The canyon walls closed around Bellacrux like the throat of a giant, swallowing them deeper and deeper into shadow. Lysander glided behind them, and Sammi flew above.

Then, abruptly, they came to a dead end. A sheer cliff face as wide as Fortress Lennix—and five times as tall—stood before them. Carved into it were many windows and doors and balconies, through most of these were half-collapsed. They were made of the same red rock as the cliff, and just a sliver of light shone on the structure from above, illuminating the massive main doorway between two pillars of stone.

The dragons alighted on the rocky ground before the library. Allie jumped down and heard her footsteps echo along the canyon walls behind them. Then complete silence fell; not even the wind could reach this strange place. All around them were scattered bones—dragon and human alike.

Joss immediately checked on Lysander's wounds, which were healing well thanks to the athelantis they'd been applying every few hours.

"Tashiva Lhaa," said Bellacrux in a low, reverent tone. "The most ancient structure in this world, where our ancestors buried all our secrets."

Swallowing hard, Allie resisted the temptation to jump back on Bellacrux and fly away. Something about this place made her want to flee it. She had the strangest feeling that if they walked through the gaping black doorway into the library's interior, they would never walk out again.

"Why is it so dangerous?" she asked. "Why call it a *killer* library?"

I do not know, said Bellacrux. *I never had reason to come here before now, and I've never known any dragon who dared it.*

"It looks like Petra," said Sirin, studying the library. "That's a place on Earth, an ancient temple in a country called Jordan."

"Come on," Allie said, before Sirin could draw Joss into another one of her Earth stories. "Let's get this over with."

Wrapping a strip of cloth torn from her cloak around an old dragon bone, she then held it up for Bellacrux to light. It took only a tendril of fire from the dragon's tongue, and the makeshift torch blazed.

The library's entrance was so wide and tall that it was clearly built with dragons in mind. Indeed, all around it had been carved fantastic dragons in flight, their tails and necks intertwining, their fearsome claws still sharp despite the wear of centuries. Allie stood a moment in the doorway, listening the eerie echoes and sighs coming from within, and tried to work up the courage to go another step.

Wait, said Bellacrux.

Allie stepped back and looked up, above the door, where her Lock was staring. There was some sort of writing carved there, strange runes she didn't recognize. They weren't like human writing, but rather enormous slashes that could only have been done by a dragon's claw.

"Can you read it?" Joss asked Lysander, and the Silver shook his head.

It is Talonfari, Bellacrux told Allie. *A form of dragon writing that is nearly lost to us. Only a handful of dragons are old and wise enough to still know it.*

Great, Allie groaned inwardly. *So now we have to find a dragon who can read it?*

Bellacrux snorted indignantly, then breathed a wash of fire over the runes. The kids gasped and jumped back at the wave of heat. Where the flames hit the stone, they turned to smoke, but within the deep slashes of the runes the fire held and burned, so the ancient words glowed orange.

"*Lehemenn fin Lhaa*," Bellacrux read aloud. "*Lehemenn tek makaa.*"

"Silence in the library," translated Allie. "Silence . . . or death."

They all exchanged looks.

"I think," said Sirin at last, "that we had better be very, *very* quiet."

13

Silence in the Library

The moment she set foot through the door of Tashiva Lhaa, Sirin felt a chill run down her spine.

Sirin loved libraries. She'd spent loads of time in them back home, always snug in some corner with a whole stack of books at her elbow. It was a rare week indeed in which she and her mother hadn't checked out a bucketload—always adventures and fantasy and sci-fi for Sirin, and romances and historicals for her mother. Libraries were special places—*safe* places.

But by that standard, Tashiva Lhaa was no library at all.

There was no tidy counter with a smiling, slightly frazzled librarian behind it. There was no friendly sign directing her to the juvenile section or the reference stacks. There was no corkboard listing local book clubs, movie nights, or author signings.

Instead, there were rows and rows and *rows* of stone columns fading away into total darkness. In the columns, crammed into recesses, nooks, slots, and holes, were enormous scrolls taller than Sirin herself. She stared at the nearest ones and realized, with a sort of sinking sensation, that the parchment was rolled not over wooden spindles, but *bones*.

Sirin had felt safer a thousand feet in the air atop a

fire-breathing dragon in the middle of a hurricane than she did in this dark, dusty place.

"Look at those," whispered Joss, pointing upward. Allie raised her torch.

The ceiling was so high that Sirin couldn't even see it. There were only the columns, fading upward into the black. There were a good many stone walkways crooking overhead, wide enough for even a dragon as large as Bellacrux to walk comfortably. And beneath them, carved into the supporting corbels, were dragons— *stone* dragons, like the gargoyles she'd seen back home. These stone dragons were much larger than their Earth counterparts, with wings and claws and everything. Their blank eyes seemed to watch the visitors' every move.

"Remember," said Allie sternly, "the sooner we find the scroll about the Banishing, the sooner we can find the Skyspinner's Heart. So don't make a sound. We must all be very, very qui—"

"A-*CHOOO!*"

Everyone froze.

And stared at Sammi, who herself looked completely shocked at the volume of her own sneeze.

The sound of it echoed through the library: *achoooOOoooOoooOOOooo . . .*

No one moved for a whole minute; even Bellacrux stood locked in place, her big eyes stretched as wide as they could go. Sirin looked all around, hardly daring to breathe. Her heart pounded so violently that she was certain it was making its own echo. She wasn't sure what she expected would happen—maybe the floor to open under their feet, dropping them into a pit of sharpened stakes like in some sort of Indiana Jones film.

But nothing did happen.

No creature stirred, no trap sprang, no cardigan-sporting, bespectacled librarian popped out from behind a column to shush them.

"Well," said Sirin shakily. "We're not dead."

"Yet." Allie rolled her eyes. "After the things I've survived, dying because a baby dragon couldn't stifle her sneeze would just be embarrassing."

"She's only a baby," Sirin said. "She didn't do it on purpose."

"Maybe you and Sammi should wait outside and leave this to us."

"I can help!" Sirin protested. "If there's one thing I know, it's libraries." Not that this placed really counted as a *library*; it was more in the realm of *ancient tomb probably stuffed with mummies and bones and girl-eating spiders*. But she squared her shoulders and looked at Allie straight on, unwilling to be left behind.

Allie looked unconvinced by her bravado.

"C'mon," said Joss, bravely taking the first step forward. "Let's just get what we came for."

"Yeah," said Allie. "About that . . . How are we supposed to find one scroll in all of *this*?"

Everyone looked around uncertainly. It was a good question. Sirin felt it safe to assume this library didn't abide by the Dewey decimal system.

"Spread out," she suggested. "Start at the bottom, work our way up. And be careful. I've read about stuff like this in books. This place is probably booby-trapped. Watch out for pits full of snakes."

"Oh," said Allie, groaning. "Well, if that's what your *books* say."

"Sirin's right," said Joss. "We should be careful. Being cranky about it won't help."

Grumbling, Allie turned away and marched to the nearest column. Sirin was starting to get the feeling that Allie didn't much like her.

But this wasn't the time to argue. They'd come here to find a scroll about the Banishing, and who knew how much time they had. What if someone had seen them flying this way and told the Raptors? And it wasn't like there was anything to eat around here. They had a little bit of seaweed left, but no water. By nightfall, they'd all be starving and thirsty and crankier than they already were.

Sirin struggled to pull a scroll from its alcove. She tried not to think about the fact she was tugging on somebody's *bone* to do it. But despite her efforts, the scroll was firmly wedged in place.

Finally, she exhaled in frustration and put her hands on her hips. "This is nuts," she said. "Allie's right. We'll be here the rest of our lives and still probably never find the right one."

Bellacrux pulled scrolls from the higher alcoves and spread them on the ground, while Lysander flew to the high walkways and wandered around, as if trying to decide where to start. Joss opened a scroll so ancient the entire thing crumbled to dust at his feet, and he was left holding the pair of femurs the parchment had been wrapped around—femurs which, Sirin grimly realized, were definitely human-size.

"What would help," said Allie, putting back another useless scroll, "is if there were a little more *light* down here."

"What would help," Sirin added, "is if the scroll we needed were lying right out in the open, waiting for . . . for us to . . ." Her voice faded away.

"For us to what?" asked Joss.

"For us to find it," whispered Sirin. "Kind of like . . . *that*."

She pointed down the row of columns, at a scroll lying on the floor, all alone but clearly out of place. Every other scroll in the library seemed to be stored in its proper alcove. So why was *this* one sitting out?

They gathered around it at once, Lysander leaping from walkway to walkway before landing lightly on the ground. Allie held her torch over the scroll.

For a long minute, they just stared.

Then Joss said, "Someone's going to have to open it."

With a grunt, Bellacrux extended a single claw and unrolled the parchment. The bone holding it together rattled on the stone floor.

"Weird," said Allie. "There are only two sentences written on it. The rest is blank."

She began to read aloud from the scroll: *"This being the total and true account of the Tale of the Banishing of the Dragons from Earth."*

"It says Earth?" interrupted Sirin. "Not the Lost Lands?"

"That's what it says," Allie replied. "But . . . there's no tale at all. Just this one last line: *Enter two and two alone; part not till the tale is done.*"

"What does that mean?" wondered Joss. "Enter *what*?"

Allie shrugged. "Maybe—"

She was cut short by the rustle of parchment and clatter of bone, as the scroll began to *move*.

Sirin jumped back, stifling a shout with her hands. The others drew back as well as the scroll began to unroll *itself*. The bones clacked and bounced over the stone floor, then one of them shot up into the air, drawing the roll of parchment with it like a banner.

Joss was pale as a sheet. "What the—"

"*Shh!*" hissed Allie. "Everyone stay quiet!"

The scroll parchment began to bend in midair, zigzagging upward like a staircase. Then it stretched high, and on the blank, creamy surface, dark blotches of ink began to swirl and spread, as if someone were pouring a bunch of inkpots onto it. The black patches then coalesced—into the shape of a doorway.

Sirin stared. The scroll didn't just look like a staircase. It *was* a staircase, leading to that black, inky portal that led to who knew where.

"Right," said Allie. "Enter two and two alone."

"You're not thinking of going *in* there, are you?" squeaked Joss.

"Someone's got to do it. You in?"

"I'll go," said Sirin, the words leaping from her mouth before she could stop them. She didn't even know *why* she said them.

"Fine," Joss sighed. "I'll go with Sirin."

"What?" Allie shook her head. "No. No way. I'll go with you."

"You're forgetting the Banishing took place on *Earth*," Sirin pointed out. "*My* world. If anyone goes through the creepy ink door, it should be me. Anyway, I read about something like this before—"

"This is *not* one of your storybooks!" said Allie loudly.

"*Shh!*" Joss and Sirin both said.

High, high above them, they heard a groan, like shifting rock. Allie pressed her hands over her mouth. The only other sound was the light crinkle of the parchment stairs rising before them.

They waited even longer than they had after Sammi had sneezed, but nothing more happened.

"I'm going," whispered Allie. "Joss, you come with me."

"Okay," he said, though he looked uneasy.

Allie planted her foot on the first step. The parchment, which should have torn, instead held firm. Still, Sirin held her breath until Allie reached the top, well above their heads. She paused only a moment in front of the black, inky portal, then glanced down at Joss.

"Here goes," she said.

Then she stepped through the doorway and vanished.

"Whoa," said Joss. "My turn, I guess."

But the moment he set foot on the staircase, the scroll crumpled. With a gasp, he jumped back. The scroll rolled itself up as quickly as it had unfurled, until the two bones clacked together.

"Allie!" Joss grabbed the scroll and tried to pry it open again, but it refused to even part an inch. Bellacrux plucked it from him with her talon and frantically tried to force it apart, to no avail. She looked at Joss with wide eyes.

"You're her Lock. Can you hear her?" Joss asked Bellacrux. "Can you sense her at all?"

The dragon shook her head no.

"I don't understand," said Sirin. "It said two must enter. But only Allie went in!"

"Wrong," said another voice from behind them.

They all whirled.

From behind one of the stone columns stepped a girl. Sirin vaguely recognized her.

"You attacked us!" she said. "Your dragon injured Lysander!"

"No," said the girl. She was shivering, her arms wrapped around herself. "That's my twin, Tamra."

"Mirra Lennix!" said Joss. "What—"

With a terrible snarl, Bellacrux lunged forward, putting herself between Joss, Sirin, Sammi, and Mirra. At first Sirin thought this a bit over the top, considering the girl was only barely taller than they were, but then she glimpsed the pair of red eyes burning in the darkness behind the Lennix girl.

The Red Raptor emerged slowly from the shadows, and Sirin could swear the creature was *grinning*. Her scales glimmered like dark, polished ruby as she moved, her long claws gouging the floor.

"*Valkea!*" hissed Bellacrux.

The Red dipped her head in a mocking greeting. The two dragons began circling each other like alley cats, their scales prickling and their lips pulling back to reveal their fangs. The library echoed with the sound of snarls.

"*Quiet!*" warned Sirin. She looked up anxiously. She'd always been one to respect the rules of libraries, but this was the first time her *life* had depended on it.

"Calm down, Valkea," Mirra said, also looking nervous. The two big dragons hadn't struck at each other yet, but they looked on the verge of ripping out each other's throats.

"This was a trap!" said Joss. "Where are the rest of you?"

Mirra Lennix shrugged. "It's not a trap. Just me and Tamra are here. Or Tamra *was*, before she went into the scroll, like your sister. I . . . opted to stay behind."

Meaning she was too scared to follow her twin, Sirin could easily guess.

They all turned to stare at the tightly sealed scroll on the floor.

"Wherever Tamra and Allie are," said Mirra, "they're there together."

14

The Tale of the Banishing

Allie swam through ink, forcing herself not to panic. She'd already tried going back to the scroll door but found only swirling black liquid. Eyes squeezed shut, she pointed herself in the direction she hoped was *up* and swam with all her strength. Memories surged through her, of swimming in the sea by her family's old village, searching for pearl oysters and pretty shells to take back to her mother. The water had been clear and warm, nothing like this strange, inky sea in which she now found herself.

Finally, she burst through the surface and saw a pale shoreline ahead. Allie dragged herself out of the black water and found, to her shock, that she was completely dry.

The world around her looked like nothing she'd ever seen—there was no sky, no land, no walls. Only endless beige blankness, a world of parchment. She swallowed hard and looked back, to see the water she'd swum out of shrinking, swirling inward until all at once it was *gone*.

Bellacrux? Bell, can you hear me?

She got no reply. She couldn't sense anything of her Lock.

It was a nightmare. It had to be. She must have hit her head in the library and now she was stuck in some awful dream world. Where was Joss? He didn't surface from the inky sea as she had.

What if he'd drowned? What if something had gone wrong in the library? What if, what if—

Focus, Allie, she told herself. *You can't help anyone if you're panicking.*

She had to keep it together or she'd break apart completely. So what if she was alone? Joss was probably sitting comfily against Lysander, waiting for her to get back. They were all waiting for her, counting on her, *trusting* her . . .

Allie felt panic spike in her chest again.

And again she forced herself to breathe it out.

The sooner she figured out where the Skyspinner had died, the sooner they could all leave Raptor territory and disappear into the Lost Lands. There, at least, they wouldn't have Raptors on their trail everywhere they went.

Shivering, Allie began to walk. There didn't seem to be much else she could do. Her steps crinkled, as if she were stepping on paper.

"You're not Mirra," said a voice.

Allie looked around, and behind her, having appeared from nowhere, stood a girl.

"Tamra Lennix!" Allie's heart skipped a beat. She wished she had a weapon, a knife or even a rock to hold, but all she could do was raise her clammy fists. Glancing around, she waited for more Lennixes to come scurrying out of hiding, like cockroaches. But all was still. "Stay away from me! Or I'll—I'll—"

"What?" Tamra scoffed, her arms folded on her chest. "What'll you do, Allinson Moran?"

"You tried to kill me!"

"You stole our Grand."

"After you tried to *feed me* to her!"

Tamra snorted. "Looks like you didn't take too much damage."

"How did you get here?" Allie asked, her scalp prickling. She still wasn't convinced Tamra was alone. She didn't lower her fists.

"Same way as you, I would imagine. Creepy library, magic scroll, a door made of ink . . . Been waiting a couple of hours, I'd guess. Mirra was supposed to come in after me, but I'll bet she chickened out. Typical."

"Mirra's in the library?" Allie felt a chill of alarm. "Are there more of you in there?"

Tamra just smirked.

Allie imagined Joss surrounded by slavering Raptors. The library had seemed empty when they'd arrived, but it was so vast, who knew what was hiding in the shadows. She hoped Bellacrux and Lysander would be enough to defend her brother until she returned . . . *if* she returned at all. She had no idea how to escape the scroll, and even if she figured it out, there was still Tamra to deal with.

Allie felt nauseated with fear. She had to get out of here *now*.

"Why are you here, anyway?" asked Allie. "What do you care about the Banishing?"

Tamra scowled. "I'm not telling you anything. If it weren't for the whole *two and two alone* thing, I'd be wringing your neck right now."

"*Together till the tale is done*," Allie remembered, groaning. "I guess we do need each other. But why? And what are we supposed to do now? How do we get out?"

"No idea," Tamra growled. "This day just keeps getting—*Whoa!*"

All at once, a dragon swooped over their heads.

Tamra and Allie yelled, ducking low. The dragon, which was made of swirling, smoky ink, swooped and dived but didn't seem to notice them.

"Look," said Allie.

She pointed down, where below them a coastline was taking shape as if painted by an invisible hand. It made it look as though Allie and Tamra were standing on a high cliff, the jagged line of the bluff's edge just inches from their feet. Little blade of grass sprang up under Allie's shoes and all around, sweeping away to a tall forest of pine trees behind them. The colors were faded and watery, the lines like black brushstrokes.

"There!" said Allie. "More dragons."

Ahead of them, in the parchment sky, a battle was taking shape. Dragons clashed and clawed, while papery flames crinkled from their jaws.

"This must be the Battle of Banishment," said Tamra. "The final dragon battle in the Lost Lands."

Allie studied the inky dragons, wondering which one was the Skyspinner. According to the legend, she fought and died in this battle.

Hearing a rustle of paper to her left, Allie turned and got a shock—a Green was standing on the cliff beside her, so close that she could see the individual brushstrokes of his inked outline. He snorted out two streams of watercolor smoke and looked at her.

Have you come to bear witness?

Allie started; she heard the dragon the same way she heard Bellacrux—like another voice in her head. "Um . . . I suppose I have." Allie hesitated a moment, then put her hand on the dragon's side. His scales were washed in light green and felt like parchment paper.

Throwing caution to the wind, Allie climbed onto the paper-and-ink dragon and settled into the rider's dip.

"What are you doing?" Tamra gasped.

"C'mon. Like the scroll says—together till the tale is done."

"I'm not riding on a dragon with *you*!"

Allie clenched her fists. "You're not exactly my first choice either. But we're in this together, like it or not. If we're going to get out of here, we have to do it as a team."

"I'll come," said Tamra. "But we are *not* a team. And I'm riding in the front."

Allie groaned but scooted back to make room for her. Tamra sat stiffly, her black hair twisted into a severe braid, but a few curls had escaped and tickled Allie's chin.

"So . . . now what?" said Tamra. The dragon just stood there, his talons curling over the edge of the cliff.

"I don't know," said Allie. "It's not like I've done this bef—*ooohhhhhhhh!*"

The paper dragon didn't take off from the cliff so much as *fall* off. It dived straight down toward the rocky sea below, then spread its wings with a crackle of parchment to lift up again.

"What," said Tamra, "is *that*?"

A shadow had begun to darken the sea below, as if a massive cloud were moving across the sun.

But when the girls looked up, they saw not a cloud—but a dragon.

The largest dragon Allie had ever seen.

It was easily twenty times the size of Bellacrux. Her Lock

could comfortably carry three humans if she wished; *this* beast could carry a *city*. Its scales were obsidian black, its wings so wide they seemed to touch either horizon. The talons curled beneath its belly were each larger than Fortress Lennix.

The Skyspinner! thought Allie. She was certain this was the dragon from the legend, the great queen born in a star, with a heart full of magic.

All around them, in the Skyspinner's shadow, dragons battled viciously. Some fell from the sky, blazing with flames, and when they hit the water the fire extinguished and great plumes of smoke rose up. The air stank of smoke and blood and death. Allie could taste ashes when she inhaled. She had lived through two dragon battles, and neither of them had been anything like this. This was a full-scale war.

The Skyspinner screeched suddenly, a sound that drowned out all else. Allie and Tamra clamped their hands over their ears until it ended, but even still Allie reeled at the immensity of the sound.

Several flights of Raptors—Allie made out their tattooed bellies—had peeled away from the battle and begun an assault on the Skyspinner, harrying her like bees. The dragon queen's size made her slow and unwieldy in the air; she grabbed a few Raptors from the sky with her talons and hurled them into the sea, but most buzzed around her, out of reach of her claws and teeth. Then they darted in and raked their own talons into her vulnerable points, then filled the gashes with dragonfire. From her wounds, rivers of dark blood spilled.

"They're killing her," said Allie, her heart breaking.

Allie would have expected Tamra to take savage delight in the Raptors' destruction of the queen, but the girl was quiet and wide-eyed.

In the corner of her eye, Allie saw a blur of movement—a dragon hurtling toward them. "Watch out!" she cried.

Without even thinking of what she was doing, she grabbed Tamra and pulled her down, just as an out-of-control Blue zoomed over their heads. If she hadn't grabbed Tamra, the girl would have been knocked into the air.

"Let go of me!" Tamra snapped.

"I saved your life!"

"Don't expect a thank-you."

"Trust me, I don't." Wishing she'd just left the girl to be smashed by the Blue, Allie looked down to see the dragon tumbling snout over tail through the sky. Then she saw why—his wings had been torn off entirely. The poor thing couldn't fly. But as Allie watched, the dragon managed to straighten itself, and it dived like an arrow into the sea. Moments later, it popped up again and swam away, undulating through the waves. Blues were, she remembered, as at home in the sea as in the sky.

Another trumpeting screech sounded from the Skyspinner, and again Allie covered her ears. This time, the dragon queen's cry was racked with pain and agony. It was the most horrible thing Allie had ever heard. It tore at her very soul.

Then a strange thing happened: The queen began to shine. Her black scales flooded with light, and she burned whiter and hotter until Allie was forced to look away. The Skyspinner shone like a star, and from her mouth and eyes and the tips of her claws, brilliant beams of light shot out. They lanced through the sky, and every dragon they swept over jerked in the air. Then they turned and fled, high, high into the air. And there they . . . *vanished*.

Into portals, Allie realized. She recognized the pops of light where the dragons disappeared. But she tore her eyes from them and looked instead at the Skyspinner, whose light had begun to dim. As quickly as she'd shone, she flickered out. The only light that burned in her a moment longer was a bright red glow in her chest—*her heart*.

"She's banished them," she whispered, horror knotting in her throat as the great queen's heart finally faded. Then she fell, plummeting into the sea like a crumbling mountain, sending up an enormous splash. The wave bore down on the girls' dragon.

They didn't even have time to scream.

15

The Librarians

Bellacrux did not once take her eyes off Valkea the Red.

The Green was furious with herself for having not noticed the dragon the moment they'd arrived at the library. How could she have failed to detect the stench of savagery that clung to Valkea like a miasma? When they'd come slinking out of the shadows, Bellacrux's instinct had been to spread her wings and reduce them both to ash in a torrent of dragonfire.

But the gleaming runes above the library door burned brightly in her mind: *Silence in the library.*

So she had stilled her rage and let it harden instead, like a hidden dagger ready to be pulled the moment she sniffed aggression from the Red.

Now they all sat in a circle around the Scroll of the Banishing, waiting, in the flickering light of the bone torch that Joss now held.

They had, remarkably, struck a temporary truce.

"There's nothing to be done but wait," Bellacrux had pointed out in dragonsong, and though she could see it made Valkea furious to agree, the Red had no choice. Both of their Locks were trapped in the scroll, and neither of them could abandon them there.

Joss was beside himself. The boy wouldn't stop pacing, and his constant movement was grating on Valkea.

And though Bellacrux would never show it, she too was growing anxious.

She had no idea what ordeal Allie might be going through, but the girl was brave and quick-witted and likely to survive whatever the scroll held in store. Whether she would survive Tamra Lennix, on the other claw, was more in doubt. That girl was bad news. She was the fiercest and strongest of the Lennix brood, as Bellacrux well knew. After all, it had been an act of Tamra's unspeakable villainy that had first brought Allie to Bellacrux. Tamra had meant to feed Allie to the Grand; instead, the Grand had Locked with her intended victim. And now Allie was trapped in some other place with her would-be murderer. It chilled Bellacrux's very scales.

Valkea watched Bellacrux with venomous, scornful eyes.

"Feshi me'lakti kefaan?" snarled the Red. *What are you looking at, traitor?*

Bellacrux snorted disdainfully and turned her gaze away, though she never quite let Valkea get out of her sight.

"So why are you here?" Joss asked Mirra. "What's your interest in the Banishing?"

"I don't know," Mirra said. "Tamra wouldn't tell me. But I think it has to do with—"

"*TSSSS!*" hissed Valkea, baring her fangs at the Lennix girl.

Mirra swallowed and pulled her legs to her chest. "Never mind."

Bellacrux watched Valkea very carefully. What had Mirra been about to say? Could it possibly have been *the Skyspinner's Heart*? Bellacrux thought it highly unlikely the Raptors would have been searching for the same thing, given how few dragons knew of its existence. Even Bellacrux hadn't known what it was, until they'd met Ash.

No, Bellacrux decided. It must be something else they were after. Something also related to the Banishing, and probably quite horrid, but not the Heart.

Under no circumstances could she let them learn of it.

"You know, Mirra," said Sirin, "where I come from, girls our age just go to school and eat loads of junk food and play video games and stay up way too late reading."

"Where do you come from?" asked Mirra, eyes wide. "And what's a video game?"

"I come from Earth," said Sirin. "You call it the Lost Lands."

"Really!" Mirra gasped. "What's it like?"

"Very different from here. There are *loads* more people, for starters."

Bellacrux noticed how Valkea's eyes glowed at that. The Red did all but lick her chops.

"And it's beautiful," said Sirin. "Green forests and white beaches and sparkling cities—and more books than you could read in your life, and the most wonderful food, like chocolate cupcakes and extra-cheesy pizza and hot chips you get by the seaside. But of course, I guess that'll all be over soon."

"Over?" echoed Mirra, whose eyes also now held a hungry glint.

"When you Lennixes and your Raptors take over." Sirin sighed. "All those wonderful things will burn up. Your dragons will destroy everything, even though long ago, they lived peacefully on Earth with us humans. I suppose my world will soon look like yours—everything scorched and dying, and the few free people and dragons left will go into hiding."

Joss looked between Sirin and Mirra, holding a half-eaten fish by its stick skewer.

"Yeah," he said slowly, catching on. "Too bad you Lennixes hate everything and everyone."

"We don't *hate* everything," Mirra protested. "We just . . . My ma . . ."

"Oh, right," said Joss. "I forgot. Whatever D'Mara wants, the rest of the Lennix clan does."

"Not true!" Mirra scowled. "I do what I want."

Valkea began to growl; she didn't like that Sirin and Joss were trying to sway Mirra's allegiances. Bellacrux made no sound, but pulled back her lips, showing her larger fangs. Valkea glanced at her and fell quiet, but her fury seemed to shimmer on her scales like heat.

"Is Valkea your Lock?" asked Sirin.

"No!" said Mirra hurriedly. "She's Tamra's Lock. I only rode here on her because this is an all-important mission for Ma—"

"T'lehemenn!" snarled Valkea, ordering Mirra to be silent.

"No!" Mirra said back, startling them all. "No, I won't be silent. You're not my Lock, and you're not my boss. You can push Tamra around—I know you do, though she won't admit it—but not me. So *you* shut up!"

"Faka labint," hissed Valkea.

"I am not a *stupid girl*," shouted Mirra. "You and Tamra and Ma are all the same—everyone thinks I'm stupid! Well, I'm not! I know Tamra's lying about this mission. I think Ma might not even know about it! And I saw the scale Tamra's got hidden in her pocket."

"Scale?" echoed Joss. "What kind of scale?"

Mirra didn't seem to hear him. She kept yelling at Valkea. "Tamra thinks she's *so* clever, but guess which one of us got herself stuck in some booby-trapped scroll? Not me!"

With a roar, Valkea lunged at Mirra, and the girl screamed. Whether the Raptor was intending to simply scare her into silence or truly bite the girl in two, Bellacrux did not know. They didn't find out, because high above them, a gong sounded.

CLAAANNNGGGGGG!

They all froze, even Valkea. Mirra choked off her scream. Instead of fading away, the gong's tone grew stronger and louder, until the scrolls in the alcoves began to flutter and the temperature in the library seemed to drop.

Then, from all directions, came the sound of groaning and moaning and splintering stone, like the sound of corpses trying to escape their tombs.

With a growl, Bellacrux stamped out the torch, throwing the library into darkness. She pulled Joss, Sirin, and Sammi into the shelter of one wing and spread the other over the scroll that had swallowed Allie. If it were destroyed, her Lock might never find her way back.

"There!" shouted Joss, pointing. "Something moved!"

"Over there too!" said Mirra, looking in the other direction.

Valkea loosed a sudden burst of dragonfire that scorched the columns and destroyed dozens of invaluable historical scrolls.

In the light of that red fire, the library brightened suddenly, and they saw all around them had gathered scores of dragons. *Stone* dragons. Bellacrux recognized them as the carved statues that had been fixed atop the columns. Even now, she saw more of the stone dragons break away from their posts with splintering, cracking sounds, and they stretched open their gray jaws with deep groans and dropped to the floor. They formed a tightening circle around the intruders. Their voices—which sounded like rustling paper—whispered sibilantly. "Lehemenn, lehemenn, lehemenn . . . !"

Bellacrux and Valkea stood back to back, the humans under their wings, the Scroll of the Banishing stuck to the floor between them. Enemies they might be, but they would fight together to protect their Locks.

For they had broken the library's first and only rule.

And now the librarians had come.

16

Escaping the Library

Tamra Lennix was drowning.

She'd never learned to swim. There weren't any lakes or rivers around Fortress Lennix that were safe to set toe in; the water was usually choked with ashes and debris from one of the wildfires the Raptors had set, or else stank of rotten eggs due to the sulfur abundant in the mountains. So she'd grown up with a fear of water deeper than her bath.

Now Tamra sank like a stone in an ocean that wasn't even *real*. Which made her angry. It wasn't fair to die in a make-believe world. That would be like dying in a dream. *Stupid*. She clawed at the pale blue water, while all around her, slain ink-and-paper dragons dissolved into dark smudges.

Then a pair of hands grabbed her beneath the arms.

She squealed and went still as Allie Moran swam powerfully for the surface.

The parchment sky was now empty of dragons; those who had been slain disappeared into the sea. There was no sign of the girls' dragon guide. Allie treaded water, holding up Tamra with one arm.

"The exit!" said Allie. "Look!"

There on the ink shoreline, a black doorway had appeared. It looked exactly like the one Tamra had gone through to reach this wretched place. It was a fair swim away though.

Tamra, seized with sudden fear, met Allie's eyes. "Go on, then," she snarled. "Swim to it."

Allie stared at her, her mouth a grim, hard line. "Do you really think I'd leave you to drown?"

"I think we both know you have a score to settle. So just get it over with."

But Allie didn't shove her away. Instead she began kicking her legs, her arm still tight around Tamra's torso.

"You're *saving* me?" Tamra said.

"I'm not like you," Allie said, now breathing hard from the effort of swimming one-handed, Tamra's weight making her work twice as hard. "I don't kill people for fun. Or revenge."

"That doesn't make you better than me! It makes you weaker." Tamra tightened her jaw and said no more; she held grimly on to Allie until they reached the shore. There they both collapsed onto papery land, coughing and gasping. Allie looked exhausted, but she still managed to reach her feet first and sprint for the door.

Gritting her teeth, Tamra charged after her.

They reached it at the same time and fell through the inky black curtain—

—to nearly be scorched in a blaze of dragonfire.

Tamra yelped and ducked, covering her head. Her knees had landed on the hard stone floor of Tashiva Lhaa, but the library was not the silent, dusty place she'd left. Now it was a scene of battle, with burning scrolls and splintering stone falling everywhere. She heard a clatter as the Scroll of the Banishing landed on the ground beside her, rolled tightly once more. It must have opened to spit them out.

"Mirra!" she yelled, looking up. There was her twin, seated atop Valkea. It was the Red's fiery breath that had nearly set Tamra on fire. Now her Lock snarled at her.

Get on!

Stumbling to her feet, Tamra ran to climb atop her dragon.

"Move!" she said to Mirra, shoving her back and taking her seat in the front. "What's happening?"

"We made too much noise," said Mirra in a frightened squeal.

All around them, murky in the shadows, stone dragons hissed and scraped claws over the library floor, sending up sparks. They didn't seem capable of breathing fire, but they were still nearly as large as Valkea and struck like snakes, darting in to rake their stony claws over the Raptor's scales. Valkea whirled and growled, swatting them aside and building up another blast of fire in her belly. Tamra felt her Lock's sides heating up beneath her legs.

In the illumination of Valkea's next fireblast, Tamra saw a familiar Green Grand several rows away, also battling the stone dragons. Bellacrux, the traitor. And the Silver was with her.

"Valkea!" she screamed. "Get them!"

A little busy! her Lock hissed, the thought sharp as a lash in Tamra's mind.

With a roar, Valkea grabbed a stone dragon in her jaws and hurled it; it crashed into a column and shattered—but so did the column. Above, the ceiling of the library began to dangerously groan.

Val, get us out of here! Tamra ordered.

Call me Val again and I'll make sure you never leave this place! But the Red recognized the danger and started toward the door.

The way was blocked by a horde of stone dragons.

There was something more terrifying about their blank stone eyes than if they'd been real dragons. Utterly soulless and wholly intent on destroying the intruders, they advanced like a wall of living rock, clambering over one another in their eagerness to kill.

Bellacrux bellowed and tried to barrel through their midst, stampeding past Valkea. The Green's steps rocked the library. More columns, already weakened by the fighting, crumbled with thunderous crashes, filling the air with dust. Tamra choked and coughed.

Back, back! she said. *There must be another way out.*

Stone dragons were piling atop Bellacrux. That's when Tamra realized she'd lost sight of the Silver and the Morans. Twisting around, she spotted them—vanishing into the deeper recesses of Tashiva Lhaa.

They'd had the same idea as her—find another way out. Bellacrux was buying them time to do just that.

Follow! Tamra told Valkea, but the Red was one step ahead, already giving chase.

A few stone dragons slipped past Bellacrux and pursued them as Valkea bounded through the columns. Atop the Silver, Allie looked back and saw them. Her eyes connected with Tamra's for a second, then she turned back around and the Silver picked up his pace.

With an ear-shattering series of cracks and groans, splinters webbed through the floor and ceiling and up the remaining columns.

The entire library was on the verge of caving in.

Tamra's heart stopped as Valkea launched herself into the air. The Red swerved wildly through the crumbling columns, and

Tamra felt her Lock's panic sizzling through her own mind. Valkea tore at the air, while all around them, stone dragons slithered up the columns and lashed out with their claws. They couldn't fly, but they moved with unnatural speed, flocking over the ceiling and floor like chittering cockroaches. Valkea weaved in and out, her wings pumping furiously. Just ahead of them, the Silver was doing the same.

Tamra leaned low and shut her eyes. She didn't want to see the ceiling come crashing down on their heads.

We will not die here, Tamra Lennix! Valkea roared in her thoughts. *I smell fresh air!*

Daring to hope, Tamra lifted her head.

She saw nothing but the faint glimmer of the Silver's wings, heard nothing but the roar and crash of the collapsing library. Great slabs of stone fell from above and shattered around them, forcing Valkea to veer steeply. Tamra and Mirra barely hung on.

A stone dragon leapt out of the darkness and landed on Valkea's neck, teeth gnawing on the Red's scales. Tamra lunged forward and kicked it hard, knocking it loose. Another dropped onto Valkea's back and bit down on Mirra's cloak.

"Tamra!" she screamed. "Help me!"

But Tamra was more focused on holding on to her Lock.

Valkea shook her tail, throwing off the stone dragon, who nearly took Mirra with her. But the girl unclasped her cloak just in time, and it tore away in the dragon's maw.

Ahead, a burst of sunlight blinded Tamra's eyes. The Silver had found the back door and broken through it, and seconds later, Valkea shot out too. Tamra looked back and saw a humble stone door broken from its hinges in a dingy gray cliffside; it was nothing like the pompous entrance of Tashiva Lhaa. She probably would never have noticed this back door if she'd walked right by it. All around rose the high walls of the canyon, reaching to a dim blue sky.

Valkea landed awkwardly, exhausted. The Silver had set down a few yards away and looked just as tired. The three riders on his back watched the door anxiously.

Bellacrux was still inside. Even Tamra felt a moment of panic for the Green, before remembering she was a dirty traitor who *deserved* to have a million tons of rock dropped on her head. But still, she watched the doorway with her breath held, waiting to see if Bellacrux would make it . . .

"C'mon, Bell!" Allinson Moran cried out. "*Please!*"

Seconds ticked away. The stone wall shuddered and stones crashed in the darkness within. Still the Green did not appear.

Tamra started to laugh. "I guess that's the end of old—"

The wall exploded outward and Bellacrux burst through, bellowing sparks. The former Lennix Grand looked half-mad, her eyes rolling and her fangs bared. She still had a dozen stone dragons clinging to her hide. With a trumpeting, furious roar, the Green planted her claws on the ground and shook.

Stone dragons went flying, crashing into the canyon walls and shattering into shards and dust.

With a great crash that shook the canyon, the library caved in at last, the doorway filling with boulders. All those scrolls and knowledge were buried for good.

A minute of silence passed, filled only by the heaving breaths of the winded, beleaguered dragons. All three were covered in scratches and dented scales, and the Silver's belly was bleeding where Valkea had torn it open in their last meeting. Allie Moran slipped from his back and ran to Bellacrux, running her hands over the Green's scales and then embracing her neck.

Tamra was the first to recover from the mad escape from Tashiva Lhaa.

"Stop them!" she snapped at Valkea. Behind her, she heard Mirra sigh.

The Red made a half-hearted effort to breathe fire, but was simply too worn out. The Silver, however, lifted into the air with an angry snort.

"Seriously?" called Allie, who was climbing onto Bellacrux's back. "After what we just went through, you're *still* trying to capture us?"

Tamra smirked. "Only because I want to watch when Valkea bites your limbs off one by one. But whatever. Fly away. I don't care. We don't even need the Silver anymore." She relished the shocked looks on their faces and couldn't resist adding, "That's right. I know *another* way to reach the Lost Lands, boneheads. So go on—slither off through one of your magic portals and hide. We'll just catch up to you on the other side."

Bellacrux opened her mouth and a funnel of flame came flashing toward Valkea. The Red jumped clear, and when Tamra had blinked away the blinding spots dancing in her vision, Bellacrux and Lysander had taken off together.

She opened her mouth to order Valkea to the chase, but at that moment, the air rippled and the two dragons and their riders vanished through a portal.

Gritting her teeth, Tamra took the Silver's scale from her pocket. She'd nearly been drowned, crushed, and roasted, but by blood and bone, she'd gotten what she'd come for. The memory of the Banishing burned in her mind, filled with Raptors opening portals across a parchment sky—glowing Silver scales gleaming on their brows.

"We lost them," Mirra groaned. "Tamra, what are you talking about? Another way to reach the Lost Lands? That's impossible!"

"Shut up, Mirra," she said. "You don't know anything about it. *This* is all I need. And now I know how to use it."

Then she smiled, and if she'd had a mirror handy, she would have seen how in that moment, she'd never looked more like her mother.

"Enjoy your freedom while you can, cowards!" she called to the spot where the others had disappeared. "Oh yes. We'll see you *very* soon."

17

The Land of Fish and Chips

Joss hung grimly to Lysander as the Silver hurtled through a tunnel of light. Lightning prickled all around, and Sirin's arms around his waist were tight as a shackle. Sammi was crushed between them, and the little Green's claws dug painfully into Joss's back. His whole body hummed, the way it had during the storm over the Blue islands. It felt as though he'd swallowed a thunderbolt.

Crossing portals was not something he thought he would ever get used to, and he was very glad when Lysander finally shot through into a clear evening sky.

The Silver's wings spread and caught the air like sails. Bellacrux, who had been flying close behind, her nose touching Lysander's tail tip, swooped low, flying beneath them. Joss leaned over and gave Allie a thumbs-up, which she returned. Everyone had passed through safe and sound.

"Joss!" Allie called. "Did you hear her? Did you hear what she said?"

Joss swallowed. "About another way to reach the Lost Lands? She was lying, Allie. That's impossible. Only a Silver can open portals, and Lysander's the only Silver alive."

"She seemed pretty sure to me!" Allie replied.

"Let's just stop and catch our breaths," Joss said. "We were almost crushed to death in that place." He shuddered; when he closed his eyes, he could still see the stone dragons scurrying in the darkness, hissing. He, Sirin, Allie, and the dragons were coated in fine gray dust from the collapsing library, and judging by the way they were all coughing, they'd breathed in just as much.

"Do you know where we are?" Joss asked Sirin.

She released Sammi, who wriggled free and lurched into the air, falling a moment before finding her wings. She wobbled alongside them, looking ill from the crossing.

Sirin spotted a large road sign and squinted, barely making out the letters. "Oxford, I think."

She pointed to a large cluster of buildings to their right. It was not as large a city as the one they'd found Sirin in—Lon-Don, he remembered—but it was still bigger than any city in the Dragonlands. Directly below them, the ground was a great green quilt, broken up by lines of trees and shrubs. In the dimming light of day, the world seemed tinted purple.

Joss.

Lysander's thought was so weak that Joss nearly didn't hear him at all. *Lysander?*

I need to rest, Joss. And eat.

The Silver opened his mind a little more, and Joss reeled at the pain and exhaustion emanating from his dragon. His wound, which had been healing, had been reopened in the battle with the stone librarians. And opening the portal while wounded had drained his energy.

"Let's find somewhere quiet to land," Joss said to Sirin.

She nodded and, a few minutes later, pointed to a strip of wooded land by a river. "There. Under those trees."

Lysander needed no convincing. He landed roughly in the brush, while Bellacrux lowered herself more gently beside him. They were in a small wetland, enclosed by trees and scrub, but Joss had seen from the air that it was completely surrounded by houses and buildings.

Allie turned a full circle, staring around them. "Everything's so . . . *green* and fresh. No ashes or smoke or bones."

"Feel that?" said Joss, spreading his arms wide.

"What?"

"*No Raptors.*" He grinned. "That, my dear sister, is what *safe* feels like."

Allie shook her head. "Not for long, if Tamra was telling the truth. She must have found something in the library. But *what*?"

"I told you," Joss said. "She was mad we got away, so she was just telling lies to try to scare us."

Allie only shook her head, unconvinced. She looked up at the clouds suspiciously, which annoyed Joss. They were supposed to be *safe* here. He wanted to go for a day where he didn't have to keep watching the sky in dread and terror. And despite his words, he was worried Tamra *had* been telling the truth. He just didn't want to admit it, not even to himself.

"Raptors or no Raptors, we're still not totally safe," Sirin reminded them. "If someone here found the dragons, they'd be taken away. Locked up. Experimented on."

Joss and Allie stared at her, horrified.

"We just have to keep a low profile," said Sirin. "Don't mention dragons around other people. Don't speak at all, if you can help it. You're in my world now, so let me do the talking. The minute an adult gets suspicious of us, they'll phone the police, and it's all over from there—for us, the dragons, and everyone back in your world that you're trying to save. Got it?"

It was a sobering reminder of why they were here, and what they stood to lose. Would they ever be truly safe? Would they ever find a world where they could just *exist*?

"We're not idiots," said Allie resentfully. "You don't have to tell us what to do."

"This *is* Sirin's world," Joss pointed out. "We should probably listen to her."

"Let's find somewhere to eat," said Sirin. "It'll make us all feel better."

"Eat!" Allie stared at her. "We don't have time for that! This isn't a vacation! We should talk about what I saw in the library scroll and what we should do next. If Tamra was telling the truth—and we *have* to consider she was—then we're not safe here. *Nobody* is safe here. We have to act as if Raptors could drop out of the sky at any moment. Which means we need to move faster than ever and find the Heart before the Lennixes launch whatever plan they're cooking up to reach this world."

Joss sighed. All he really wanted just then was a nap and a chance to wash off the dust that was itching inside his clothes. But he knew Allie was right. They'd never really get a chance to rest until this was all over and the threat of the Raptors was dealt with for good. Especially if they did have another way to reach the Lost Lands. Maybe Tamra had been lying, but Allie was right—they had to act as if she weren't. Everyone was depending on them, in the Dragonlands and in this world too.

"That's all true, Allie," said Sirin. "But we're not the only ones who are hungry. The dragons need food too."

Allie let out a long breath, then nodded, her shoulders slumping. "I guess we can take a few hours to plan what happens next. But no more than that."

"Right." Sirin squared her shoulders. "Into town, then. Sorry, Sammi. You'll have to stay here and mind Bellacrux and Lysander. Promise?"

Joss wasn't sure he liked the idea of leaving Lysander. They had only a little athelantis left, and he carefully applied some to his Lock's cuts, trying not to gag at the awful smell. He wrapped the last pieces of the pulped plant in its oilskin wrapper and put it in his pocket.

Go, Joss, sent Lysander. *I will be here when you return.*

I'm a little scared of this place, Joss admitted. *All those people and buildings. It's so strange here.*

Lysander pressed the fine arch of his brow against Joss's chest. *If you can survive Fortress Lennix, you can survive anything.*

Joss drew a deep breath. "All right, Sirin. Lead the way."

Lysander, if you smell Raptor, you let me know right away.

Go, Joss. I will keep watch on the skies.

They followed a dirt path through overhanging trees. All around, birds chirped and fluttered. It didn't seem so strange a place then—not unlike the hills around the Zolls', where Joss had tended sheep.

But then they stepped out onto a hard stone road. With the woods behind them, they now faced a row of brownstone buildings, like little castles, and a bridge crossing a small river.

"Stay on the sidewalk!" warned Sirin, putting out a hand to keep Allie from crossing to the other side. "There's a car!"

Joss sucked in his breath and flattened himself against the

railing of the bridge as the thing called a car zoomed by. It made a loud, snarling sound. He had liked hearing Sirin's stories about cars; he thought he liked the real thing much less. To his surprise, Allie—ever brave Allie—grabbed his hand and squeezed it tight, looking as spooked as he felt. He squeezed her hand and tried to put on a brave smile for her.

Everything was very neat and fancy; little signs announced the names of the roads: *Frenchay* and *Bainton* and *Hayfield*, though he didn't see any signs of hay or fields anywhere. In the windows of the houses, lights were being lit, and he saw silhouettes of people moving about inside them. Across the road, an old man strolling along gave them a curious look. Joss wondered what they must look like, three kids covered in stone dust and dirt and sweat, all evidence of their recent adventures.

"Those houses . . ." Allie murmured. "So much wood on them. They'd burn in a snap if a Raptor came through."

Sirin grimaced.

"No Raptors here," Joss reminded his sister.

"*Yet*," she said.

"Even if they come," Joss said fiercely, "we'll find the Heart and stop them. And one day, Allie, I promise, we'll live in a house just like these ones."

To his surprise, Allie giggled. "Yes, and I can get Bellacrux one of those." She pointed at a miniature house beside one of the big ones; a glum-looking dog was sitting inside it, blinking at them.

Joss laughed, imagining Bellacrux squeezed into that tiny house, and beside him, Sirin started chuckling too. It didn't totally untangle the knot of dread and nerves in his belly, but it helped a bit.

They found a kid standing in front of one of the brown houses, playing with a black-and-white ball. He was a little younger than Joss, with hair as orange as a torch's flame, and was kicking the ball skillfully, never letting it touch the ground even though he wasn't using his hands. When he saw them, he caught the ball and stared.

"What're you guys supposed to be?" he asked, lifting an orange eyebrow. "Some kind of cosplay club?"

"Yep," said Sirin. "Cosplayers. That's us. Here for the . . . um, convention. Is there somewhere to eat around here?"

"There's a fish and chips place that way." The boy pointed. "*Nerds.*"

"Hey, if you see any funny, fire-breathing lizard shapes in the sky," said Joss, "just a word of advice: hide, don't run. They like it when you run."

"Uh . . ." The boy backed away slowly, staring at Joss like he'd grown a third eye. "What convention are you here for, exactly?"

Groaning, Allie grabbed Joss's arm and hauled him away.

"What?" he whispered in protest. "It's not like I said the *word* dragons!"

Soon they found themselves following a larger, busier road. Joss slowly began to relax and not cringe so much when cars rumbled by. They passed buildings much larger and grander than the houses. These places were like fortresses. Many of them, according to Sirin, were schools. There were schools for toddlers and schools for kids a little younger than they were, and ones for their age and ones for kids a little older. There were even schools for grown-ups.

"Do you do *anything* here except go to school?" he asked, astounded. "Seems as soon as you finish one, you're packing off to another."

Sirin sighed. "Exactly. It never ends. Unless, I suppose, you get carried off by a dragon."

She looked glum, but Joss thought nothing would be more fun than going to school with other kids. He'd heard of schools before, but most in the Dragonlands had been burned down or raided.

After walking nearly twenty more minutes, Sirin led them up to a glassy building that smelled *delicious*. It had pictures on the window of sandwiches, soup, and fish. A little bell rang when they opened the door.

"We don't have money," said Allie. "Are we going to *steal* the food? What if we get caught? I don't think this is a good—"

"Relax." Sirin pulled a card from her pocket. "My mum made sure I would have a little bit of spending money after she . . ."

A blur of sadness, anger, and panic passed over Sirin's face, as it always did when she spoke of her mother. Joss had quickly learned not to ask about her mum. Sirin seemed determined not to talk about her. He remembered feeling similarly after his parents had been killed.

Inside the *restaurant*, as Sirin called it, they sat a table with a smooth, shiny red top. Pictures on the walls showed scenes of castles and sheep, which were probably meant to be nice, but they reminded Joss way too much of Compound Zoll.

A young man with bright orange hair—he *must* have been related to the boy they'd passed earlier—asked them what they wanted. Joss and Allie stared like owls, until finally Sirin said, "Fish and chips for three, please, and Cokes."

In minutes, food arrived in baskets lined with paper. Joss didn't even mind that it was too hot; he began stuffing it into his mouth. He was a little more wary of the black, sparkling liquid called Coke—it looked like it might be poison. But when he tried it, it tasted sweet and slightly spicy and filled his mouth with bubbles. He laughed so hard it shot out his nose. Sirin grinned and handed him a paper napkin.

"Dingbat," scolded Allie. She eyed her food suspiciously, then took a tentative bite of the chips.

Everything was delicious. The *most* delicious food, in fact, that Joss had ever tasted.

Yes, it certainly seems you're enjoying yourself.

Joss nearly choked on his fried fish when Lysander's wry words popped into his head. He swallowed guiltily.

I'll bring you the biggest helping ever! I promise.

You better, or I might have to eat Sammi. The little pest won't stop biting my tail!

"Right," said Allie, slamming down her cup. "Time to talk."

"Fine." He sighed. "What did you find in the scroll?"

"I saw *her*," said Allie. "I saw the Skyspinner. She was . . . enormous. Like a flying mountain. But there were Raptors everywhere too, attacking her. I saw her banish them, and then she fell into the sea."

"Did you see anything that might tell you where she fell?" asked Sirin.

"There was a coastline, with cliffs and trees. It was . . . cold, I think."

"That's it?"

"That's all I saw! It was a little chaotic, all right? Dragons battling everywhere, and Tamra Lennix of all people hanging on to me, apparently figuring out some other way to—Joss, are you even listening to what I'm saying?"

"Huh?" He blinked; he'd been staring at a family that had come into the restaurant. They looked so happy, two parents and three little kids. Should he warn them that Raptors might appear in the sky any moment and burn down this nice fish and chips place and everyone in it if they weren't prepared to fight for their lives?

"Can you draw the coastline?" asked Sirin. "Maybe we could match it up to the real place."

"I could try," said Allie, looking doubtful.

Sirin chased down the orange-haired man and got a pen off him, which she gave to Allie. Scrunching her nose and nibbling her lips, Allie began to draw on one of the paper napkins. Joss drained his Coke and let the bubbles tingle on his tongue before swallowing.

When Allie finished, she showed them what looked to Joss like senseless scribbles.

"Like I said," she reminded them, "it was chaotic."

Sirin frowned and took the napkin. "This doesn't look familiar, but then, I was never much good at geography. That's all right. We'll go to a library tomorrow and look it up on a computer."

"A library?" echoed Joss, with alarm.

"Don't worry," said Sirin. "There's no library in *this* world that ever tried to murder anyone. At least, not that I know of."

"We still need to get dinner for the dragons," Joss reminded her.

"Right. Waiter!"

The orange-haired man came back, eyebrows lifted. "Miss?"

"We'll take twenty orders of fish and chips to take away, please." Sirin handed the astonished man her money card, thought a moment, then added, "Actually, make it *forty*."

18

Shadow Twin

Mirra Lennix was quiet nearly the whole way back to Fortress Lennix. She thought her sister might have forgotten she was even there. Valkea flew high and fast, through turbulent mountain air that made Mirra's stomach queasy. But she said nothing. She already knew neither the dragon nor her twin would listen to her.

She kept reliving the moment in the library when one of the stone dragons had nearly dragged her off Valkea. She'd almost *died*, and Tamra hadn't done anything to help her. Would her twin have even noticed if Mirra had fallen off? Would she have cared?

Probably not. She'd probably be glad to have their room all to herself, finally.

Mirra's thoughts churned like a cauldron of bitter poison, sickening her even more than Valkea's rough flying.

She tried to blame the sheep boy and the Lost Lands girl. Their words had crawled into her ears and begun rearranging her brain until she wasn't sure of anything anymore. But she found her anger kept turning to other targets—to her ma, to Tamra, to herself.

She was desperately unhappy.

When Fortress Lennix finally came into view, clinging to its mountain like an oyster on a rock, Mirra had never been more confused to see her home. She wished, suddenly, that Declan was there waiting for them. She had a feeling he would be the only person in the world who might help her understand the tangle of thoughts in her head.

Valkea angled sharply for the landing yard, and Mirra finally spoke up, murmuring in her twin's ear as she held tightly to her middle.

"Tamra, are we . . . *bad guys?*"

Her sister snorted. "Blood and bones, Mirra. You know what ma says. There's no such things as good guys and bad guys. Only—"

"I know, I know. There's only Ráptors and sheep." Mirra sighed.

"Sometimes I wonder how we're even related. You really are stupid."

There's a difference between quiet and stupid, Mirra thought.

With a roar to announce their arrival, Valkea tilted her wings to slow her descent, then her talons threw sparks as they dragged along the floor of the landing yard. Mirra waited until just before the dragon stopped completely to jump down.

Her sister leaped off next, gave Valkea a pat on her nose, then strode off toward the loggia and their mother's tower sanctum.

Gritting her teeth, Mirra hurried to follow. She'd risked her life in that library. She wasn't about to get left in the dark again. So she darted behind Tamra like her twin's shadow. It seemed like she had always been doing just that, forever lurking behind her sister, never getting her own place in the sun.

Tamra just gave her an annoyed look but didn't tell her to

shove off. So together they climbed the long stair to D'Mara's tower, where they found their mother sticking sharpened sheep-bone pins into a leather map on the wall. It showed all the lands around the fortress, and Mirra guessed she was monitoring the search parties scouting for the Silver. By the dark look on her face, she also guessed those search parties had turned up zilch. On her desk were scattered writing instruments and beeswax candles; it looked like the workstation of a madwoman. Messy ink spills had left dark stains everywhere, and who knew how long that half-eaten leg of lamb had been sitting on top of those maps and charts.

Without even asking if they could enter, Tamra marched in and slammed the Silver scale onto D'Mara's desk, making all the quills, parchments, and inkpots on it rattle.

"I know what we have to do," she said breathlessly.

D'Mara scowled.

Afraid they might begin fighting, Mirra tucked herself into the corner to watch, standing between a small dragon skeleton assembled with strings and a suit of scaled metal armor.

"Where have you been?" D'Mara demanded in a dangerously calm voice.

"Tashiva Lhaa," said Tamra, not quailing a bit.

Mirra noticed her sister didn't mention that the very Silver their mother was hunting had also been at the library. She knew why, of course. D'Mara would be furious with them if she learned they'd let their quarry slip through their fingers again. Besides, it wasn't like the Silver was still in Raptor territory, and thus within their reach. She had seen it vanish with her own eyes, Bellacrux too.

Then Tamra said, "I have the key to the Lost Lands, Ma. And this time, I know how to use it."

Mirra unfolded her arms and leaned forward. Tamra had refused to tell her what the whole library trip had been about, and what she intended to do with the Silver scale, but Mirra had figured it was some sort of plot to breach the portals.

She really *wasn't* stupid.

You think more than you talk, Declan had once told her. And he'd been right. So now Mirra listened, and thought, and said nothing at all.

D'Mara looked like she was about to bite Tamra's head off, but then she glanced at the map on the wall, and all those pins that may as well have spelled out FAILURE. Then she sighed and sat in her desk chair, which was wood covered in gray wolfskins.

"Go on," she said.

Tamra looked ready to combust with smug self-satisfaction. "I figured if there was ever a time Raptors needed to open portals, it would have been when they left the Lost Lands. It was a mass exodus—thousands and thousands of dragons all flooding from that world to this one at once. I thought, How many Silvers could there have been? Surely there was another way for them to access the portals. So I found the story of the Banishing in Tashiva Lhaa, and guess what? *I was right.*"

D'Mara leaned forward, looking truly interested now. She picked up the Silver scale and turned it over; it reflected the gleam of her candles and sent glittering flecks of light bouncing around the chamber.

"What did you see?" she asked.

"I saw a scale just like this one embedded on the forehead of every single Raptor. Not just worn, like a headpiece—but *forged* onto their own scales. And I realized, that's how the scale worked for Valkea and me before. Just before we went through the portal, that traitor Bellacrux blasted us with fire. The flame must have been hot enough to partly melt the scale onto Valkea's, and that gave her the power to use it. I pried it off later, having no idea that I'd just made it useless again."

Their mother leaned back, still turning the scale in her fingers.

"If this works, we will enter a new era, girls. The Lost Lands would be *ours*, after years and years of dreaming and planning and disappointment." Her eyes began to shine, as if she were already gazing upon the wildfires set by their dragons. Mirra remembered what Sirin had predicted: Raptors razing her lush green world, destroying it as they had destroyed this one.

"I can test it," said Tamra. "I'll take Valkea to that blacksmith whose family we imprisoned. He'll do anything we ask. Valkea's already agreed."

"No," said D'Mara. Her hand closed around the scale, and she stood, her eyes gleaming. "Not Valkea."

Mirra smirked as the color drained from her twin's face. Surely Tamra hadn't thought their mother would give such power to *her* and Valkea. If the scale really could open portals, D'Mara would keep it all to herself.

But Tamra wasn't ready to give up. "You—you can't use Krane!" she spluttered. "His scale fever's flaring up again."

D'Mara nodded. "I'll use Zereth."

"That hothead? He's Kaan's dragon."

"They haven't Locked. Actually, I'm starting to think there's not a dragon alive who *will* Lock with that useless boy. Zereth is strong and fast, and he'll jump at the glory in being the one who leads us to our true home."

Mirra was sure there was much more to her mother's choice than that; there were always layers and layers to her scheming. Not that Mirra particularly cared what D'Mara's reasons were. It was enough simply to see Tamra turning red with frustration. Served her right. She'd always been D'Mara's favorite. No matter how harsh or ruthless Mirra tried to be, it was never enough to best Tamra, as Tamra herself loved to point out. So Mirra took particular delight in watching her sister be put in her place by their mother.

"Fine," said Tamra. "Take it, then, like you take everything. But I want something in return."

"Since when do *you* make bargains with *me*?" hissed D'Mara. "I am your mother, and head of this clan! You'll do as I demand and you'll be grateful I notice you at all!"

She strode past Tamra and out the door.

When her twin turned around, her fists clenched and eyes furious, Mirra laughed outright.

In two steps, Tamra crossed the chamber. She slapped Mirra hard across her face.

With a gasp, Mirra held a hand to her cheek, and tasted blood where her sister's hard silver ring had cut her lip.

"There," said Tamra nastily. "That took the smirk off your face. Now get out of my way, idiot."

She stormed out after D'Mara, leaving Mirra trembling and blinking away tears of pain. She sank down to the floor, listening to the screech and roar of the Raptors at dinner below.

"They were right," Mirra whispered. "We *are* the bad guys."

19

A Blue Clue

Joss and Allie emerged from their respective dressing rooms in jeans and trainers, looking bit dazed but now dressed like any other normal kids. Well, except for Joss's T-shirt, which was two sizes too big. Yawning, Sirin sent him back in to change it.

She had not slept well the night before, curled in the park with Sammi's bony wings jabbing her back. They'd set out at sunrise, stopping first at a bakery for jam-filled donuts and directions to the nearest library. The clothing shop had been a last-minute detour.

"They itch," Allie said, tugging at the collar of the navy sweater Sirin had found her. "I don't get why we have to waste time buying clothes. We should be figuring out where to find the Heart."

"Did you see how people were looking at you two? We're supposed to be *avoiding* attention, not shouting for it. If we walk into a library looking like hobbits, people are gonna notice. Now you fit in, just regular Earth kids."

"We're neither regular *nor* from Earth," Allie protested. "What's a hobbit? And why are these trousers so tight?"

"They're called jeans. And you look nice," said Sirin. "Just one last thing . . ."

She hunted a bit, then returned with a hairbrush and pack of scrunchies. "Want me to . . . ?"

"I can brush my own hair," snapped Allie, grabbing them. "We're not *idiots*, you know. We might not have grown up in this fancy, weird world of yours, with your fish and chips and zippers and . . . whatever *these* are." She waved the scrunchies. "But we're not helpless babies."

Sirin stepped back, feeling a prickle of heat on her face. "I never said you were stupid! Remember how I stumbled around when I first arrived in *your* world? If it weren't for Joss, I'd never have managed it all. He helped me, and so I'm trying to help you."

Allie scowled. "You want to help? Fine. You can help by figuring out where the Skyspinner fell. No more, no less."

"I know what your problem is," said Sirin. "And I get it. This is all overwhelming. You're trying to save *two worlds*! Anybody would be feeling stressed."

"I'm not stressed! I can handle this."

"Of course you can! But that doesn't mean you have to be so strong and bossy *all* the time. It's okay to admit you're a little—"

"Bossy! Just because *I* am trying to focus on our mission, instead of always stopping for snacks and shoes? Ever since we got to the Lost Lands, *you're* the one who's gotten bossy!"

Sirin gasped. "I have not! I'm just trying to—"

"*Help*, I know, yeah, yeah. I forgot this is all some storybook quest to you." Huffing, Allie turned away, leaving Sirin to fume in silence. Honestly, what was the girl's problem? Why couldn't she just admit she was feeling in over her head? And Sirin *was* only trying to help.

Joss came out again, his clothes right side out this time. He looked suspiciously between the girls, as if suspecting they'd been arguing. In a slick red windbreaker and gray hoodie, he appeared as if he might be on his way to school. He grinned at his own feet, shod in the high-top sneakers of neon yellow so bright it hurt Sirin's eyes to look at them.

"They're ridiculous," said Allie. "A Raptor would spot them a league away."

Joss folded his arms. "I have been nearly burned, crushed, buried alive, *eaten*, and struck by lightning in the last week. I deserve these shoes. I'm keeping them."

Allie and Sirin exchanged exasperated glances; for that moment, it almost seemed as if their argument had never happened.

"Fine," Allie said, throwing up her hands. "At least if it gets too dark, we can use them as a torch."

Sirin paid for the clothes, relieved when the transaction went through. Then they filed out of the shop and onto the sunny street, and already Sirin felt more at ease. No one stopped to stare at them anymore.

A new pair of shoes can make anyone's day brighter, whispered a voice.

Sirin stiffened, at first thinking it was Sammi. But no, it came from a deep place within her own mind.

The voice was her mum's.

It had been years since she'd said it to Sirin, and years since Sirin had remembered it. But now the memory was so sudden and tangible that it stole her breath away. She'd been knocked down at school by bullies, who'd then torn up the painting of her house she'd made for her mother's birthday. So her mother had taken her, still sobbing, to the nearest shop, where she'd bought her the most lovely pair of sparkling red shoes. And her mum had been right. Sirin had danced home in those shoes and worn them until the soles tore.

"What's that, Sirin?" Joss asked. "Did you buy it in the shop?"

She blinked away the memory, feeling gutted. "Huh?"

He pointed to her hand, which was clutched at her throat. Without even realizing it, she'd pulled the dragonstone from under her shirt and was now gripping it tightly.

"Oh," she muttered. "It's nothing. Just an old piece of jewelry."

Her hand dropped to her side, letting the pendant slipped back under her shirt. Tears bristled in the corners of her eyes; she stubbornly dashed them away and steeled her jaw.

"Right," she said. "Library."

Crossing the street, they went into the big glass-and-concrete building, and straight toward the reference desk.

"So many books," whispered Allie, looking around.

"Are we sure we're in a hurry?" asked Joss mournfully, gazing at a display of picture books about buses.

"Don't worry," said Sirin. "Once we've defeated the Raptors, you'll have all the time you could want to visit libraries."

Behind the reference desk, a librarian was sorting piles of books. She looked like a kind granny, with fluffy gray hair and a large, glittering bumblebee brooch, but when they approached, she scowled.

"Yes?"

"Hello," Sirin said brightly. "We'd like to find this, please."

She put down the napkin with Allie's drawing on it.

The librarian blinked at the napkin, then at Sirin. "What?"

"We have to figure out what bit of coastline this drawing shows. We're doing a . . . geography project, for school."

"Yes, school!" Joss added happily.

Sirin sighed, while the librarian stared at the beaming Joss.

"Don't mind my cousin," said Sirin, fixing a rigid smile on her own face. "He's from . . . out of town. Out of country, actually."

The librarian muttered, "I swear, it's something new every day. All right, then, wait a moment."

Her computer keys tick-tacked for a few moments, while she muttered and shook her head and made various guttural noises that soon had Sirin exasperated.

"Anything?" she asked.

The librarian peered at her. "No matches that I can find. It's just not enough to go on. Do you know the scale of this drawing? What hemisphere, even?"

Sirin looked at Allie, and Allie shrugged.

"Thanks, anyway." She sighed, reaching for the napkin. But the librarian tapped it thoughtfully.

"Now, this, though, does look familiar."

"What!" Sirin squinted at the line she'd indicated. It looked like nothing to her, just a random squiggle. "What is that, Allie? Waves?"

"It's a . . ." Allie glanced at the librarian, then whispered, "A *Blue*."

"A what, dear?" asked the librarian.

"It's nothing," Allie said. "At least, it's nothing that can help us find out where this is."

"Then why'd you draw it?" asked Sirin.

Allie shrugged. "Maybe because it nearly smashed me out of the sky? Look, it's just some Blue dragon whose wings got ripped off by Raptors, and it fell into the ocean and swam away."

"I *beg* your pardon?" The librarian removed her glasses in order to better peer at them. "Is this some sort of game? Are you wasting my time on purpose?"

"I—I meant to say—" stammered Allie.

"Honestly!" huffed the librarian. "As if I haven't got enough to do without delinquents making games of me! Where are your parents? And why aren't you in school?"

"Oh," Sirin said. "We, um, we *are* in school. This is a history project."

"I thought you said it was for geography." The librarian scowled. "I'm calling your teacher."

"No! We're sorry!" Sirin said hastily, trying to push Allie and Joss along. "And we're off, see?"

They retreated to an enclosed reading nook padded with brightly colored pillows. There Sirin made them sit while she studied the squiggle on the napkin.

"I'd rather deal with *dragon* librarians," said Joss, watching the circulation desk anxiously.

"She might have been onto something though," muttered Sirin. She kept turning the napkin around, looking at it from all angles. "Allie, you're *sure* you saw a wingless dragon swim away from the battle?"

"Are you saying I'm lying?"

"No! It's just . . . how would it have got through the portals to the Dragonlands, if it couldn't fly?"

Allie tilted her head. "I guess it couldn't have."

"So it must have been left behind."

"I suppose."

"And if it *were* left behind . . ." Sirin's heart began thumping. It seemed a ludicrous idea, but then, the very existence of dragons had seemed ludicrous to her just weeks ago. "It might have been spotted by humans. They might have told stories of it, long after the other dragons had disappeared. Perhaps it lived on for centuries. How long *do* dragons live? How old is Bellacrux?"

Allie looked a little embarrassed. "I've never asked. But she told me once that according to legend, dragons lived longer in the Lost Lands than they do now. Something about the air being better here, and the water cleaner. And in our world, they can live to be over a thousand."

"So it's possible the Blue *is* still alive. And if we could talk to it, it could tell us *exactly* where the Skyspinner fell!"

The Morans exchanged looks.

"Well . . ." Joss stammered. "Your world seems pretty big. Even if it were alive, how would we know where to find it?"

"It could be anywhere," said Allie.

"That's the thing," said Sirin, so excited she jumped to her feet. "See this squiggle? The librarian was right—it *does* look familiar. It looks just like some old pictures I've seen in books. And if I'm right, then I know *exactly* where this Blue dragon has been hiding for the last two thousand years."

"Where?"

Sirin grinned. "How would you like to visit Scotland?"

20

The Forging of Silver

D'Mara would have preferred to keep her mission to reach the Lost Lands a secret, at least until she knew whether or not it would turn out to be a success, but it was not to be. It must have been Valkea who'd talked, spreading word of the Silver scale's power to the other Raptors. And so, when D'Mara reached the landing yard and found them gathered, buzzing with the news, she gritted her teeth and decided to pretend this had been the plan all along.

"Tamra," she said. "Send for the rest of the clan."

Her daughter, who was still sour-faced after losing her bid to make Valkea their first Forged Raptor, did as she was told. D'Mara knew the girl demanded watching; she was getting too independent, with too many *ideas*. Normally she'd have sentenced Tamra to some terrible post—such as scouting the wastelands or standing sentry atop Mount Lennix—as punishment for running off on her own mission like that, especially at such a crucial time for the clan. But the possibility of the scale's power was too great to be ignored. D'Mara could not postpone testing it.

In the future, however, she would have to keep a closer eye on her ambitious daughter, particularly since she'd Locked to their most ambitious Raptor. Tamra and Valkea made for a formidable pair, and they could be magnificent indeed—so long as they remained under D'Mara's control. If they went truly rogue and turned against her leadership, she would be in grave trouble. This was certainly a big reason why she could not allow Valkea to be their first Forged. That would be too much power in the hands of Tamra and the ferocious Red. The rest of the Raptors could very well desert her entirely if that were to happen.

In moments, Tamra returned with Edward and Kaan, while Mirra came slinking down from the tower, a bright red spot on her cheek. D'Mara barely noticed it; she watched the dragons, and let them watch her, waiting for her to speak. Silence was a powerful tool when wielded well, and she allowed it to rope the Raptors into her control. They quieted one by one, their eyes turning to the head of the Lennix clan.

"My brothers and sisters," she said at last, when the yard was quiet. "By now you've heard the news."

She nodded to Valkea, who stared back at her with gleaming dark eyes. D'Mara was sure Tamra had relayed to Valkea that she would not, in fact, be the one to be forged with the Silver scale. Clearly Valkea was not happy with this decision, but she seemed to be holding her tongue for now.

"Behold," D'Mara said in a strong, clear voice. She raised her hands, clenching the scale above her head. The Raptors chuffed and growled at the sight of it, flashing silver in the sun. "This is the scale of a Silver, and according to legend, it may be our key to the Lost Lands. But nothing is certain, and this legend bears testing. And so I personally will embark on a mission to discover the truth, and I must have a dragon of strength and cunning to accompany me."

Across the throng, she saw Krane lift his head.

I am sorry, my love, D'Mara sent to him. *Not this time. You know why.*

Krane only gazed at her in a way that ripped her heart.

Unsettled, D'Mara had to gather herself before she could speak again. "Where is Zereth?"

A murmur rippled through the Raptor ranks. Scaly heads turned to look around, but there was no sign of the young Red.

Then Valkea spoke, her dragonsong clear and steady. "Tragically, young Zereth was wounded this morning in a training exercise. His wing was injured. He won't fly for weeks, poor creature."

D'Mara stared at Valkea, working very hard to show no emotion, even though shock and fury were exploding in her head. *Accident, my left boot*, she thought. Obviously Valkea was behind this. She must have learned through Tamra that D'Mara intended to forge the Silver scale onto Zereth, and so she'd arranged for the Red to meet with an accident. That was a bold move. *Too* bold. Striking down another Raptor in D'Mara's own fortress? Valkea was on the verge of a full-scale revolt. D'Mara couldn't possibly go on a journey to the Lost Lands and leave Valkea here to scheme behind her back. No, there was only one thing D'Mara could do, though she hated being backed into a corner like this.

Valkea watched D'Mara hungrily, no doubt fully aware that D'Mara was thinking through all of this.

"Ah," said D'Mara, scrambling to recover. "That is too bad, because I was going to tell Zereth to take charge of the next mountain patrol."

Valkea tilted her head, eyes gleaming. She knew—they all

knew—that that was Valkea's primary responsibility. Glancing to her left, D'Mara saw Tamra watching her with narrow eyes.

"Yes," D'Mara continued. "Because I have been watching you, Valkea, and you have proven yourself to be a worthy Raptor indeed. Therefore, I have chosen you to be our harbinger, the first Raptor to enter the Lost Lands since our exile began. We will fly together, you and I."

More than a few Raptors looked at Tamra, probably thinking how unconventional it was for a human to fly with another's dragon Lock. Tamra, to her credit, held her tongue, but D'Mara didn't miss the look that passed between her daughter and Valkea. If she had to guess, she'd say the Red was telling Tamra to stay out of it.

D'Mara couldn't let her rage at being outmaneuvered show. Instead, she had to turn this to her own advantage. Fine, she would fly with Valkea—but Tamra would stay behind. She had to keep them separate, at least until she figured out a way to curb their ambition permanently.

Feeling the weight of both Tamra's and Krane's betrayed gazes, D'Mara lowered the scale and beckoned Valkea nearer. "We will go now to the smith, who will forge this scale onto your brow. Do you accept this mission, Valkea the Red?"

Valkea gave a single nod. D'Mara could have sworn the Raptor was smirking at her.

"Then we will delay no longer." D'Mara climbed onto Valkea and settled into place. Tamra turned and disappeared into the fortress without a word, but she was clearly unhappy with this arrangement.

"Clear the yard!" D'Mara ordered, and the Raptors withdrew

to either side, opening a clear path to the runway. With a snarl, Valkea threw herself forward. D'Mara leaned low and held tightly on as Valkea reached the end of the cantilevered platform and launched into the sky. She caught her breath—the Red really was a strong flier. She hadn't realized how old and infirm Krane had gotten until she felt the power of this young Raptor beneath her. Valkea roared, circling over the fortress in a superfluous show of pride, then winged south, toward the village where the blacksmith was.

Farrelara me soll, sa nar Mifra a te, whispered Krane in D'Mara's thoughts. *Farewell, my soul friend; may the spirit of the air be with you always*. It was a strange message to send, given that it was usually only spoken upon the death of one's Lock.

I wish it was you, she returned truthfully.

Then she and Valkea were out of sight of the fortress, and her connection with Krane weakened. If he replied, she did not hear it.

21

Escape from Oxford

Sirin, Joss, and Allie were halfway back to the park where the dragons were hidden when the bus they'd caught suddenly braked. With startled cries, the passengers looked around and demanded an explanation. This was not an ordinary stop, and traffic jammed on both sides of the street.

Sirin couldn't have explained why, but her stomach dropped. Dread flooded her system, until she felt glued to the hard plastic bus seat.

"Something's wrong," said Joss. "Sirin?"

Her mouth dry, Sirin leaned across him to look out the window. There were two uniformed policemen approaching the bus, waving for the driver to open the doors. The driver did, and the policemen came aboard. They showed a piece of paper to the driver, who nodded, turned in his seat . . . and pointed directly at Sirin.

"Oh," whispered Sirin. "Not good."

"Who are they?" asked Allie.

"Police. That librarian must have called them. I *knew* I should have worn a disguise!"

"Sirin Sharma!" called the first policeman, who began edging through the crowded bus toward them. "You've had a lot of folks very worried. If you'll just come with us, then, like a good girl."

Sirin turned to the others. "Upstairs! Quick!"

They scurried out of their seats and darted for the stairs, Sirin taking the rear. She was nearly grabbed by the collar, but the policeman was a second too slow.

"Hey!" he shouted. "Blasted delinquents. There's no way out up there!"

"Go, go, go!" Sirin yelled. They burst onto the upper deck, which was even more crowded than the lower, and pushed through the students and tourists crammed in.

"Where are we going?" asked Allie.

Sirin pointed up.

The emergency hatch was overhead, just out of Sirin's reach. Without a word, Allie pointed to her own shoulders, and ducked so Sirin could scramble up. She wrestled with the hatch, while adults yelled at them to cut it out. The first policeman had reached the top of the stairs and was trying to push his way through to them.

"Back off!" Joss yelled. He pulled from his pocket the last remaining wad of athelantis, wrapped in its oiled leather pouch. When he opened it, the rancid, rotting smell filled the bus. Gagging, cursing passengers scrambled to back away from the smelly, sticky, dripping mass in Joss's hands, which he swung around, flinging gross-smelling droplets everywhere.

"I will use this!" he warned.

The press of passengers blocked the policeman's path and gave Sirin time and space to wrench open the hatch.

"Let's go!" she shouted. She stood on Allie's shoulders and pulled herself up, then, lying on her stomach, extended her hand downward. Allie climbed up next, using the backs of the seats to clamber out. Joss was last out of the bus. He tossed up the stinking athelantis first, which Sirin caught with a groan. She held her breath, trying not to wretch from the ghastly stench, and stuffed the wad of leaves into the side mesh pocket of her new backpack.

Once they were all atop the bus, they slammed the hatch shut. All around, cars were honking and drivers yelling, and another policeman stood in the road, shouting at them to not move.

"We have to get away from here," said Sirin.

"They're after *you*," Allie pointed out. "Not us."

"We're not leaving her!" Joss said, staring incredulously at his sister.

Allie scowled, but at least she didn't press the possibility.

"Oh no," Sirin moaned as the sound of sirens reached their ears. "More police are coming."

"We're trapped!"

Desperately, Sirin looked around and spotted a tall van stopped next to the bus. It was still a fair jump, but she thought they could make it.

"This way!"

Without waiting to explain, she leapt from the top of the bus and onto the van; the vehicle rocked beneath her when she landed. Allie and Joss jumped to either side of her, leaving sizable dents in the roof.

Then they were off again, jumping to the next car, then the next. Then their feet hit the sidewalk and they took off at a run.

"We have to lose them before we can circle back to the dragons!" shouted Allie.

"Duh!" said Sirin.

They cut left down an alley as the sirens grew deafeningly loud—and Sirin realized the police were already cutting off the exit. Skidding to a halt, she panted for breath and looked around.

Suddenly Sammi's voice burst into her head. *Sirin! What's wrong? I am coming!*

Panicking, Sirin turned left and pelted down the sidewalk, knocking over a café sign and nearly tripping over a startled cat. *Stay put, Sammi! I'm fine!*

You don't feel fine. You feel afraid!

Stay put! We will come to you when it's safe!

Then, around the corner just ahead, three officers appeared, blocking the way to the park. Sirin skidded to a halt, her legs tangling with Joss's, and they both fell hard. Allie tripped over them and landed with a grunt.

In a pile of limbs, hair, and still-attached clothing tags, the three of them looked up in dismay as the police casually closed in. There were two men and one woman. They shook their heads at the children.

"You just had to do a runner, eh?" panted the one who'd nearly caught them on the bus.

"Still," said the woman, "good effort."

Sirin, Sammi sent again. *Watch the skies.*

Sirin met Joss's eyes. He looked at her steadily, then his gaze flicked to Allie's. Allie looked back and gave the tiniest nod. They'd gotten the same message as her.

"Now get up and play nice," said the first officer. "We'll sort out who's who at the station. Miss Sharma, there is a very frantic social worker looking for you."

Just like that, the real world came grasping for Sirin, trying suck her back into the black vortex she'd barely escaped from the night she'd met Joss, Lysander, Allie, and Bellacrux. And Sammi. Her Lock. She couldn't leave Sammi. She couldn't go back.

Sirin's temper flared.

She *wouldn't* go back to Life Before.

She was a dragon's Lock. She'd traveled between worlds. And she was on a very important mission with two people who needed her.

"All right." She sighed. She extricated herself from Joss and Allie and stood. "You got me. Fair is fair."

"Good girl," said the first policeman. "Come along, now, and no more games. I've got a cramp in my leg already, and I'll be very cross if you—"

"Do this?" asked Sirin.

She bolted left, into traffic.

The police shouted; she didn't stop. Cars slammed on brakes and blasted their horns. Sirin slid across the hood of a little green car while the driver leaned out the window to yell at her. She heard Joss and Allie behind her and knew the police would be steps away.

Running down the center stripe of the street, Sirin felt her heart pounding in her ears. And even with cars screeching to halts all around her, she kept her eyes fixed on the sky.

Until she saw them—three dark shapes descending from the clouds, wings whipping up a gale.

"SAMMI!" she yelled.

Up and down the road, people began screaming. She saw a man get out of his car and fall to his knees, pulling the cap off his head. Children poked their heads out of windows and gaped. A window washer, stunned by the sight, dropped his sopping brush onto the head of a teenage girl.

The dragons swooped so low their wing tips brushed the buildings on either side of the street. First came Sammi, dipping and diving like a hawk. Then came Lysander, gleaming bright and baring his fangs. Behind him soared Bellacrux, who let loose a roar that rattled every window for blocks around. People on the sidewalk covered their ears or ran screaming. The great Green's shadow darkened the street.

Sirin leapt, planting one foot on the fender of a van and using it to vault into the air, where she caught hold of Bellacrux's outstretched talon. Allie caught the other, and Joss was plucked up by Lysander.

Allie climbed up quickly, then extended a hand to help Sirin.

"Thanks," Sirin said.

She looked down. The police were staring wide-eyed. One had taken out his baton and held it up uncertainly, as if it were a sword and he were Saint George.

But once their riders were settled in place, the dragons swooped upward, their wings blasting a gale that sent hats, papers, coats, and even a small cat tumbling away. As Bellacrux's wingbeat overturned a flower cart, petals and blossoms went spiraling over the street, making the whole thing look like a strange and magnificent parade.

"That was *awesome*!" Joss yelled.

Sirin laughed. "We made it!"

"This time," muttered Allie.

As Oxford shrank away and a cool northern wind rose to meet them, Sirin's spirits rose too. She'd escaped again. The real world had receded for now. The black, hungry vortex of rage and sorrow that had opened up in her mother's hospital room wouldn't have her yet.

"Right," she said. "Next stop: Scotland."

22

Out of Exile

D'Mara supervised the forging closely, watching every movement the smith made. Melding dragon scales together was a delicate process, even more so when the scales were still attached to a live dragon. It had to hurt quite a lot, but Valkea bore it silently, her eyes shut and her only sign of pain a thin tendril of smoke that curled from her nostrils. D'Mara was impressed by the dragon's fortitude.

The smith embedded the Silver scale in the center of Valkea's forehead, where Tamra said the ancient Raptors had borne theirs. To fit it, the smith first had to pull out one of the Valkea's own scales, and a trickle of dark blood ran down the Red's snout from the procedure. But not once did Valkea grumble or complain.

"There," said the smith at last. He was a brawny man with a large black beard and a bald head, but despite towering over D'Mara, he quivered at her approach. "Mistress Lennix, if you're pleased with my work, perhaps you'd consider freeing my family now? I beg you."

D'Mara almost snapped at him to shut up but bit her tongue. "If this scale works," she said, "and the Lost Lands are opened to us at last, then of course your family will be returned to you."

She had no idea what state the man's family was in. For all she knew, they'd already been made into Raptor snacks. But it didn't matter. Nothing in this world would matter once she reached the Lost Lands. She might well never return here again.

But the smith's work was admirable. The Silver scale looked as if it had grown there on Valkea's skin. It was held in place by small points all around it where the smith had welded the metal of her other scales to it. The only way it would ever be removed would be if half the scales on Valkea's face were pulled out by their roots.

D'Mara laid her hand on the Silver scale, and Valkea let her. She shut her eyes and tried to feel its power, but it only felt cold.

"We will return to the fortress," she said. "And then you, Valkea, will lead the First Flight into the Lost Lands."

"Somarla lessa," said Valkea. *Let it be so.*

They flew in a line, ten dragons connected nose-tips-to-tails. The flight was short two—wounded Zereth was limping around the landing yard, looking more injured in spirit than body, and Edward and Decimus remained to oversee patrols and other Lennix business.

They had departed the fortress in a frenzy of roars, trumpeting calls, and jets of celebratory flame as the other Raptors wished them luck and good fortune on their mission. Valkea flew high and proud, clearly basking in the attention. The rest of the First Flight drifted into formation, a long line of dragons that snaked through the air. Eventually the fortress fell behind them and they steadied enough that each one could reach out and gently take the tip of the next one's tail in their teeth, linking together. Valkea led the line, piercing the sky at a steady pace, intent on finding the first portal she could. D'Mara leaned forward in anticipation, her heart hammering and her palms sweaty. She hadn't felt this nervous or giddy since she was a little girl. It was hard to believe that after generations of Lennixes, *she* would be the one to finally lead them all home.

Out of exile.

At last.

They flew only ten minutes before Valkea suddenly tensed. The spines along her crest seemed to ripple, and she let out an excited, high-pitched bugle. D'Mara glanced over her shoulder to see the other Raptors still neatly lined up behind them.

This was it.

All at once, the scale on Valkea's forehead lit up like a beacon, and then the sky at her nose began to part. It twisted and pulled back, and next thing D'Mara knew, they were shooting through a tunnel of light. Her skin prickled and her hair rose. She gasped and clung tightly to Valkea, not blinking for a moment. It felt as if they had dived into the heart of a tornado. Valkea seemed to be struggling, smoke streaming from her nostrils, her muscles seizing. D'Mara leaned forward and saw the Silver scale was burning so hotly it was giving off smoke.

Had something gone wrong? Had Tamra's instructions been faulty?

Alarmed, D'Mara looked back to see how the other Raptors were faring—but they were alone. No other dragons darkened the tunnel of light twisting behind them. The other Raptors hadn't made it through.

"Valkea!" yelled D'Mara.

But the Red didn't seem to hear her, and instead released an earsplitting roar. She pumped her wings furiously, snarling, as if she might reach the Lost Lands by force of sheer fury alone.

Then they burst into blue sky, over a quilted landscape.

It had *worked*.

The world below was not D'Mara's. It was green and lush and—blood and bone, there were several hundred fat, lazy sheep waddling around just below! D'Mara had never seen so many in one place.

"The stories were true," she said. "All the stories were *true*. Valkea. We're home."

"Fala Terrana," confirmed Valkea. *The Lost Lands.*

"It's beautiful," D'Mara whispered. "And soon it will all be *ours*."

She felt the sting of tears in her eyes, which startled her. Blinking them away, she looked all around as Valkea spiraled to the ground. There was a settlement nearby, and a few small houses, but mostly they were surrounded by hills of green. She wished Krane were here to see it. Tentatively she reached for her Lock, wondering if she would send him a mental picture of what she saw, but she felt no connection to him at all. That left her feeling hollow and uneasy, as if she'd left behind half of herself.

"I need to eat," said Valkea. "And rest. The passage . . . it was not easy."

The Red did look unsteady on her feet, her eyes slightly unfocused. The Silver scale still glowed faintly, like a star on the dragon's brow.

"Very well," said D'Mara. "Then I shall have a look around."

Leaving Valkea to take her pick of the unattended sheep,

D'Mara began hiking toward the town she'd seen. She had to think, and decide what to do. Because clearly, there were limitations to crossing portals with only a Silver scale. The other Raptors had failed to make the crossing. D'Mara could well imagine what had happened—her and Valkea vanishing while the rest of them scattered in confusion, still trapped in their own world. They'd have returned to the fortress by now and told the others. A Forged dragon *could cross* through a portal, but only alone.

Nonetheless, as D'Mara picked her way across the field, avoiding piles of sheep dung, she considered this mission to be a success. They'd reached their goal. Now they just needed a way to get the rest of the Raptors through.

They would need more scales.

Which meant they still needed the Silver dragon after all. The search wasn't over. But where could he be? In D'Mara's world, hiding out with the Red or Yellow clans? Or might he and his wretched boy, Joshua Moran, be in the Lost Lands too?

"Where are you, Lysander?" she muttered.

The town slowly came into view, and D'Mara circled it before entering. She watched the humans walking around, getting in and out of strange, horseless carriages that spit black smoke from pipes and made a terrible racket. Children shouted and kicked a ball around in the street, until an elder yelled at them to clear out. A mother pushed a baby in a little wheeled contraption while taking loudly into a small metal tablet she held to her ear.

Some of the things they used looked strange to D'Mara, but the people looked like any other people she'd seen. How much fun would it be to drop into their midst atop Valkea, spreading flame and smoke and destruction? She savored the image a moment, then stepped out from behind the fence she'd been hiding behind and strode boldly into the street.

A few people glanced at her curiously, but no one spoke or called out. In her own world, D'Mara's presence would be met with screams of terror and people throwing themselves down for mercy. But here, she was no one. It was like being in disguise. These country folk had no idea their future *queen* was walking among them. D'Mara laughed aloud at the idea, and that got her a few more odd looks.

Then D'Mara's laughter cut short, as she stopped in front of a building with a large glass window. It had a sign that read THE WINKING SHEEP TAVERN & RESTAURANT. Inside, people were sitting at a counter, drinking from mugs, and large glass tablets on the wall above them glowed with magic. D'Mara kicked open the door, startling the patrons. She ignored their grumbles and instead watched the shining magic tablet. On it, pictures moved and people spoke, looking as real as if they were truly trapped inside the glass, but D'Mara figured this was some Lost Lands sorcery at work.

But there was no doubting what she saw on that glass.

"It's a prank, obviously," said one of the patrons, an old man with several empty mugs in front of him. He gestured at the picture-glass. "Some publicity stunt."

"My cousin lives in Oxford," said another man. "He saw the whole thing!"

"But *dragons*?" said the first man. "Really, Harry, you'll believe anything."

D'Mara watched the picture-glass as it showed a shaky view of three undeniable shapes—each of which D'Mara was intimately familiar with.

A Green hatchling.

A Silver dragon.

And the traitorous, black-hearted swine of a former Lennix Grand, Bellacrux.

They were swooping over a crowded street, picking up three children. D'Mara recognized Allinson and Joshua Moran right away.

They were *here*, in the Lost Lands! And there, on Lysander's gleaming hide, were the shining scales D'Mara still so desperately needed. Forget the Silver himself. With his scales, she could rescue the entire Raptor population out of exile.

"You!" snapped D'Mara, grabbing the one called Harry by his collar. The man choked, eyes wide. "You said your cousin lives in this *Ox Ford*, where the dragons were spotted. So tell me—how do I get there? Speak fast, man, or I'll prove to your friend that dragons can be very, *very* real indeed."

She listened closely while the terrified man stammered out directions. The other people in the Winking Sheep Tavern & Restaurant watched them with expressions of shock and confusion.

Soon, D'Mara Lennix would finally have the Silver in her grasp. No bumbling children or husbands or Raptors would mess it up this time. She would take care of it herself, swiftly and decisively.

She would have the Silver . . . and every one of his gleaming scales.

23

The Dragon in the Lake

Allie was glad to be on Bellacrux again. The smell and crush of the city had been suffocating to her. All those people, and those rumbling cars, and Joss looking around as if they'd reached paradise . . . She couldn't stand it. And then, of course, there was Sirin, smugly pushing them around from one shop to the next, gloating in her familiarity with this world. Rubbing in the fact that they were outsiders here. Calling Allie *bossy*! Honestly!

Is that quite fair? asked Bellacrux. *You have been on edge ever since we got here.*

Allie grumbled under her breath and glanced up at the silhouette of Lysander, flying above them. All she could see of Joss and Sirin were the soles of their shoes. Sammi flew alongside them, her small wings fluttering like a moth's compared to the Silver's long, gliding form.

The land below spread like an endless quilt, pleasantly green and wrinkled with shimmering rivers. Town after town appeared, some no bigger than the village Allie had grown up in, others a hundred times as big. The larger ones they avoided, so she only saw them in the distance. She wondered if news of the dragons' appearance was spreading.

All the more reason to find the Heart as quickly as possible. They were running out of time.

They flew low, to avoid being detected by what Sirin called *air-planes*, and so their pace was slower due to the more turbulent air. Sirin had said they could probably make it to this Scotland place in six hours flying at their fastest, but at this pace, it would take twice that. Allie saw several air-planes above, silver birds rumbling and snarling through the air. They made her shudder.

Near evening, Sammi zipped down to squeal at them. Still lacking the gift of dragonsong, the hatchling's high-pitched voice was mere babble, but it was the signal from Sirin that Allie had been waiting for. It was time to land.

Lysander took the lead, following instructions from Sirin. She had a large map purchased from the library shop earlier and had been navigating their trip. Now Allie saw her point to a lake below. Long and very narrow, its waters seemed to shift in color, gray to blue to green. The dragons angled for its shore, flying fast and silent.

They landed on the sloping western bank in a tangle of trees and brush. The wind howled over the water, sending choppy little waves breaking over its rocky shore. It was easily the wildest spot in the Lost Lands Allie had yet seen. She'd been starting to wonder whether there was any true wilderness left in this world.

"Well," said Sirin as she as Joss walked over to Allie, "here we are. Loch Ness, home of the Loch Ness Monster, or if we're lucky, the Loch Ness *Dragon*."

"Do you really think there's a two-thousand-year-old Blue hiding out down there?" asked Joss.

Sirin shrugged. "All I know is that that squiggle Allie drew looked *just* like the old photos people said they took of the monster. Some of those photos were proven fake, but not all of them. And there are hundreds of stories, people claiming they saw it. Sometimes it was in the water, sometimes it was in the trees or crossing the road."

"This lake is *massive*," said Allie. "Where do we even begin?"

I think, my Lock, Bellacrux sent, *it is time for us dragons to take over for a bit.*

Bellacrux exchanged looks with Lysander, and the Silver nodded. Sammi squealed and darted into the air, as if eager to begin.

"Right," Allie said. "You three probably know best."

"How will they do it?" asked Sirin.

In response, Bellacrux tilted her head back and released a long, ululating trumpet. Allie had heard a similar sound echoing across the Blue islands, when the dragons had been calling to one another. It was not a roar, which would be throaty and terrifying; instead, Bellacrux's call was more like dragonsong, musical and articulate, warbling notes that might have come from a bird, had the bird been the size of a house.

After a moment, Lysander joined in, and then Sammi's high, young voice also joined in, though her notes weren't quite on key.

Allie, Joss, and Sirin moved closer together, watching their Locks with wide eyes.

"Incredible," said Sirin, speaking loudly to be heard even though the Morans were standing shoulder to shoulder with her. "They're magnificent."

"Yes," said Allie. For once, they were in perfect agreement.

After a few minutes of calling, the three dragons fell silent. They stared at the dark water and waited.

And waited.

And waited . . .

Until ten minutes had passed and nothing—dragon or monster—appeared.

"It's not here," whispered Allie, first to break the disappointed silence. "It probably never *was!*"

"No, I swear there are stories!" insisted Sirin. "There's *something* here, there has to be! If people can tell stories about dragons for hundreds of years, and *those* stories can turn out to be true, then surely this one can too!"

"Stories!" retorted Allie. "Of course it's all just *stories* to you!"

"What is that supposed to mean?"

Joss put up his hands. "Allie, Sirin, don't fight! Not now!"

"I want to know what she means," said Sirin, still glaring at Allie.

Allie crossed her arms. She wanted to unleash it all on Sirin right now, tell her *exactly* what she thought. She was about to do just that but was stopped by a snort from Bellacrux.

Listen, the Green told her.

I don't want to listen! Allie sent back. *I've listened to her too long. We should be back home, looking for the Red or Yellow clans to see if they know anything about the Skyspinner, not chasing Lost Land legends at the word of a girl who still treats all of this like some storybook adventure!*

No, you hotheaded hatchling of a girl. LISTEN.

Allie frowned and looked toward the lake.

The water was rippling more than it had been . . . as if something were moving toward them. The waves lapping the shore got stronger and harder, slapping the gray-and-black rocks and even reaching high enough to break on the trunks of the slender trees.

"What," said Joss, "is *that*?"

Looking from the shore to the lake, Allie saw a high wave rushing toward them. It was taller than even Bellacrux and moved too swiftly for them to possibly outrun. Allie yelled, remembering the wave in the Scroll of the Banishing that had swept her and Tamra from their dragon guide's back. She turned and grabbed Joss, trying to shield him, as the water finally dashed over the bank and washed them all off their feet.

In the chaos of the miniature tsunami, Joss was ripped from Allie's grasp. She tried to scream but the wave was receding into the lake and dragging Allie with it. She rolled roughly over the rocks and roots and brambles, the wind knocked from her lungs and her limbs scraped and bruised. Then she was pulled into the cold lake and dragged under, and that's when she realized it wasn't the wave gripping her—it was a pair of *jaws*.

Bellacrux! she called out silently. *Help!*

Don't move, Allie! Bellacrux replied. *Go limp! Like a dead sheep!*

Allie did as she was told, letting her arms and legs go wobbly, though her heart continued to race against her chest. She saw bubbles streaming all around her, but beyond them, the water was too black to reveal anything more. The jaws were clamped around her hips, and though she stared through wide eyes, she saw only the occasional oily gleam of scaled lips around yellow, stubby teeth— the teeth of an old dragon, worn nearly down to the gums.

Then Allie was pulled upward, as the creature holding her

reared its head from the water and rose, high, high above the bank, its sinewy neck towering over the three dragons and Joss and Sirin below. Allie was hanging facedown, so it wasn't till she worked up the nerve to turn her head that she saw the thing holding her.

She saw the underside of a powerful jaw, and the gleaming dark blue scales lacing the dragon's throat, and when it cocked its head slightly, she caught one glimpse of a gleaming, coal-black eye. Below her, churning in the shallows of the loch, was the rest of the dragon's body—oily coils of scales and flesh and legs, and two wretched stumps where its wings had once been.

It *was* the Blue Allie had seen in the story. Only this time, the dragon was definitely not made of paper and ink, but of scale and bone and the *worst* dragon breath she'd ever smelled.

"Stehfa, malki, shefini lon tarralan," said Bellacrux. *Excuse me, friend, but that human is mine.*

The Blue snarled and released a hot cloud of putrid, fishy breath that rolled around Allie and made her gag.

In dragonsong, Bellacrux added, "We honor your territory, old one, and beg your forgiveness for our trespassing here. But our need is great. Please release my human. She is small, but she is mine."

Allie felt the Blue's jaws tighten, its stubby teeth pressing against her ribs, and she gasped. It would bite her in half with barely an effort! Below, Bellacrux and Joss both stepped forward, her brother's hands raised.

"Please!" he called, before switching to dragonsong too. "Lafaarla!"

"Lafaarla," repeated Bellacrux, and then the Grand did something Allie never dreamed she would see: The great dragon lowered her head to the ground, eyes shut, then rolled onto her back, exposing her vulnerable white underbelly.

It was the ultimate sign of submission, baring one's weakest point.

Opening her eyes, Bellacrux rumbled, "Leshi tamar lak asha-fetarla."

We come in the name of the Skyspinner.

At once, Allie felt the Blue's jaws slacken. The dragon seemed to sway, as if dizzied, and then a long, low moan sounded in its throat. Allie braced herself as another wave of hot, stinking breath rolled over her.

Then the Blue gently lowered its head and let Allie drop onto the bank in front of Bellacrux. The Green rolled over, shaking mud and leaves from her scales, and then she quickly pulled Allie behind her wing.

In a voice as old as mountains, rumbling like distant thunder, the Blue spoke.

"Ness, old pal," it rasped, as if it hadn't spoken in hundreds of years. To Allie's surprise, it spoke not in dragonsong, but in *human* speech. She'd never met a dragon who could speak it. "Are these . . . what I think they are?"

Then, in a higher voice with a strong accent, the Blue replied to its own question: "Ach, no, Thorval, they cannot be!"

Just as quickly, the Blue switched back to the first, deeper voice. "But, Ness—"

"How many times have I told you?" he interrupted himself, changing tones yet again. "There's no such thing as dragons. Obviously these are fakes. If anyone should know what a fake looks like, it's us! God knows how many phony monsters have been dropped in our loch."

"So you've said, Ness, so you've said," rumbled the dragon, in its first voice. "But still . . . that sound they made . . . I could swear it made me remember something . . ."

The Blue dragon continued arguing with itself, switching between the two voices so quickly and effectively that if Allie weren't seeing it with her own eyes she would have thought it were two different dragons entirely. All the while, the lake's waves lapped over the Blue's tail and hindquarters, and the three humans and their dragons stood blinking and silent on the rocky shore.

I fear, Bellacrux sent to Allie, *that this will not be easy.*

24

The Monster and the Dragon

It took about ten minutes of the Blue dragon's rambling before Allie had had more than enough.

"QUIET!" she shouted.

The Blue dragon's jaw snapped shut. He stared at Allie.

"I'm sorry," she said. "But we're in a bit of hurry here. We just have a few questions and then we'll leave you alone."

The Blue grimaced. "If that's what it will take to be rid of you, then ask them quick, before old Thorval loses his temper. I really can't be responsible for him when that happens."

"I saw you," Allie said hurriedly. "In the last battle against the Raptors, before all the dragons were banished from this world. Well, I didn't *see* see you, I saw you in a scroll, in a library, and—oh, never mind. Just tell us, *please*, where did the Skyspinner fall?"

The Blue snorted, then spoke in the higher, strongly accented voice. "I don't know what you mean, lassie. In fact, I shouldn't be talking to you at all. My brother, Thorval, came running the moment he heard your phony dragons here bleating to the skies, the poor fool."

"Your *brother*?" Allie asked. "It's just you here!"

"Nonsense."

"But—but I am *looking* at you! Nessie, Thorval, whatever your real name is. *One* dragon!"

"Dragon!" The Blue made a hissing, choking sound that Allie slowly realized was laughter. "There is no such thing as dragons, small human. I am a *monster*. In fact, I am *the* monster, I'll have you know. Humans come from all over the world to look at my lake."

I see, sent Bellacrux. *This one's mind has split. Thorval is the dragon we seek, but losing all his brethren two thousand years ago must have broken his mind, driving him mad with loneliness. So he invented this monster, Nessie, and now they think they are brothers.*

"It's Thorval we have to talk to, then," Allie muttered. She turned to the Blue dragon, then started over again in a more tempered tone. "Nessie, perhaps you could let your brother, Thorval, tell us a story about a great many dragons battling in the sky? And a dragon queen who fell into the sea?"

With a shriek, Nessie withdrew slightly, sliding deeper into the water. "Not that story! That story frightens poor Thorval. Thorval doesn't like to remember it. In fact, he has forgotten it entirely."

"Surely he can remember *something*?" Allie smiled, trying to look encouraging. "How about you let us ask him?"

Nessie shook his head. "He's gone now. Back to our secret caverns deep, deep below. It's better this way. He is safe there, away from these poking, prying humans with their camera phones and noise."

With a shudder, Nessie slid even deeper into the water. Now his whole back was submerged and only his long neck stuck out of the water.

Careful, Allie, Bellacrux sent. *If he goes under, we may never see him again.*

Then Sirin stepped forward. "Hello, Nessie. I'm Sirin. I'm a great admirer of yours, you know."

"Oh?" Nessie preened a little. "How lovely to meet a fan. But no pictures, please."

"How clever you are," said Sirin. "And so brave and noble too, protecting your brother, Thorval."

Nessie narrowed his eyes, as if growing suspicious of her motives. "Yes, I am quite noble."

"I also know how difficult it is to talk about things that have . . . hurt us." Sirin's voice sounded a little rougher. "Sometimes, it seems better not to talk about them at all, so that we don't have to feel the bad feelings they stir up. Believe me, I know. I . . . I know what it's like to lose everyone you love and feel all alone in the world. It's the worst feeling of all."

Allie watched Sirin, her own heart hurting at the sudden memory of her parents being snatched away by Raptors. She felt a hand take her own and turned to see Joss at her side. She squeezed his hand.

Boldly, Sirin stepped forward and put her hand on the Blue's nose. He startled a little, but then let her hand remain.

"Thorval," Sirin said. "It doesn't have to go on like this anymore. The dragons—*your* own kind—are ready to return to this world. They need to return to it, because terrible things are happening to them where they are now. We need to bring them back, Thorval, us and our Locks and *you*. To do that, we need to find the Skyspinner. Please, tell us where she fell."

"I . . ." The Blue dragon shivered, then suddenly dropped his head onto the rocky shore. "I can't. I don't want to remember them."

"Remembering is . . . is how you keep them with you."

The Blue dragon looked as sad as any creature Allie had ever seen.

"They left me," he said. "All of them. My brothers and sisters, my clan. They *left* me."

Sirin nodded and stroked his nose. "It must have been awful."

The daylight was fading fast. Long shadows stretched over the narrow loch, its murky waters turning opaque black. Fewer and fewer cars drove along the road across it. And up on the hill above them, Allie thought she saw a shadow move. She peered hard at the spot, but it was too dark to make much out. Had a human heard the dragons' calling after all, and come to investigate? If they had a camera, Thorval would vanish at once.

"Sirin," Allie whispered. "Hurry."

"Thorval," Sirin said, "we don't have much time. Now is your chance to do what even the Skyspinner couldn't do—save the dragons. All of them."

"It's her Heart you want, isn't it?" Thorval asked.

Sirin nodded.

With a deep, rumbling sigh, Thorval said, "Then know she fell off the coast of a continent west of here. They call it the *Oosa*."

"Oosa?" echoed Sirin. "Wait—you mean the USA?"

"Like I said, the Oosa."

"Do you know where on the coast the Skyspinner fell?"

"I only know that centuries later, humans began to build a great city there. I swam back once—I have tunnels down below that lead to the sea, you know—and I saw it. Great tall buildings, so many boats and humans with *cameras*, and a giant green woman standing on the same island where the battle began. Honestly.

How rude! It ought to have been a memorial to all the dragons who died there."

"A giant green woman," said Sirin, her eyes widening. "I know where that is!"

"Then go," said Thorval. "I don't want to talk about it anymore."

"You've been brilliant, Nessie—er, Thorval. Really! Thank you!"

He snorted and began to withdraw, his neck sliding into the water. "I don't know why you want the Heart though. If you know the story of the Skyspinner, surely you know what the Heart truly does."

"Truly does?" echoed Allie. "What do you mean? It controls the minds of dragons."

"Aye," said Thorval, with just the top of his head still above water. "But at what cost?"

Then he vanished into the black lake with the smallest of ripples and was gone.

They stared at the spot he'd been, but he made no reappearance. Allie didn't think he would. He'd probably gone back to his deep caverns, to forget his own past all over again. She almost wished him luck; it had been clear in his ancient, sad eyes how much sorrow he'd carried over the centuries.

Farrelara, ancient one, she heard Bellacrux say. Her Lock gazed at the lake. *May you find peace.*

"May we all," Allie murmured. Then she turned to Sirin. "So. You know where the Skyspinner is, then?"

"Yes," said Sirin. She still looked shaken from her conversation with Thorval, but there were no more tears in her eyes. Instead she looked at Allie with steely resolve. "I know exactly where to look. It's called New—"

Sirin was cut short by a thunderous roar from atop the hilly bank.

They all spun just as a massive Red dragon came barreling toward them. There was no time to react. No time to think.

All Allie could do was scream as Valkea and D'Mara Lennix fell upon them in a storm of claws and fangs and dragonfire.

25

The Ultimatum

Sirin had been facing the lake, so when something slammed into her from behind, at first she thought it was Sammi fooling around. She landed hard on her stomach, and quickly rolled onto her back—only to see a dragon's claw come pressing down on her, pinning her to the damp earth. There was no mistaking the Raptor tattoo on its belly. A moment later, the dragon released a jet of fire, spraying the bank. Sirin gasped and covered her face with her hands, her new coat barely protecting her skin from the intense heat.

She heard screams and roars around her. *Sammi!*

Her Lock replied only with a ferocious growl. Sammi was unharmed but scrambling to avoid the Raptor's next blast of fire.

Then Bellacrux hurtled from the left, slamming into the Raptor and pushing it off Sirin. Sirin leapt to her feet, gasping for air. The two great dragons rolled and clawed at each other, knocking over trees and sending rocks rumbling into the lake with great splashes.

Sirin saw Joss and Allie standing by Lysander, and started to run their way, but then a hand grabbed her from behind. Before she could react, she found a blade nudged beneath her chin and a chilly voice in her ear. She could only move her eyes, which she tilted upward to see a tall, black-haired woman standing over her. Nearly as terrifying as the Raptor, the woman looked to Sirin like an evil sorceress from a story, her eyes glinting with terrible intention.

SIRIN! screamed Sammi.

She sensed her Lock nearby, still hidden, but vibrating with the urge to defend her. *No, Sammi! Stay back. I can handle this.*

"Keep still, little girl," said her captor, "and you might yet live."

"Wh-who are you?" Sirin whispered shakily.

"Your future queen, that's who." The woman laughed, then called out, "Well, well! If it isn't my ex-son. Hello, Joshua."

"D'Mara Lennix," said Joss. "Let her go!"

"How did you find us?" demanded Allie.

"Oh, that," said D'Mara, waving a hand. "That was easy, given that everyone in Ox Ford could talk of nothing but the three dragons they'd just seen. From there, it was simply a matter of sniffing you out. It's as if you *wanted* to be found." She pulled something from her pocket, and Sirin recoiled at the familiar and pungent odor wafting from it.

An athelantis leaf.

Sirin gasped and looked down. The mesh pocket in her backpack, where she'd shoved the leaves after Joss had thrown them to her on the bus, had torn open. She must have left a trail of the reeking leaves all the way from Oxford to Loch Ness—a trail that would have been invisible to most, but not to a dragon like Valkea with her superior sense of smell.

"But how did you get through the portal?" asked Joss.

"It is astonishing, is it not, what one can discover in a library?" said D'Mara. "For example, my Tamra discovered the power of a Silver's scales to open portals, when forged onto a Raptor's own skin. But clearly, she missed the even *bigger* story."

"She heard everything," whispered Allie in horror.

"The Skyspinner's Heart," said D'Mara, tasting each word as if it were a delicious piece of chocolate. "A jewel with the power to control dragons' minds. How *intriguing*. You know, I'd heard stories when I was little, rumors of ancient dragons born out of stars and endowed with miraculous powers . . . but perhaps they were more than just stories."

Behind them, Sirin could hear the battle between the Raptor and Bellacrux growing ever more ferocious. Snarls and bright blasts of fire filled the gloaming sky.

"There's no proof of that," said Joss. "It probably *is* just a story."

"Well, if I've learned anything this week, it's that there is more truth in stories than one might believe. After all, here I am!" She gestured around them with her sword, before quickly returning it to Sirin's throat. "So, you're the girl from the Lost Lands. You're the one who knows where to find the Heart."

"Sirin, don't tell her anything!" ordered Allie.

D'Mara pressed the sword harder against Sirin's skin, until she felt blood running down her neck.

Sirin! I will bite off her head! I will chew on her bones!

No, Sammi! Stay!

"Stop!" cried Joss. "We'll tell you everything, just let her go!"

"No!" Allie said. "Joss, we can't let her get the Heart at *any* cost!"

"Not at the cost of Sirin's life!"

"Enough!" ordered D'Mara. "Sirin, is that your name? Well, Sirin, it's your life. It's your choice."

Sirin swallowed, but her throat felt like it was stuffed with sandpaper. "Will—will you let the others go, and not harm them?"

"You can't trust her," said Allie. "Sirin, be quiet!"

Sirin breathed harder, her skin cold, her heart galloping. "Please," she whimpered, tears running from her eyes. "Please, don't—*umph!*"

Something crashed into Sirin and D'Mara, knocking them both over. Sirin rolled down the bank, stopping herself from falling into the water by grabbing a sapling just in time.

Above her, she saw Sammi attacking D'Mara Lennix. The small dragon scratched like a cat, but the woman clearly knew how to handle an angry hatchling. She jabbed Sammi at a nerve point beneath her jaw, and the little Green fell limp.

"SAMMI!" screamed Sirin.

D'Mara threw up her arm. "Valkea! To me!"

The Red disengaged from battling Bellacrux and thundered to them. She shot a blast of fiery breath to hold Lysander at bay while D'Mara climbed onto her back. With Bellacrux closing in from behind and Lysander roaring ahead, the Lennix leader seemed torn about what to do. Then her eyes briefly connected with Sirin's, before looking down at the unconscious Sammi in her arms.

"One day!" she shouted. "You have one day to give me both the location of the Heart . . . and the Silver."

She pointed her sword at Lysander.

"You know where to find me. One day, or the hatchling dies . . . *slowly.*"

With an earsplitting screech, the Raptor launched into the sky. Bellacrux didn't even wait for Allie to mount up before giving chase, but in seconds, a flash of light above signaled the opening of a portal, and the Raptor, D'Mara, and Sammi vanished.

26

Brimstone Lake

Triumph tasted oh so sweet.

D'Mara resisted pumping her fist in the air, and instead held on tightly to her small, scaled prisoner.

Valkea flew quickly over the ravaged Raptor lands; they were leagues from the fortress, but at this pace, they'd reach it in a few hours D'Mara had until then to plan her next move. She reminded herself that victory was not quite in hand, though she felt buoyant as a leaf on the wind.

The Skyspinner's Heart!

All the dragons that had slipped through her fingers or defied Raptor law, even *Bellacrux*, would be hers again. And this time, the Green would be utterly obedient—after D'Mara made her suffer awhile for her treachery. Oh, the very image was enough to fill her with glee!

So enraptured was she by her visions of a glorious future that D'Mara didn't realize Valkea was landing until the dragon was touching down. Lurching forward at the impact, D'Mara nearly dropped Sammi.

"Valkea!" she snapped. "What are you doing?"

They'd landed on a small, rocky island in the middle of Brimstone Lake, a sulfuric pit of yellowish water—that was boiling hot. Acrid steam choked D'Mara's nostrils, the rotten smell strong enough to even wake Sammi. The hatchling shrieked in terror at the sight of the boiling-hot water all around them and the putrid steam clogging the air, and she didn't even try to fly away.

"Valkea!" roared D'Mara. "What are you doing?"

"Thinking how best to tell the woeful tale of D'Mara Lennix, and how she fell gloriously in battle against Bellacrux in the Lost Lands."

D'Mara's skin went cold. She swallowed, her mind racing.

"I will not kill you, D'Mara," Valkea said in a taunting tone. "You are a warrior, and I honor that. So I will instead leave you here to decide your own fate."

It was clear what Valkea meant: D'Mara could sit on this rock until she starved, or she could attempt to cross to the shore. But the water would boil her alive in minutes. It *was* a death sentence, and a particularly cruel one. She tried to call out for Krane, but though she felt her Lock, it was as if he were a sparrow on a distant mountain—barely seen, and certainly too far away to notice her. Even if her Lock went searching for her, he might never find her in time to save her life.

"So," she said, her voice calm. She met Valkea's gaze. "You've finally worked up the nerve and made your move. You are very fierce, it is true. But how long will it take for you to oust Decimus and my husband and all our *loyal* Raptors? There will be bloodshed, of course. How many followers will you lose? And look at you, you're still battered from your tussle with Bellacrux."

Valkea snorted, but watched her warily.

"Valkea. Listen to reason. It is clear you are a born leader of dragons—"

"I will be *queen* of the dragons! Only I may enter the Lost Lands! I will claim the Skyspinner's Heart and all her power!"

"Yes, yes," said D'Mara, flapping her hand as if waving off the insensible shouts of a child. "That is . . . unless Bellacrux claims it while you're busy fighting Decimus and his Raptors. After all, those Moran brats know where it is. You'll become Bellacrux's puppet."

Valkea snarled, and D'Mara knew she'd painted the worst possible picture in the dragon's mind. If there was anyone Valkea hated more than D'Mara, it was Bellacrux.

"But if *I* name you as the Lennix Grand," D'Mara said slowly, "no one will question it. Not even Decimus."

Clearly this caught Valkea by surprise. The Red was momentarily speechless, but then she shook her head. "I don't trust you."

"Of course you don't, no more than I trust *you*. But we could be great together, you and I, if we stopped working against each other. We were pretty great back in the Lost Lands, weren't we?"

Valkea made a throaty noise of assent.

"Still," the dragon said. "I would need more than your word. I would need your ultimate trust."

"Very well." D'Mara knew the dragon hadn't fully discarded the idea of leaving her for dead, and for her life, D'Mara could bargain anything. "What can I do that will make you trust me?"

"You can make me your Lock."

The words slammed into D'Mara's like a cascade of rocks. She reeled.

"I—I am already Locked," said D'Mara, her mouth suddenly dry. "As are you!"

"To weaker partners. Krane is old and sick. Tamra is fierce but young and foolish."

"Is such a thing even possible? I've never heard of a dragon or human taking new Locks while their old ones lived."

"There is a way. There is a ritual. Like you said: We could be great together, you and I."

"I can't do this, Valkea. Krane is . . . Krane is everything to me." He was her life's only love. He'd been with her since she was a child. He knew her better than anyone, and what's more, he loved her back.

He *trusted* her.

"No," she whispered. "I'll give you anything, Valkea. But not this."

"Then," said the dragon, "I suppose this is farewell, D'Mara Lennix. If I must take command of the Raptors the hard way, then so be it. My reign will be all the stronger for it."

Valkea's wings stirred the sulfuric steam, making it swirl like a tornado as she rose into the air. D'Mara gaped, while Sammi cowered behind her. The Red was really doing this—leaving her to die. How had this happened? Minutes ago, everything had been in D'Mara's grasp: the Lost Lands, the Skyspinner's Heart, ultimate power, and an unbreakable crown. Yet in the space of a few heartbeats, she had lost it all. Even her life was being taken from her.

"Valkea! I'll give you anything else—anything at all!"

But the Red was already vanishing, as the steam wrapped around the rocky island and cut D'Mara off from the outside world. She felt as if she were suffocating. Calling again for Krane, she found only silence.

D'Mara had never felt terror like this before.

Dropping to her knees, she thought of Krane. Her Lock, her love, her only friend. The only good thing she had in this world.

She remembered what her mother had said to her: *Are you a Raptor or a sheep?* And years later, when her mother was dying and she'd been passing rule of the fortress to D'Mara: *Command will cost you everything, daughter. But power is only forged through sacrifice.*

Despite herself, she began to imagine what Locking with Valkea would achieve. She'd no longer have to watch her back for betrayal within the Raptor ranks. The Raptors would be united at last, at their strongest, just in time to raid the Lost Lands. And Valkea was strong, fierce, ambitious—all the things D'Mara admired most in herself. They wouldn't be a great match . . . they would be a *legendary* one. Together they truly could rule two worlds.

All it would cost her was the one she loved most.

Are you a Raptor, D'Mara Lennix, or a sheep?

Well, she was no sheep.

There was only one thing D'Mara could do.

She put her trembling hands to her cheeks and felt tears there. Her heart pounded, unwilling, but her mind overruled it.

Power is only forged through sacrifice.

I am no sheep.

I am a Raptor.

D'Mara Lennix stood up. She drew a deep breath. "Forgive me, my love," she whispered.

Then she called out, "Valkea!" It felt unnatural and twisted, as if she were bending all her joints the wrong direction. But she forced herself to do it anyway.

"Valkea! I . . . I will do it. I will accept you as my Lock."

For a moment, she heard only silence. Perhaps she was too late. Perhaps she really was too weak. All around her, the stinking fumes of the Brimstone Lake swirled and coiled.

Then, two red eyes materialized in the mist. Wretched in a sulfuric cloud, Valkea stalked toward her.

"Then come with me, D'Mara," she said. "And let us perform the Rite of Sundering."

27

A Flight Divided

In the stunned silence that followed D'Mara's attack, Joss thought it might have all been a dream. It had happened so fast, with no warning, and then all at once it was over.

But Sammi was gone, and that had been no dream.

"Sirin," he gasped out at last. "Sirin, are you okay?"

Sirin had fallen to her knees, her eyes wide, staring at nothing. It was more frightening than if she'd been sobbing uncontrollably. She looked . . . *empty*.

Joss skidded down the bank to her and took her shoulders in his hands. "Sirin?"

The shock is great, Lysander told him. *Being separated like that, so suddenly . . .*

Joss nodded. He remembered what it had felt like when Lysander had been taken from him at Fortress Lennix. While Kaan had flown on *his* dragon, Joss had been locked in a cell, feeling like his heart had been torn from his chest. Whatever it was that connected a human to a dragon, that bond was stronger than any other force in nature. So having it torn or stretched too far hurt like having your lungs pierced.

Sirin drew a deep, shuddering breath, and finally focused her gaze on Joss. "She's gone," she rasped. "Sammi!"

"We'll get her back."

"Everything gets taken away," said Sirin. "Everything and every-one. My dad when I was little, my mum just *days* ago, and now Sammi. Why do I always end up alone?"

"You're not alone. I'm here. And we will rescue Sammi."

With a hiccup, Sirin lifted her head. "*Please*," she whispered. "Joss, it hurts."

"I know," he said. "C'mon, stand up. We'll set things right, so don't give up hope yet."

They stood, Sirin leaning on Joss. He'd never seen her like this, so fragile. She'd been so strong, jumping into their world and all its dangers with both feet and never complaining. But now she looked thin and hollow.

"Joss," said Allie, with a look of warning, "you know how bad this is, right? The Raptors have found a way to cross *portals*. And now, even worse, D'Mara Lennix knows about the Skyspinner's Heart. It's just a matter of time before she finds it, with or without our help. We *have* to find it first. Our world and this one *literally* depend on it!"

"It'll take days to reach the city Thorval told us about," said Sirin. "I know where to look now, but it'll still take time to find the Heart. And Sammi will . . . Sammi will be gone before then."

"She won't hurt Sammi," said Allie. "That hatchling is her only leverage. She's bluffing."

"You can't know that!" Sirin shouted. "If it were Bellacrux's life in danger, would you risk it?"

"We could all go now," said Joss. "Stage a rescue. With Lysander and Bellacrux working together—"

"Against scores of Raptors?" Allie shook her head. "It's madness."

"But we could *try*."

"You're being an idiot, Joss."

"You're being heartless, Allie!" said Joss, looking hard at his sister. "We are family. We stick together. And Sirin's one of us now, and so is Sammi. If it were me in that fortress, you'd tear it apart to rescue me."

Allie looked down; he was right and she knew it.

"Bellacrux agrees with me." Allie put a hand on the Green's shoulder. "She says the Heart is the most important thing, and we cannot risk the Raptors finding it first."

Bellacrux nodded.

Joss, said Lysander. *We have to save Sammi. That little eggbrain is a pest, but she's a member of our flight. Our family.*

I agree, Lysander. But how do we convince Allie and Bellacrux?

The Silver sighed and couldn't offer a reply.

"You're *glad* she took Sammi, aren't you?" said Sirin suddenly, narrowing her eyes at Allie.

"What?" Allie's jaw dropped open.

"You *are*! All along, you've been looking for a way to get rid of me. You think I'm too soft, that I'll just slow you down."

"I . . ." Allie reddened. "Well, it's more complicated than that. But it doesn't change the fact that the Heart—"

"The Heart, the stupid Heart!" shouted Sirin. "I'm sick of it! Ash was right. It's more trouble than it's worth."

"It's the answer to all our problems."

"It's not the answer to Sammi's problem! Which is, oh wait, I remember: *getting killed!*"

"Sirin, just tell us where the Heart is. The sooner we find it—"

"I'm not telling you anything."

"What happened to you being a member of the team?"

"Oh, so *now* you want me to be on the team?" Sirin threw her hands in the air. "*Now* you want to listen to my ideas?"

"Stop!" Joss said. "Both of you!"

They ignored him and kept arguing, their voices getting louder and louder until even Bellacrux was groaning.

Joss walked away. He couldn't listen anymore. He agreed with Sirin, but he also saw Allie's point. With the Lennixes now hunting the Heart too, there was more at stake than ever before.

Joss.

Stopping, Joss sighed and turned to his Lock. Lysander had followed him, and though they could still hear the girls shouting, Joss couldn't make out the words anymore.

I'm tired, Lysander. I'm tired of the running, the fighting, and I'm sick of Allie and Sirin always arguing. How do we fix all this?

When hunting two prey, the flight may divide.

Joss stared at the Silver dragon.

"Lysander," he whispered. He knew at once what his Lock was thinking.

Joss chewed his lip and watched his sister and friend as they yelled at each other.

I trust Allie, he sent. *And I trust Sirin. And I trust* you, *if you think this is the only way.*

Lysander nodded. *And I trust you, Joss. Always.*

Then let's not wait any longer. If we do, I might chicken out.

I was thinking the same thing, my Lock.

Joss climbed onto Lysander's back and settled into the rider's dip, his stomach tumbling. This was by far the stupidest thing he'd ever done, but he also knew it was *right*.

I'm sorry, Lysander. I wish there were another way.

I'm not sorry. We have unfinished business with the Lennix clan, anyway.

"Allie!" Joss called out. "Sirin!"

They didn't even seem to hear him.

So Lysander roared a roar to flatten the very grass under their feet. Startled into silence, the girls stared at them.

"Joss?" Allie took a half step, raising her hand. The color drained from her face. "Joss! What are you doing?"

"What I have to do. I can save Sammi, while you two save the world."

"Joss! NO!"

"Find the Heart!" Joss called out. "I'll find you when we've escaped Fortress Lennix. Again."

Allie's next shout was drowned out by the *whoosh-oosh* of Lysander's wings as he lifted into the air. Bellacrux trumpeted, but her size slowed her down as she attempted to launch herself in pursuit.

By the time the Green was airborne, with Allie shouting desperately on her back, Lysander had opened the portal, and then he and Joss were gone.

28

The Rite of Sundering

D'Mara Lennix stood on a stone ledge just below the top of a massive volcano, Valkea beside her, the hostage hatchling limp at her feet.

Smoke wafted from various cracks and pits in the volcano's slopes. Despite their elevation, the air was hot enough to make D'Mara sweat in her leathers. She stared at the place Valkea had brought them to.

Before her loomed a cave just large enough for a dragon to squeeze through.

This was the place where, according to Valkea, they would sever the links with their current Locks and form a new bond—with each other.

The hostage hatchling had given up struggling, thanks to D'Mara's belt, which was now wrapped around its nose as a make-shift muzzle. D'Mara had tied her wings together with a bit of leather lacing she'd pulled from her coat cuff. The little Green shivered, too tired now to even shoot angry looks at her captor. She would go nowhere while D'Mara and Valkea went in to perform the ritual.

Would Krane feel it the moment their connection was severed?

D'Mara shivered and pulled her coat tighter.

I'm doing this for the bigger picture, she reminded herself. *For the clan. For my children.*

Really? whispered a voice; if she didn't know better, she'd think it was Krane's. *Or for yourself?*

D'Mara scowled. *Yes, for myself too! And what's so wrong with that?*

Squashing the fear inside her, D'Mara squared her chin. "All right, then. Let's get it over with."

She strode into the cave first, before Valkea tried something stupid like *ordering* her to. Then D'Mara would just have looked like she was obeying the dragon, and she thought it very important that they established early that D'Mara would be ordered around by no one, not even her Lock.

Valkea followed, her tail scraping the stone as it dragged behind her.

Inside the cave, D'Mara found not darkness and damp, but a fiery-orange glow that scorched the walls and heated her skin nearly to blistering. She walked past bulbous mounds of black rock that had once been roiling magma, then stopped and let out a long, low whistle of awe.

Before her flowed a river of bright red lava. It bubbled and slurped as it moved lazily through a channel of stone, flowing deeper into the mountain. And like a trail of stepping stones, pillars of rock rose from the lava and marched down the center of the river.

On the stone walls ran deep gouges that could only have been made by dragon claws. She wondered how long ago they'd been carved there. It looked like whatever dragon had made them had been trying to claw its way out of the lava. Judging by the scattering of large bones around her, D'Mara guessed it had not succeeded. In fact, it looked like many dragons had died here.

"Is it not glorious?" hissed Valkea. "I grew up not far from here. Before I joined the Raptors, of course. My clan used this place as a rite of passage. If a young Red traveled the length of the fire river, they were made full clan members. Of course, many failed." She sneered at the bones.

"How can this place sever the bond between Locks?" D'Mara whispered. "Even if you separate them for years, the bond will still exist. Death is the only true and final separation."

"If you would find out, enter Hama Sarath," intoned Valkea.

D'Mara's heart thumped hard and fast. Hama Sarath was dragonsong for *The Jaws of Death.*

"Well, what you standing around waiting for?" she said, and then she jumped to the first stone pillar. It was just wide enough for a dragon's claw to stand upon, so there was plenty of room for D'Mara. Without slowing, she jumped to the next stone.

The pillars led all the way down the tunnel of searing lava, but where it ended, D'Mara could not see. Still she leapt onward, building momentum as she hopped from stone to stone. The heat was merciless and hungry. The lava slurped as if it were anticipating swallowing her whole.

But D'Mara was nimble and quick; she'd been training all her life at swordplay and knifework, and it paid off now. Her feet flew, her steps were sure. Before she knew it, she'd landed on solid ground—the other end of the deadly pathway. A stone tunnel stretched away before her, into shadow.

After a short walk, lit occasionally by cracks in the wall that revealed more pockets of simmering lava, they came to a large round chamber. A moat of lava encircled the space, and they crossed a small stone bridge that arced over it. In the center of the chamber rose a rocky pedestal, and on the pedestal sat a stone.

But not just any stone.

D'Mara approached it carefully. Its surface swirled and shifted, as if it contained a legion of living shadows. It seemed *aware* of her, and she shivered.

"What is it?" she whispered.

Valkea replied, "My clan called it the memory stone. There were even rumors that it was once the heart of an ancient dragon queen, brought over when we were sent into exile."

"Like the Skyspinner's Heart," said D'Mara.

"Perhaps so."

Was this dark, glistening stone truly the heart of an ancient, star-born dragon, one of the first of their kind? D'Mara yearned to touch it, even as it frightened her as nothing ever had before. It was full of power, that much was undeniable.

"What do you mean, *memory* stone?" asked D'Mara. "How could that sever a Lock's bond?"

"You can't be bonded to someone you never met," said Valkea.

"But I've met Krane." D'Mara thought of that day in the fortress, running scared for her life, while hungry Krane hunted her. The sacrifice of the servant man, Krane's offer to be her Lock.

Are you a sheep or a Raptor?

"You will have," agreed Valkea, "until you touch that stone."

"It will make me forget him? And that will sever us?"

"As surely as death. My clan called it sundering. They discovered that the memory stone could break Locks' bonds by erasing all memory of the human from a dragon's mind, and it's why they sent us to this place when we came of age. Locks made by hatchlings are usually rash and poorly chosen. If a young dragon chose a human Lock too early, it could sunder that bond here and choose a new, stronger Lock after completing the Rite."

"How do I make it work?"

"It requires only a little blood to bond with you," said Valkea. She opened her jaw, grinning, clearly offering her own fangs for D'Mara's use.

Scowling, D'Mara pulled a dagger from her belt and drew its blade over the heel of her hand. Scarlet blood welled and ran down her arm.

D'Mara ground her teeth together. She'd already made up her mind about this. There would be no second-guessing, no regrets. And in a way, she was glad this was how the sundering was done. If she forgot Krane, she couldn't miss him. She couldn't feel guilty for what she was about to do.

But still, as she reached out to touch the stone, her stomach soured and her heart twisted, as if trying to pull her back. Betrayal tasted like rotten fruit on her tongue.

D'Mara pushed through it and touched the memory stone. Her hand, slippery with her own blood, gripped the hard facets of the jewel tightly.

At once, she felt its presence in her mind like a thousand whispers. She couldn't make out words, only the feeling of *hunger*. The stone was ravenous, and it wanted her memories.

So she gave them to it. She thought of Krane the day she'd met him, starving and full of rage and cunning. The stone seized upon the memory and began to pull it, and behind it followed a great string of images, scenes, words. Every moment D'Mara had shared with Krane was sucked from her. She gasped. She wept. She did not remove her hand, even though it felt like the stone was draining her very soul. She remembered the context of the memories—she could recall old battles, but the face and name of the dragon she'd ridden in them blurred into anonymity.

The very last memory to be stolen from her was of her final parting with Krane, and his last whisper in her mind: *Farrelara, me soll.*

Farewell, my soul friend.

As if he had known.

When it was done, a shock sparked on D'Mara's outstretched hand, and she stumbled back. Her head was thick and clouded. She looked around the lava-lit chamber and knew she'd come here for something important, but she couldn't quite remember what. Valkea, beside her, extended her snout and touched it to the stone. D'Mara watched in confusion.

They'd come here to . . . to sunder old Locks . . . She managed to recall that much, but the rest slipped away. It was as if there were a wall put around D'Mara's thoughts, one she couldn't breach no matter how she tried. A pit opened in her stomach and she felt the sense that she'd done something terrible, surrendered something dear . . . but then the feeling was pushed away by a new voice.

D'Mara. D'Mara Lennix.

She looked up, into the eyes of the Red dragon.

Valkea?

The dragon's lips curled into the sort of smile only Raptors could make.

Hello, D'Mara. Hello, my Lock.

29

Sirin Alone

Sirin stared at the empty sky, her mind struggling to interpret what her eyes had seen.

Because surely, *surely* she hadn't just watched Joss and Lysander return to the Dragonlands without them. She scrubbed at her eyes, but the scene didn't change: There was no Joss; there was no Lysander. Only the first few twinkling stars of night in the space where they'd been seconds ago.

Bellacrux landed heavily on the bank, and before Sirin was half aware of Allie running toward her, the girl shoved her hard with both hands. Sirin stumbled back, nearly falling.

"This is *your* fault!" yelled Allie. Her face was red and tears poured down her cheeks. She shoved Sirin again, and Sirin let her. "He's going to get himself killed, because of *you*!"

Sirin stared at her, unable to speak.

"And there is nothing we can do about it!" Allie said. She grabbed Sirin by her shoulders and shook her. "Don't you see? We're *stranded* here without Lysander, Earth girl! We can't get back! We can't save him! And it's *your* fault! All your talk of acting normal and not drawing attention in this world—but it was *you* those police were chasing, it was *you* the dragons had to come rescue while the whole world watched, and it was *you* who led D'Mara straight to us!"

Sirin's teeth rattled from being shaken. Finally she pushed Allie off and stepped back.

"I—that's not fair!"

"Not fair?" Allie's voice cracked. "You know what's not fair? Watching my parents get snatched by Raptors was not *fair*. Working until my hands bled for the Zolls was not *fair*. Losing my brother because some girl couldn't stop crying is not *fair*. You're too weak and soft for this! I knew it all along!"

Sirin sniffled and clenched her fists. She could think of a few things that happened in her own life that weren't fair either. Her life hadn't been all charmed and happy like Allie thought.

Mum, thought Sirin. *Oh, Mum!*

The tidal wave of grief that Sirin had been holding back threatened to break loose at last. She swayed on her feet at the sheer force of it. But still she held back. With everything else going on—losing Joss, losing Sammi, Allie's accusations—Sirin couldn't afford to break down now.

Allie interpreted Sirin's stony expression in an entirely different way. "You're not even *sorry*!" she said. "You still see this as some pretend story, don't you? Some cool adventure you can go tell your *real* friends about later!"

"Of course not!" Sirin had no real friends. Not anymore.

"Was any of this ever real to you?" asked Allie. "Do you even care what happens to Joss?"

"I *do* care!" shouted Sirin. "I do, I do, more than anything! You're right, okay? Everything you said is the truth. When I met you it was like a chance to run away from my problems, from . . . from what happened to my mum. With you and Joss and Sammi, I didn't have to think about her. I could . . . I could pretend everything was okay back home. Or maybe I thought if I just kept running, it would never catch up to me." Her voice dropped to a whisper. "But you're right. This *is* my fault. I'm sorry I led D'Mara right to us. I'm sorry I brought my curse on you and Joss."

Allie's chest was heaving from pent-up sobs and anger. She glared at Sirin. "Your curse?"

"I'm bad luck, that's what I am. I'm cursed. I should have known this would happen."

Because I always end up alone.

Everyone left. Parents, cats, dragons, friends. Maybe this was just how life was. Maybe she'd been a fool for ever thinking it would be different with Joss and Allie.

"I have to find the Heart," said Allie. "It's Joss's only hope. Where is it, Sirin?"

"New York City," said Sirin quietly. She still had the world atlas she'd bought, and now she pulled it out and opened it. "There."

She handed the map to Allie.

"Go," Sirin said. "Just go. I won't slow you down anymore."

She was so very tired of trying to fit in where she wasn't wanted.

Allie hesitated, then rolled up the map and stuck it in her coat pocket. She turned toward Bellacrux.

"I'm sorry," she said. "Maybe after I find Joss . . . Good-bye, Sirin."

Sirin looked away, at the dark lake below, and rubbed her arm where Allie had shoved her. She said nothing.

She heard rather than saw Bellacrux take flight. In moments, the whisper of the Green's wings faded away altogether.

Then Sirin was alone.

Perfectly, utterly alone on a ruined bank beside Loch Ness.

She was hollow inside, like every feeling and thought had been scoured away. She felt like a puppet whose strings had been cut.

But as the night deepened and the waters endlessly lapped at the stones, she did begin to feel. She felt the great wave inside her sloshing and rising, like floodwaters. She knew if she let it loose it would drown her, because now she'd lost so much more than her mum. There was Sammi and Joss too, and even Lysander and Bellacrux and Allie. With them, she'd been able to forget. Constantly running for your life was a surprisingly effective distraction from one's other problems. But now all of that was over, and Sirin was alone, and there was nowhere left to hide from the past.

Who had she thought she was, running off on *quests*, trying to save the world? As if she could help anyone. As if she didn't always make everything worse. She'd tried so hard to be useful, a strong member of the team, figuring out clues and plotting how to outsmart the enemy. But it had all fallen apart, and it was her fault. Why *would* Allie and Joss want her along after this? Who had ever really wanted her, besides her mother? And her mother was gone.

"Little human," said a rumbling voice, startling Sirin. She looked up to see a pair of glittering dark eyes watching her.

Thorval! For it was his deep, ancient voice speaking now, not Nessie's. His head rose just above the water.

"You came back," Sirin whispered.

"I felt the trembling of the earth from my deep caverns and knew there was a dragon battle above. But it seems I have come too late."

"They're all gone."

"Ah," said Thorval.

"And it's my fault," Sirin added.

"Is it?"

Sirin leaned over and buried her head in her arms. She was shaking all over.

"I have been remembering," murmured Thorval. "Your words rattled memories out of me like rocks tumbling down a hill. I remember when I too found myself all alone."

Perhaps Sirin would crack like Thorval had and invent another person to help stanch the flow of painful memories.

"I'm sorry," she said. "I shouldn't have made you remember. It's awful, to remember."

"Yes," agreed Thorval. "But if I had not remembered, then I could not have aided you on your quest. And if I had not remembered, then who would be left to tell you *how* to use the Skyspinner's Heart once you found it?"

"How to use it?" Sirin looked up.

"But surely you are not interested in that," said Thorval. "It looks to me as if you have given up. Trust me, I know what that looks like. Over the past two thousand years, I've become very good at giving up."

"Well," Sirin admitted. "It's not as though there's much else I can do. I am alone, with no way to help anyone. And besides, it's not as if they want my help. I only make things worse. It's like I'm cursed, Thorval. Everyone I love . . ."

The wave inside her churned, pressing against the unfeeling dam she'd built. She fell silent.

"Everyone you love *what*?" asked Thorval.

"I don't want to talk about it anymore. Or *think* about it."

"Why?"

"Because! It—it hurts too much. I'd rather feel nothing at all than remember her."

"Her?"

"My . . ."

Thorval tilted his head. "A wise person once told me that remembering is how you keep the lost with you."

Sirin squeezed her eyes shut. She sobbed once.

And that was all it took.

The dam broke.

"Mum," Sirin whispered. "Oh, Mum, I miss you so much."

The dragonstone pendant under her shirt seemed to burn into her skin, and finally she drew it out and held it tight in her palm.

She began to sob, and sobbed harder when she felt Thorval nudge her foot with his nose. She threw her arms around the ancient dragon's neck and cried into his shimmering blue scales.

Sirin remembered her mother as she'd been before the sickness, bright and energetic and full of whimsy. She remembered her packing Sirin's lunches so that when Sirin opened them, the food was arranged in a silly face that always made her laugh. She remembered her mum cooking for three days straight when their neighbor's kitchen flooded, so that they could take over a dozen casseroles for them. She remembered her mum best of all snuggled in Sirin's bed, reading to her even though Sirin was almost a teenager and fully capable of reading herself. But she never would have dreamed of telling her mum to leave. She could still feel her mum's frail, sickening body, but her spirit as large and vibrant as it had ever been.

She even remembered her in the hospital in the last days, fading before her eyes, but still smiling.

All the sorrow that had been building up inside Sirin flooded out. She'd never wept so hard in her life or felt so wretched.

But as she cried, deep, deep down, Sirin began to feel as if a great weight had been lifted from her chest. She felt lighter and lighter with each tear that fell, until she had no more left to give.

30

Tamra Alone

When the blast of the signal horn sounded over Fortress Lennix that night, announcing the return of an important Raptor and rider, Tamra was lying in her room, having just vomited. She'd been ill all morning, and no one could figure out why. It had started with a sudden pain out of nowhere, right in the center of her chest, and Tamra had been aching and dizzy ever since.

But no illness would stop her from being in the landing yard when her mother returned.

Valkea? Are you back?

When her query received no reply, Tamra frowned. Maybe it wasn't Valkea and D'Mara back from the Lost Lands. But why else would someone be blowing the signal horn? It wasn't used for ordinary recon and scavenging missions.

Shoving aside the servant who attempted to help her out of bed, Tamra stumbled through her room and down the stairs to the yard, clutching her chest. Every few steps she had to stop to catch her breath. Honestly, what was *wrong* with her? The pain was like she'd been impaled with a firestik between her ribs. Blinking away tears, Tamra pushed on, but she was still the last Lennix to reach the landing yard. Edward, Mirra, and Kaan stood at attention with the First Flight, while the other Raptors crowded behind them eagerly.

There had been much confusion when the First Flight had returned without D'Mara and Valkea. They'd reported that the Lennix leader had vanished along with the Red, through a portal that had closed to the rest of them. It had been Tamra who'd first realized what had happened, and that the Silver scale forged onto Valkea's brow must have only been powerful enough to let one Raptor through the portal.

Still, her Lock and D'Mara should have been back hours ago. What if the scale had stopped working, and they were trapped in the Lost Lands? What if something terrible had befallen them while they were there? Tamra didn't know; her connection to Valkea had all but ceased the moment they'd gone through the portal.

She wished she'd been more assertive that morning and demanded that *she* be the one to ride Valkea through the portal. But her dragon had insisted it would be fine, and Tamra had believed her.

"There!" shouted Kaan, pointing to the sky. As usual, he was the first to spot the returning dragon. "It's Ma!"

Tamra squinted and saw he was right. Valkea bore down on the fortress with a roar of undeniable triumph.

What happened? Tamra sent. *Did it work? What did you see?*

Still Valkea made no reply, but the pain in Tamra's chest sharpened. She bent over, gasping. *Valkea, something's wrong with me.*

She'd heard that Locks could feel each other's pain, but Valkea didn't even look at her.

Valkea!

Why was the Red ignoring her? Tamra started to walk to her, but Valkea swept away, up the loggia and after D'Mara.

Valkea? What's going on? Valkea! Can you hear me?

"Tam?" Mirra glanced at her, frowning. "What's wrong?"

"Nothing," Tamra rasped. "I'm fine! Mind your own business."

Mirra rolled her eyes and turned back to the approaching Raptor. Valkea landed hard, her claws sending out a spray of sparks as they scratched the stone. D'Mara vaulted down, holding a squirming hatchling.

"Edward!" she shouted. "Hold on to this whelp. And all of you pay attention! I intend to announce the new Lennix Grand."

Edward took the little trussed-up Green, then exchanged a smug look with Decimus as more Raptors crept into the landing yard, their interest piqued by D'Mara's announcement.

Tamra knew everyone expected the new Grand to be Decimus. Edward looked as pleased as a hatchling that had just caught a rabbit. He stood with his chin high and his shoulders squared. Even if it wasn't him receiving the title, being the Lock of the Lennix Grand was an honor in and of itself. He would hold almost as much sway as D'Mara over the Raptors.

"Raptors of the Roost," D'Mara said loudly. She spread her hands wide. "I am pleased to report that the mission to the Lost Lands was a success. As you've guessed, we will require more Silver scales before a full raid can be launched, but I have already set wheels in motion to ensure we are supplied with as many as we need. Which brings me to our second announcement: We have gone far too long without a Lennix Grand, and it is high time we purged the stench of that traitor Bellacrux from the Roost for good, by honoring our *new* Grand."

Everyone looked at Decimus, who preened.

"Raptors," called D'Mara, "I present to you your new Grand—and *my* new Lock! VALKEA!"

Tamra's heart stopped.

Instead of roars of adulation, the Raptors looked around in confusion. D'Mara's new Lock? But Krane was still alive! And so was Tamra.

As Valkea reared onto her hind legs and screeched and spat flame all over the sky, Tamra reeled. She backed away, out of Mirra's reach, and bumped into a stone column supporting the loggia.

Valkea? What is going on?

Valkea didn't even seem to hear her. For that matter, now that Tamra really reached for her Lock, she found it was like grasping at a shadow.

In the spot where her Lock had been, now Valkea simply *wasn't there*.

"Grieving sickness," whispered Mirra, turning to her twin. She stared at Tamra with the one thing Tamra had always despised most: *pity*. "You've got grieving sickness."

Tamra had seen it before, the pain that followed the death of a Lock. Dragons and humans alike experienced it, and it lasted for days or even weeks depending on how strong the bond had been.

But Valkea wasn't dead.

Valkea had *broken* their bond.

Which was way, way worse.

And even worse than *that*, she'd broken their bond in order to Lock with D'Mara. The link between human and dragon was the strongest in nature, a joining of mind, heart, and spirit. It was the ultimate form of trust . . . and Valkea had betrayed all of that. She might as well have torn out Tamra's heart and crushed it in her jaws.

"Tam?" Mirra put out her hand, her eyes full of concern. "Are you—"

"Don't touch me!" Tamra snapped.

She wrenched away and pelted into the fortress. Behind her, she heard the Raptors begin to roar, taking up the chant led by D'Mara.

"*Val-kea! Val-kea! Val-kea!*"

31

Joss Alone

Fortress Lennix.

There it was.

The last place Joss had ever wanted to see again. It clung to its mountain with the long lip of the landing yard extending outward in dark greeting. Joss set his jaw and glared at it, wishing the whole thing would just break off and tumble into some abyss, never to be seen again.

Second thoughts? asked Lysander.

Of course not. Let's go save Sammi.

But despite this bold statement, Joss's stomach sank lower the nearer they got to the fortress. There appeared to be some kind of ceremony happening. He heard roars and saw plumes of flame long before they reached the runway.

Lysander . . .

Yes, Joss?

Thank you.

For what?

For being my best friend and my Lock. For changing my life. No matter what happens next, I wouldn't change a thing.

Joss, this isn't the end. We will not let them beat us.

Yeah, of course. But Joss couldn't even convince himself of that. They were surrendering to Raptors, after all. He didn't think mercy was in their vocabulary.

When Joss heard the blast of the Lennix signal horn, he knew they'd been spotted. The noise in the yard faded as all eyes turned on them.

Lysander landed gracefully on the runway, then shook out his wings before folding them. Then he stalked into the yard, his neck arched proudly, as if he were a king returning to his own castle and not a renegade turning himself over to the enemy.

Too bad you haven't had your dragonfire sleep yet, Lysander. Then we could really show up in style.

Yes, replied Lysander sadly.

It was as if they'd all gathered just to witness the surrender. Every Lennix was there except Declan and, interestingly, Tamra, and almost every Raptor too. Valkea and D'Mara stood at the forefront of the throng, gloating.

"D'Mara Lennix!" Joss called out, trying to sound as proud and strong as Lysander looked. "We demand you safely release the Green hatchling Sammi! In return Lysander and I will submit to you."

The Raptors hissed and yowled, scraping their claws on the stone in a terrible frenzied show of triumph. Then D'Mara raised her hand, and they fell silent.

"Joshua Moran," she said coolly. "And the Silver Lysander. I accept your surrender. The Green will be released at once, as promised. Mirra!"

The girl jumped at the mention of her name, as if surprised to hear it. Then she nodded and scurried away to find Sammi. Joss felt a small sense of relief; he'd worried D'Mara wouldn't hold up her end of the deal.

"As for these two," said D'Mara, eyeing the Silver and Joss, "put them in separate cells below."

Well, at least it's not immediate execution, Joss sent Lysander grimly.

I'm sure they're preparing the finest cells for us, Lysander joked.

Oh, yes, with nice warm porridge and fluffy pillows.

But it was only gallows humor, and it did little to lift Joss's spirit. He slid down and held out his arms as Edward Lennix approached with a pair of manacles.

"You should never have run away in the first place, boy," Edward grumbled. Unlike the rest of them, he seemed disgruntled. "D'Mara always gets what she wants, and the rest of us might as well just give it to her. It's easier in the long run."

Joss thought he might be talking about something completely different but had no idea what it could be.

I sure did miss this place, Joss said to Lysander as they were locked in opposite cells.

The damp does do wonders for my scales. And the smell! Like dirt and pee and mold. Yum.

Joss managed a glum little laugh. At least Sammi was free—they'd passed her on the way down. She'd been squirming and snapping at Mirra's heels, pulled along on a little chain leash. At the sight of Joss and Lysander, she'd stopped dead and stared, before Mirra had yanked her along.

Joss sat on a pile of old, moldy hay and wrapped his arms around his knees. He watched Lysander circling his cell and thought of Sirin and Allie. They should have been well on the way to finding the Heart by now. He wished he were with them, seeing more wonderful things in the Lost Lands. Eating fish and chips, riding buses, shopping for brightly colored footwear.

Joss smiled at his neon-yellow sneakers. At least he still had those.

"Hey, sheep boy," said a taunting voice.

Joss groaned. "What it is now, Kaan?"

Kaan pressed his face against the bars, making sure he was standing well out of range of Lysander. "Your shoes. I want them."

Of course he did. He'd probably threaten to do something horrid like poke out Joss's eyes or make him eat sheep dung if he didn't comply. So he simply sighed and removed his beloved sneakers, then threw them at Kaan. To his satisfaction, one smacked the boy right in the face.

"Idiot," Kaan hissed. He pulled off his own boots and put on the sneakers right there, as if to rub it in. Then he walked around, testing their springiness. "Amazing! These are from the Lost Lands, I suppose. Well, soon I will be a prince of the Lost Lands and *everyone* will have to give me their shoes!"

"Yes, you're a real evil genius, Kaan Lennix," Joss retorted. "Kaan the Terrible, stealer of *shoes*."

"Shut up!" Kaan snapped. "You won't be so snarky when my ma gets down here. She's putting together a scale extraction kit as we speak."

"A . . ." Joss glanced in alarm at Lysander, who stared back at him. "But . . . but we're *here*! She has Lysander! He's way better than a bunch of scales."

"Scales don't tend to bite," Kaan pointed out. "Or run away."

Joss hadn't even considered D'Mara might try to take Lysander's scales. After all, his Lock could lead countless Raptors to the Lost Lands for her. But now he saw Kaan's point—with a scale from Lysander forged onto each Raptor, they wouldn't have to rely on the Silver at all.

Lysander!

It's all right, Joss. I knew this would happen.

But why didn't you tell me? I wouldn't have agreed—

If you hadn't agreed, Sammi might be dead now.

But—

They'll grow back, Joss. Just promise you won't watch.

Sickened, Joss clenched the bars of his cell and shook them, but they didn't budge so much as a centimeter.

Kaan, watching him, laughed.

"Oh, oh!" He snickered. "I hear footsteps on the stairs! Must be Mum. Oh, this will be fun. I hope she lets me help. It'll be like pulling off fingernails."

Joss stepped back, covering his mouth in horror.

Lysander, Lysander, what have I done?

32

Allie Alone

Allie and Bellacrux were hopelessly lost. Allie turned Sirin's maps this way and that, trying to figure out where they were meant to go, but in her panic and grief, she'd forgotten the name of the city. Was it Nork City? New Yard City? Nyorka City? Bellacrux flew in a meandering, aimless pattern over a string of islands not far from Loch Ness.

I believe Sirin said we should go west, Bellacrux told her.

Are you sure it wasn't east? Oh, I can't remember! Joss could already be dead!

A storm is brewing, Allinson Moran. We must choose a heading soon or be forced to wait out the weather.

Allie searched desperately by what dim light the moon offered. There were millions of places marked on the maps, and all the countries and islands and roads began to blur in Allie's eyes. Terror for Joss and anger at Sirin wrestled in her chest until she could hardly breathe.

We'll never find it! She shut the atlas and nearly flung it into the sky.

A peal of thunder suddenly cracked overhead, chased by a thread of white-hot lightning. Moments later, the rain followed.

Bellacrux descended, Allie gripping tightly to her as she

navigated the worsening storm. The dragon landed on a craggy island that seemed little more than a pile of rocks. It reminded Allie painfully of the place where she, Joss, Sirin, and their Locks had recovered after the Raptors had assaulted the Blue islands. Things had seemed as hopeless then as they had now—only now, it felt much, much worse. Because except for Bellacrux, Allie was alone. No Joss, no Lysander, no Sirin, no Sammi.

Rain streamed all around, and the wind sent snarling waves crashing over the rocks. Allie and Bellacrux huddled in the very center of the small island, as far away as possible from the sea. Even the dragon seemed to be shivering from the cold and wet.

I knew this would happen, Allie sent. *I knew that girl couldn't handle this. This is all her fault!*

Bellacrux grumbled when a particularly violent wave managed to drench her claws.

Allie sat against her Lock's side, sheltered a little beneath Bellacrux's wing. But the relentless rain seeped in anyway. Soon she was as soaked through as if she'd plunged into Thorval's lake. She wondered if the storm had reached Loch Ness, and if Sirin had also been caught in it. She hoped she had.

This wouldn't have happened if Joss and Sirin had listened to me. It's D'Mara Lennix all over again! Why doesn't anybody listen to me?

Bellacrux peered into the dark and said nothing.

Bell? Bellacrux?

Angry that her Lock would not back her up, Allie stood and left her wing, to stand with her back to the dragon and her eyes on the sea. Its tossing, angry waves mirrored the state of her soul.

What's wrong with you, Bellacrux? Don't tell me you're taking her side!

In a true flight, there are no sides, only one purpose, one spirit, one mind.

Allie knotted her hands into fists. "Oh, c'mon!" she said aloud. "You can't expect me to believe dragons never argue."

We do. But we are not like you humans, letting an argument fester for days or weeks. We might duel one another, wrestling until a victor is determined and his or her path declared right. But this is not common among the free dragons. It is, of course, common among Raptors.

Bellacrux let that pointed observation hang in Allie's mind for a long, uncomfortable minute.

Then she continued, *Besides, we dragons recognize the strength in all our members, even when those strengths are different from our own. We know that in order to survive, we must stay together. Nobody should fly alone, Allinson Moran.*

"I never wanted to fly alone!" Allie yelled to the sky. "That's the whole point! Me and Joss, Joss and me—that's how it's been for years! I made a promise to our parents, Bellacrux, that I would keep him safe. Someone has to be the strong one. And it's always me! I have to be the tough one, making the hard choices, and sometimes, it makes me look like a monster. But I was right, wasn't I, about Sirin Sharma? She's not tough enough, and because of her, Joss is a prisoner again!"

Again, Bellacrux gave her only silence in reply.

"Stop that!" Allie cried.

Stop what?

"Stop defending her!"

Did I?

"Well, you're not defending *me*! You're supposed to be on my side. You're supposed to agree with me."

Bellacrux's deep laugh rolled through Allie. *Little one, I am your Lock, not your groveling servant.*

"Then—then *say* something! And not some dragony proverb either. Say something real!"

All right. Bellacrux turned her head slowly to peer at Allie. A flash of lightning sent a shiver of light rippling over her emerald scales. *Here's something: I don't think you're really angry at Sirin at all.*

Allie blinked. *What?*

I think, Allinson Moran, that you are angry at someone else.

Allie backed away, nearly tripping over a cleft in the rocks. "I . . . who?"

Who do you really blame for Joss leaving?

Tears began to prick Allie's eyes, and she wasn't sure why. But a hot, rashy feeling spread through her. She felt sick with it.

Me. I'm angry at myself.

Something released in Allie's chest, and she let out a gasp. Clutching her hands to her heart, she shut her eyes and began to cry.

I'm scared that it's my *fault I lost Joss,* she admitted. *Because I wasn't strong enough or tough enough. Maybe Tamra was right in the library, when she said I was weak for saving her life. If I'd left her behind, maybe the Lennixes would never have figured out how to cross the portals. Joss would be safe. Or if I'd kept better watch on the skies, we wouldn't have been ambushed. Or if I'd stopped D'Mara from taking Sammi. Or if I'd—*

If, if, if, said Bellacrux. *Dragons do not concern themselves with "ifs." We focus on what* is, *not what might have been. That is the only way to move forward. That is the only way to find our true strength.*

Allie blinked at her Lock. *What do you mean?*

You've tried to be strong every minute. Never show weakness, never show fear, because you have to protect Joss. That makes you very brave, Allie. It's the reason I chose you for my Lock. But even the bravest must accept their limits. And accepting what you cannot change is not weakness, but wisdom, for it reveals what you can *change. It reveals the path you must take.*

But how does that help Joss? she asked. Then she said it aloud. "*How*, Bell? I'm not strong enough to save him. There. I've said it. So should I just give up, then?"

Bellacrux snorted. *After all these years, the illogic of humans still continues to surprise me. No, Allie. You don't give up. You think like a dragon. Where does a dragon's strength come from?*

"Um . . . her wings?"

Bellacrux let out a long, noisy groan.

Her flight! Allie amended. *You're always talking about strength in the flight.*

Her Lock gave a slow nod. *The flight is strength. The flight is survival. The flight is hope.*

Allie shut her eyes. "And . . . I've left a big part of our flight behind."

Shame heated her cheeks, but just like Bellacrux had said, Allie began to see the path before her, the one she *could* take.

The person she *could* save.

"Oh my stars," Allie breathed. "I've made a terrible mess of things, haven't I?"

Well, Bellacrux replied, *a little.*

"I—I left Sirin all alone on that bank."

I might have helped with that part, her Lock reminded her.

But you know it was me. It was. And I have to go back, Bell. I have to make things right. Allie pulled the sopping atlas from her pocket. *Besides, we need Sirin Sharma. We need her badly.*

She does have an eye for maps.

Even if she didn't, Allie replied, *she's a part of our flight. And more than strength, survival, or hope . . . our flight is family.*

As Allie climbed back onto Bellacrux's back, bracing to face the storm, she whispered, "And family sticks together."

33

I Do Believe in Dragons

Only a fart-breath dweebus would believe in dragons, so it makes sense that *you* would."

"I am *not* a fart-breath dweebus! You saw them on the TV too!"

"Oh, sure, it was on TV, so it *must* be true. I bet you believe in the Loch Ness Monster too, dweebus."

Sirin listened to the brother and sister arguing behind her and considered turning around and butting in. The boy, who was Allie's age, had begun to grate her nerves. The girl, younger than Sirin, seemed near tears at her brother's relentless torment. Their parents were busy across the street at the information center, loading up on pamphlets about Loch Ness, Urquhart Castle, and who knew what other touristy things. They were clearly American, judging by their accents. Sirin sat at a small outdoor café table, eating a triple-chocolate-fudge-with-sprinkles sundae. It was massive, and she'd been working on it for a while. It didn't help that she didn't have much of an appetite.

Thorval had offered to let her hide out in his hidden caverns for as long as she liked, but as appealing as a dragon's wet, fishy cave sounded, Sirin knew she couldn't keep running away from her problems.

She had taken up Thorval's offer of transport and ridden on

the dragon's spiny back across the loch. He'd left her on the shore within sight of this little town, and she'd waited out the storm beneath a picnic shelter before heading to the diner for breakfast. She'd hung around ever since, trying to decide what to do. If Joss and Lysander returned, hopefully with Sammi, they'd look for her here. Then again, if they . . . didn't return (and Sirin shuddered to think what that would mean), she would be faced with a grim alternative: taking a bus to Inverness, and from there, the train to London. Then back to her social worker and a juvenile home and everything she'd hated most about her old life.

Pushing her ice cream around as it melted into a gooey puddle, Sirin tried to ignore the clenching pain in her chest. It felt as if there were a hook lodged in her ribs, with a string attached to it, and at the other end of the string was Sammi. The farther away she got, the harder the hook pulled.

Would the pain fade eventually? she wondered. If two Locks were separated long enough, would their bond eventually break? Would she even know when it did?

With a groan, Sirin pressed her hand to her chest and shut her eyes.

Sammi? She reached out weakly, already knowing she'd only get silence in reply. Her Lock was far, far beyond her reach.

Oh, Joss. Save him, please. Then save yourself and Lysander.

But the longer time stretched without any sign of their return, the more her hopes dimmed that she'd ever seen any of them again. Allie certainly wasn't coming back. And if Joss didn't either . . . Well, then she knew she'd be mourning more lost friends than Sammi.

"How do you explain all the pictures and videos, then?" the American girl was saying behind her. "It's all over the news."

"You heard Dad, dweebus. It was a prank. Balloons or kites or special effects. Honestly, how are you this stupid?"

Sirin's fist tightened around her spoon.

"Well, I don't care what you call me," said the girl. "I believe. I do. And it just makes you mad that you can't stop me."

Inwardly, Sirin cheered the girl on.

With a sigh, she leaned back and eyed the bus station across the street. There were already a few people waiting for the next bus. The hook in Sirin's ribs pulled harder.

Then, so fleeting she almost missed it, a dark blur shot across the sky, out of one cloud and into another.

Sirin's heart tumbled.

That blur had been moving much too fast, and much too low, to be an airplane. Or a balloon or a kite or whatever other stupid thing the American boy thought it was.

Sirin jumped to her feet and slammed her spoon onto the table, then turned around. The American kids blinked at her, startled by the fact that she was glaring directly at the boy.

"You got a problem?" he said.

His sister looked near tears and lowered her gaze to her hot-pink sneakers. There were fluffy pom-poms threaded on the laces. Sirin thought Joss would highly approve.

"You should be careful what you say," said Sirin. "You never know who might be listening, and dragons are very offended by not being believed in."

The boy scoffed. "Great! Another dweebus! Honestly, this whole boring vacation has been one stupid thing after—"

He was interrupted by a ferocious roar that shook the café and the very tables they were using. Sirin's spoon clattered and then fell to the concrete floor.

The boy's and girl's mouths dropped open as a dragon dropped from the sky, landing on the street right in front of them. With her back still turned to it, Sirin grinned at the tourist kids.

"Enjoy the rest of your holiday," she said. "Oh . . . and I'd put away the cameras if I were you. The Loch Ness Dragon's sort of got a *thing* about them."

With that, she turned around and ran to the street. She was a little stunned to see Bellacrux, with Allie waiting atop her, but she was also terribly glad. As cars screeched to a halt and people tumbled out of them, screaming, Sirin sprinted to Bellacrux's side and looked up at Allie.

"I'm sorry," Allie said bluntly. "I was unfair and unkind. If you can forgive me, I can make it up to you, Sirin. I should never have left you alone. But Joss and Lysander and Bellacrux and I . . . we are your family now, if you'll have us."

Sirin stared up at her for a long moment. "You . . . came back for me."

"Yes. I need you, Sirin. I can't do this alone. I'm not strong enough. But together, we might be. *Please.*"

Allie had come back for her.

Allie *needed* her.

She'd had a family, her mum. And she hadn't been able to save her, not with all the wishes and prayers in the world.

But here was a new family that maybe, just maybe, she *could* save. They were strange and fierce and half of them were covered in scales . . . but Sirin loved them.

"Yes," said Sirin. "Yes, I want that very much. And I'm sorry too for everything I said."

"Then get up here," said Allie, grinning. "Because you're in charge of the map."

Taking Allie's hand, Sirin scrambled up onto Bellacrux. Once she was seated, she waved at the American kids. The girl waved back, wide-eyed, while the boy cowered under the table, clearly terrified out of his mind.

Bellacrux lifted off with a powerful thrust of her wings, then pulled away from the town and soared over the loch. Below them, a sinuous shape lunged out of the water, performing a spectacular leap before crashing down again.

"Good-bye, Thorval!" Sirin called. "Thanks for everything!"

Thorval poked his head out of the water and breathed a fiery farewell flame, before vanishing back into the deep with the smallest of ripples.

34

Flight Silver

All had not gone *quite* to D'Mara's plans, but she felt like a boulder rolling downhill. She was gathering momentum, and nothing would stand in her way now. So even when Joshua Moran refused to tell her where to find the Skyspinner's Heart, she found a way around it—in the form of a terrified Earth man she and Valkea snatched up during his morning jog. It had taken all of twenty minutes to open another portal, grab the man, and get the information out of him. D'Mara had been a little stunned with how easy it was. All she had to do was ask him where the city with the giant green lady was, then let Valkea snap her fangs a bit, and the man had spilled everything. Blood and bone, but these Lost Lands humans were soft, weak creatures.

New York City.

D'Mara chanted the words in her head like a prayer as she walked through the loggia over the landing yard.

New York City was their destination, and the jogger had even drawn a map for D'Mara. Really, conquering this new world would be a *breeze*, if all humans were as helpless and quivering as that one had been.

So despite this slight hitch in her plans, D'Mara was in high spirits on the morning of the biggest raid the Raptors would ever undertake. Below, the dragons assembled for a morning repast of mutton and fish, while the blacksmith—brought in from his remote village—prepared his tools and fire for the forging. D'Mara had pulled twelve scales from Lysander, and each one would be placed on the brow of a senior Raptor today. The entire First Flight would enter the Lost Lands within a matter of hours.

"D'Mara."

She stopped, irritation prickling her skin. "What is it, Edward?"

Her husband stood uncertainly in the doorway to the lower Roost. "It's Krane. He's unwell."

"Who?"

Edward blinked. "K-Krane. Your . . . former Lock?"

D'Mara stared at him. "Oh. Right. Krane, of course."

"You do remember Krane, don't you?" Edward laughed, as if he were asking if she remembered the sky was up. But then he must have seen the look on her face, because he frowned and added, "Don't you?"

"It's a bit foggy." She waved a hand dismissively. "I'm sure he was a fine Lock."

"You *don't* remember him," Edward said. He gaped at her with apparent horror. "D'Mara, what did you *do*? I didn't even know you could break a Lock's bond!"

"Well," she said, "turns out you can. And I don't have time to tend to some sickly . . . what's his name again?"

Her husband backed away, staring at her like she was a monster. "Blood and bone, woman, that's cold, even for you. Krane may be dying because of whatever you did to him. He's got grieving sickness. And what about Tamra? She didn't look too good either. Is this because you didn't want to name Decimus as the new Grand, and Krane was too ill for the job? So you went and dumped him and Locked with the most treacherous Raptor you could find?"

"Valkea is strong," D'Mara returned stiffly. "She has ambition and vision. Actually, she's quite a lot like me. Why shouldn't we be Locked?"

"Because . . . because—"

"It's *disgusting*," said a raspy voice behind D'Mara.

She turned to see her daughter leaning against the wall. Tamra's skin was sallow, her eyes sunken in and her body hunched as if she'd aged fifty years.

"Tamra! You look dreadful."

"You stole Valkea from me," Tamra said. "You wretched woman."

"Tamra," Edward said. "Don't speak that way to your mother."

"Mother!" Tamra coughed out. "Ha! That is no mother. There isn't a mother's bone in her body. She's nothing but greed and treachery and spite. She'd feed us all to her precious Raptors if she thought it would help her become empress of the Lost Lands or whatever it is she thinks to call herself."

"Enough!" snapped D'Mara. "You're clearly delirious, and unfit to join the raid. Go lie down or something, and consider how you address me!"

Tamra laughed, but it turned into a cough, and she slipped away, her feet dragging.

D'Mara turned and brushed past Edward. "What are you looking at?" she said. "Don't you have a raid to organize, you useless cretin? Go!"

He slunk away but gave her one last look. *Disgust*. She'd never seen such a thing from Edward before. As she continued on her way, D'Mara could swear she heard laughter from behind the closed doorways. Once, she stopped to kick one open, ready to execute whoever stood behind it, but the room was empty. The laughter slipped around and behind her, and she whirled, but there was no one there either.

"Ingrates," she muttered, and she kept walking.

Honestly, what was happening to her clan? They'd all thought she was getting weak, but she'd returned stronger than ever, with the key to the Lost Lands and a powerful new Lock. They were jealous, she decided. Edward had thought he'd become the new head of the clan if Decimus was named Grand. Tamra had thought she would usurp her mother with Valkea's help.

But D'Mara was more cunning than any of them. By Locking with Valkea, she'd destroyed all their treasonous plans in one fell sweep. It had been a masterstroke of genius.

By the time D'Mara reached the landing yard, she'd nearly convinced herself that Locking with Valkea had been *her* idea from the start.

Raptors crowded the yard. D'Mara found their deafening clamor comforting; the insidious laughter that followed her couldn't possibly be heard over the noise.

Only the First Flight would be departing, but no one wanted to miss the send-off. Those who had been chosen strutted proudly, displaying their new Silver scales for all to see and admire. The day was sunny, and the scales glinted like jewels, each one forged at the center of the Raptors' brows. Soon, *all* the Raptors would have Silver scales of their own, but there wasn't time for that now, so only the fiercest of them had been forged so far. D'Mara inspected each one and found them impeccably applied. If she'd been in a better mood, she might have ordered the release of one of the blacksmith's children. But after being ambushed by Edward and Tamra, she wasn't feeling particularly keen on the idea of families, and so instead, she sent a servant to bring the man a cask of her finest ale. That would have to do.

"Valkea," she said, striding toward her Lock. She spread her arms. "We are nearly ready."

Valkea gave her a sidelong look; she was having her nails sharpened by a team of three cowering human servants. *About time, D'Mara. This place lacks discipline. I will have my work cut out for me whipping these mongrels into form. You've let them all get lazy and slow.*

D'Mara simmered but let that one go.

"Flight Silver," said D'Mara, looking out across the assembled Raptors. Her heart beat with excitement. Hundreds of dragon and human eyes were fixed on her and Valkea. She wore her fiercest raiding clothes—black leathers, metal-tipped boots to her knees, an assortment of daggers and swords and firestix, and a scarlet-lined cape that billowed around her.

"Today," said D'Mara, "we reclaim what is ours. We return from our long and unjust exile, to a world ripe for the picking. I have seen the Lost Lands, and they are weak. The people there have forgotten us. They no longer watch the skies, fearing the shadow of Raptors, dreading the roar of our fury. But no more!"

The Raptors responded with eager anticipation, lifting wings, rattling scales, summoning flames that danced on their red tongues.

"Raptors," said D'Mara, "today we return! We rise! And we *conquer*!"

The battle roars that rose then shook the very mountain. The human servants cowered, covering their ears. D'Mara looked to her right and left, where Edward was seated on Decimus and Mirra was on Trixtan. Tamra was behind them, on a sinewy Yellow named Kardessa, having refused to be left behind. Only Kaan remained, sour-faced and resentful on the loggia. D'Mara had told him he would be in charge of the fortress while they were gone, in an effort to appease him, but the truth was that none of the First Flight would deign to carry him, and Valkea herself had insisted he stay. The Red was not very fond of the youngest Lennix. But no matter. Today was too important for D'Mara to concern herself with the various grievances of her spoiled children.

Today was for blood and glory.

Today was for *war*.

"Flight Silver," she called out, "to me!"

They erupted into the sky in a storm of wings, claws, and dragonfire.

35

A Grim Meeting

Two days after they left Scotland, Sirin, Allie, and Bellacrux were nearly to their destination. They'd stopped to rest twice, once on the southern tip of Greenland, then in a forest in Nova Scotia. The next stop would be New York City . . . the final resting place of the Skyspinner.

Bellacrux followed endless coastline, her shadow flickering over sandy beaches and rocky shoals. It was a tense, silent journey. Sirin's stomach felt like a buzzing hive of anxiety-ridden bees. She couldn't stop worrying about Joss. Even if he managed to escape the fortress, how would he find them again? Joss wouldn't even know where to start looking.

Allie turned around, swinging her leg over so she was sitting backward, facing Sirin.

"The Heart could be anywhere in this city. Any ideas where to start?"

Sirin chewed her lip. "Thorval did tell me more about the Skyspinner, after you . . . left. After she fell into the sea, she washed up on the shore of an island. *This* island."

She pointed to Manhattan on the map.

"It's a city now, but it used to be a swamp. Over time, Thorval said, the Skyspinner would have sunk deeper and deeper in the ground until she seemed to disappear completely."

"So . . . her Heart must be buried *under* this city?"

Sirin grimaced. "This is not going to be easy, Allie."

"No kidding," Allie muttered. She turned around again.

"Does Bellacrux have any ideas?" Sirin asked. "She *is* the dragon here, and it's a dragon's bones we're looking for."

Allie was silent a moment, apparently conferring with her Lock. Then she said, "Bell says we must move quickly. The Raptors will be out in full force soon, and it will be a race to determine the future of all dragonkind."

Sirin sighed. That wasn't the sort of helpful insight she'd been hoping for.

Minutes later, just as Sirin had predicted, Long Island rolled beneath them, looking like an arm stretching out in warning. The sky was darkening, and ahead, Sirin saw the sparkle of lights.

"Look!" Sirin said, pointing. "That must be it!"

They'd passed over many towns and cities on their journey, but now, as the day began to turn to twilight, Sirin laid eyes on the brightest, most dazzling, most terrifyingly enormous city she'd seen yet. It wasn't as large as London, but it was packed together more tightly, buildings all smashed up against one another and stretching to the clouds. Bridges stretched over wide rivers, where boats churned up the water, some as small as cars, others as big as Sirin's old school.

"We'd better keep out of sight," said Sirin. "Or they'll send fighter jets or missiles or who knows what else to try and shoot us down."

"I don't know what those are," Allie said. "But if you say so."

Bellacrux wheeled away from the city and stayed low, nearly skimming the surface of the water, where any wandering eyes wouldn't be able to pick her out against the dark waves.

Sirin stared at the distant city and felt as if she were shrinking, till she was as small as an ant. It was so much bigger than she'd anticipated. Their task, which had been monstrously difficult, now looked to be altogether impossible.

They glided past a small island, atop which Sirin spied the Statue of Liberty. The sight made her skin prickle; there was something noble and defiant about the great green lady, with her torch held high and her unblinking eyes watching the two girls and the dragon skim past. It was as if she knew the importance of their mission and was solemnly wishing them luck.

"At least we beat the Raptors here," said Sirin.

At that moment, a mighty roar shook the sky.

Sirin looked up as, one by one, dragons began to appear. They seemed to pop out of nowhere—but Sirin, of course, knew exactly where they'd come from. And from her vantage below, she could easily make out the three-pronged tattoos on their bellies. Even if she hadn't seen them, there would have been no mistaking the fiery red scales of Valkea, the dragon who'd attacked them at the Blue islands and again at Loch Ness. She terrified Sirin more than all the others put together.

"*Bellacrux!*" Allie screamed.

The Green dipped lower, hiding them between the high, rolling waves. But it was poor cover and couldn't protect them for long.

"I jinxed us," Sirin whispered hoarsely. "I jinxed us."

"I wish you had," said Allie. "We could use someone with magic powers right about now."

Just then, they were spotted.

The smallest of the Raptors—who was still larger than most dragons ever grew—let out a screech of warning to its companions. They all turned as one, like a flock of deadly, fire-breathing sparrows.

And their eyes all fixed on Bellacrux and her riders below.

Sirin's stomach dropped. They were wildly outnumbered, with no storm to disappear into this time. No Lysander to open a magic doorway to refuge.

They were helpless.

Bellacrux roared a roar to flatten the very waves, then shot upward in a powerful vertical climb that nearly unseated Allie and Sirin both. The girls held on desperately, Allie to Bellacrux's crest, Sirin to Allie's waist.

When they were level with the flight of Raptors, Bellacrux hovered on powerful wingbeats. The Raptors filled the sky all around, snarling and speeding by so close they nearly clipped Bellacrux's wings. Sirin saw the twins Mirra and Tamra among them, and a man who must have been their father. D'Mara was unmistakable—Sirin would never forget the feeling of that awful woman's blade against her throat.

Most horrifyingly of all, on each Raptor's brow gleamed a Silver scale.

Poor Lysander. Now Sirin knew her friend and his Lock must have been captured. Her stomach twisted, and her face burned with anger. What of Sammi? she wondered. She still couldn't feel her own Lock, just the twinge of pain in her chest where her bond with her was still stretched too tight.

After another few moments of the Raptors' taunting growls and dangerously close flybys, Valkea swooped in and circled them, breathing out a lazy stream of fire that left them wreathed in smoke. Sirin coughed and tried to wave it away.

"Bellacrux," said D'Mara Lennix, her expression practically jubilant. "Old friend. I don't suppose you've found the treasure we all seek?"

Bellacrux snarled and called her a word in dragonsong that Sirin guessed wasn't very flattering. D'Mara just laughed.

"I suppose you haven't," she said, "or else we would all be groveling at your feet right now, wouldn't we? The Skyspinner's Heart is *mine*, Bellacrux. I will offer you only one chance at mercy: Help me find it, and I will spare you and your human Lock." She gave Allie a mocking little wave, and Allie scowled back. But despite her defiance, the girl was trembling, and Sirin quietly squeezed her arm. She was shaking too.

"The only thing you'll get from us," Allie yelled, "is a fight!"

D'Mara laughed again. "Little fool. You'd have been better off if you'd stayed in my dungeon. Very well. As if I needed your aid anyway." She cocked her head, her eyes shifting to Sirin. "You, on the other hand, may prove useful. Come with me, girl, and you may be spared. Give me your knowledge of this world, and I will spare the life of Joshua Moran."

Joss was still alive! That was something to be glad for, even as death stared them down through Valkea's red eyes.

"As if I could ever take your word," Sirin said to D'Mara.

"Yeah, what she said," Allie added. "NOW, BELLACRUX!"

The Green, who'd been building up a massive ball of flame in her belly, the fire so hot that Sirin felt her legs warming, now unleashed it all. Valkea was forced to reel backward, and Bellacrux took the chance to dive.

The Raptors gave chase at once. Bellacrux flew as fast as her wings could pump, her neck stretched out and her tail taut behind her. Sirin leaned low, holding on to Allie tightly and looking over her shoulder at their pursuers. Valkea led them, and already the Red was closing in.

In moments, they reached the inner bay with its bustle of boats and bridges and gleaming metal towers. There would be no hiding their presence now. One dragon might have slipped through unseen, using waves for cover, but an entire flight of Raptors, all of them roaring and hissing and spitting rolling plumes of fire, had to be drawing every human eye for a mile around.

Well, Earth, Sirin thought, looking down at the gaping expressions of a ferry full of passengers on their way to the giant green statue, *the dragons are back.*

36

Old Foe, New Friend

Joss paced his cell, his hands running anxiously through his hair. The fortress, which had bustled with activity all morning, had now gone silent. He knew that could only mean one thing: the Raptors had begun their raid on the Lost Lands.

All thanks to Lysander.

He paused, his hands gripping the bars of his cell, and gazed at his Lock. Lysander was curled into a silver, scaled ball, fast asleep. He'd been that way ever since D'Mara had pulled eleven of his scales from his haunch, and Joss hadn't wanted to disturb him. Lysander had insisted it didn't hurt, but Joss knew it had stung a bit because he'd felt the echoes of the pain himself. His Lock couldn't hide much from him.

But it was hard to let Lysander sleep when Joss was desperate to talk to him. They had to work out a plan. They had to *think*. Joss knew from Kaan's boasting that they'd learned the location of the Heart, which meant the Raptors would soon be closing in on Allie, Sirin, and Bellacrux. And there was nothing Joss could do to help his sister and friends.

With a snarl of frustration, Joss kicked the bars of his cell and got a stubbed toe in return.

He glanced at Lysander, expecting the sharp burst of pain in his foot to reach his Lock and wake him.

But Lysander didn't wake.

Lysander? Lysander, are you all right? Did she hurt you worse than I realized? Alarmed, Joss switched to speaking aloud. "Lysander!"

"Shut up, already!" snapped a voice.

Joss looked over to the stairs, where he could just make out a figure leaning against the wall, hidden by gloomy shadow.

"Kaan?"

"Yeah, that's right. I'm in charge now, and if you don't shut up, I'll break your arms."

Joss blinked, then barked a caustic laugh. "Didn't make the raid, huh? Mummy left you to babysit *me*?"

"I said *shut UP*!" Kaan shoved off the wall and stepped into the light of the single torch blazing in the dungeon. He glared at Joss.

Joss glanced at Lysander, who still did not wake, and suddenly it dawned on him.

Lysander was in his dragonfire sleep.

Finally.

Quickly, Joss counted backward. From what he could determine, Lysander had been asleep for almost a full twenty-four hours. Which meant that at any moment his Lock would awaken in his full dragon strength—a true adult Silver.

Dragonfire alone wouldn't be enough to break out of this prison. It had been built to hold full-grown dragons, after all.

But it might help.

Because just then Joss spotted the dungeon key in Kaan's

pocket. If Lysander could blast fire at Kaan, maybe he'd drop it within reach in his haste to get away. Which meant Joss had to keep Kaan close until Lysander awoke, without Kaan noticing that Lysander was in a deeper-than-usual sleep. If he realized Lysander would soon wake with fire in his jaws, he would certainly keep his distance.

"I bet your ma gave you orders not to touch us," said Joss. In taunting nonchalance, he leaned his shoulder against the wall of his cell and crossed his arms. "Sucks being grounded, doesn't it?"

"I'm not grounded!" Kaan said through his teeth. "I'm in *charge*, you mudbrain. Until Ma gets back, that makes me lord of this fortress."

"Or until your father gets back, or Tamra. Or even *Mirra*." Joss laughed. "I think that makes you the bottom of the ladder, doesn't it?"

Kaan shot him a savage look. "You better stop talking, sheep boy," he said in a low voice.

"Why? What are you going to do? Come in here and punch me?"

Kaan started to reach for the door, then stopped. "You're just trying to get me to open this door! Ha! Well, shows how stupid you are. I'm not falling for it, mudbrain."

"At least I *have* a brain."

"I said SHUT UP!" Kaan screamed. He ran across the dungeon and grabbed a firestik from the supply hanging on the wall. Joss's stomach dropped. He backed away, prepared to fight tooth and nail when Kaan came into his cell, firestik or not.

But it wasn't his cell Kaan went to. It was Lysander's.

"Stop!" Joss yelled. "You leave him alone! Or I'll—"

"What?" Kaan smirked. "You'll do nothing and you know it. Like I said, *I'm* in charge now."

Kaan began to thrust the firestik through the bars of Lysander's cell, then stopped.

"Wait a minute . . ." He studied the Silver closer.

"Hey, Kaan!" Joss called desperately. "You too chicken to use that on *me*? Come try! You wouldn't get close! Kaan!"

But it was too late. Kaan turned around and laughed. "He's in his dragonfire sleep, isn't he? Is that what all this is about? You want me nearby so he can wake up and roast me alive. Well, well. Little sheep boy has more Raptor in him than I thought."

Joss stared at him, helpless and furious and disappointed. His only plan, and it had fallen through just like that.

"Good-bye, Joshua," Kaan said, tapping the firestik on his shoulder as he strode to the stairs. "It's been *so* nice chatting, but I've got loads of things to do, what with me being in charge of the fortress and all. Try not to rot too quickly. I'm sure you'll want to say hello to your little friend Sirin before I put her to work scrubbing my latrine."

Joss roared and shook his bars, but he was as helpless as ever.

When Kaan was gone, Joss sank to the dirty straw floor and put his head on his knees. *Lysander, Lysander. What now? He's right. They're going to kill Allie and capture Sirin. I can't do anything to stop them.*

Joss.

Joss raised his head to see Lysander blinking sleepily at him.

It will be all right, Joss.

"How do you know that?" Joss whispered. "Everything's gone to pieces."

Listen, my Lock.

Joss did and heard nothing but the *drip-drip* of water deeper in the dungeon, and the clatter of a brass key tumbling down stone steps.

The key!

Joss stared in shock as the bright little object came bouncing down the stairs, then landed on the floor, where it glinted temptingly. But it was still far out of reach.

"What the . . . Kaan?"

He heard a sudden scrabble of claws and a dragon-like squeal, and then Sammi burst out of the stairs and growled in triumph. She scooped up the key and darted to Joss's cell.

"Sammi!" He had never been so glad to see the little pest. She pushed the key through the bars and then bounced around like an excited puppy, her tongue lolling out of her mouth.

"Good girl!" Joss grabbed the key and shoved it into the lock of his door. It opened with a squeak. "But how did you get in here all by yourself? And how did you get the better of Kaan?"

"Well," said a new voice. "She had a little help."

Joss wheeled around, then stared.

It was a Lennix striding toward him, with one of the fortress servants at his heels. But it wasn't Kaan.

It was *Declan*.

Joss went on guard at once, holding up the key as if it might possibly defend him. Behind him, Lysander growled.

"Easy," Declan said, raising his hands. "I'm a friend. Or at least, I am now."

"What are you doing here?" Joss asked. "I thought you ran off after we escaped the last time."

"I did," said Declan. "But I've been in contact with Carli here. She told me you'd been captured, and I decided it was time I returned."

He put his arm around the shoulders of the red-haired servant girl Carli, for that's who had followed him down the steps. She smiled up at him.

"Lysander was the first dragon I ever liked," she said. "I couldn't let him rot in here while D'Mara pulled out his scales one by one."

"Yes, about that," said Declan, his face turning grim. "We have to stop my mother from taking more scales. I've been out among the hidden clans, and word is spreading that D'Mara Lennix can lead dragons to the Lost Lands. More and more young Reds and Yellows are deserting their clans and coming here, to join the Raptors. They're so tired of not having enough to eat that they're willing to turn Raptor if it means going to the Lost Lands."

Joss's eyes widened. He imagined the Raptor ranks swelling larger and larger, becoming too powerful to ever be defeated.

"What do we do?" he asked.

"Well, first," said Declan, "let your poor dragon out."

Yes, please, Lysander sent dryly. Joss hurried to unlock his door, and the Silver slipped out and shook himself. There shone a patch of vulnerable, unprotected skin on his haunch, where D'Mara had taken the scales. But otherwise, Lysander looked as healthy and strong as ever.

"Now," said Declan. "My new Lock Ramon's waiting for us in the mountains. We couldn't risk him being spotted by the others. This place is still thronging with Raptors. Kaan, the little brat, is tied up at the top of the stairs, but someone will find him soon."

"We have to get to the Lost Lands," said Joss. "It's worse than you thought, Declan. There's this thing called the Heart— Oh, I'll tell you on the way. You . . . you will come and help us, won't you?"

Declan nodded. "I can't hurt my family, Joss. Horrid as they are, they are still my parents and siblings. But I will help you stop them from destroying any more dragons. I owe it to Timoleon."

Joss's heart clanged in his chest as he raced up the stairs, passing a bound and gagged Kaan. Kaan groaned and glared, and Joss stopped just long enough to say, "Guess this puts *me* in charge, huh?"

Joss! called Lysander, from farther ahead.

One sec! Joss replied. He bent over and yanked off the neon-yellow trainers from Kaan's feet. "I'll just have these back, then."

Leaving Kaan to wriggle in fury, Joss hurried to catch up to the others, hopping as he pulled on his shoes. He threw himself onto Lysander's back without even slowing, and Declan climbed up behind him.

"Go west," Carli said. "I saw D'Mara comparing maps of the Lost Lands to our world, and she figured out that if they went through a portal over the western swamps, they'd appear right over the city they were looking for. That's where you'll find them."

"Thanks, Carli," Declan said. He reached down and clasped hands with her. "I'll come back for you. I promise. Just like I said in the letters I sent you—I'm going to get you out of here."

"Just hurry," she said. "And don't do anything stupid, like getting yourself killed."

"Right," said Declan. "I'll do my best. Now, Joss, let's pick up Ramon, then it's to the Lost Lands."

"To Allie and Sirin," said Joss.

And our most difficult battle yet, added Lysander.

37

The Battle of New York

The heat of Raptor fire washed over Allie.

They were *everywhere*.

She'd counted around a dozen, but it may as well have been a hundred for how outnumbered they were. In fact, the Raptors must have realized they didn't all have to give chase to Bellacrux. Half of them peeled away to torment the humans. Decimus landed atop the green statue, his claws leaving long scratches on the lady's arms and shoulders. He roared, spilling dragonfire all around. Below, humans ran screaming back to their boats, but Mirra and Trixtan were setting the vessels ablaze, cutting off their escape.

"We have to help them!" Sirin yelled.

Allie wanted to point out that they couldn't even help themselves but was forced to focus all her attention on keeping her seat as Bellacrux wheeled abruptly, barely escaping a jet of dragonfire Valkea had loosed.

This put them directly on course to collide with another Raptor—a Yellow named Kardessa, with Tamra on her back. Allie remembered Kardessa from her time as a servant in Fortress Lennix. The Yellow had a mean streak as deep as the sea, and was known to be a little unhinged. Half the time a servant lost a finger, it was to Kardessa's jaws.

Now the Yellow was about to set a ferry on fire, with several hundred people on board.

Bell!

I see her.

Bellacrux seized Kardessa's wing and pulled it, flipping the dragon in midair. Tamra somehow managed to stay seated, and the ferry churned away at full speed, unharmed. Bellacrux's attack sent Kardessa scrambling to recover her balance, and the Yellow screamed in fury at being robbed of her prey. She let the ferry go and instead gave chase to Bellacrux.

We cannot keep this up for long, Bellacrux told Allie.

They had Valkea and Kardessa now pursuing them plus a few more Raptors. Bellacrux didn't even try to fight back, but flew evasively, dodging jets of dragonfire and zinging firestix.

All around the bay, bells and alarms wailed. The humans scrambled for safety, but nowhere was safe. A Raptor tore the roof off a boat, and a few terrified people dived overboard and attempted to swim to shore. Screams filled the air.

We have to find the Skyspinner's Heart, Allie sent. *That's the only way we can stop them.*

I'm a little busy simply keeping us all alive at the moment! came Bellacrux's strained reply. The Green dived just as a hail of firestix, thrown by D'Mara, Tamra, and Mirra, rained overhead.

Bellacrux was tiring. Even if Allie weren't Locked with her, she would see it. The dragon's wings faltered between beats and she gasped for breath. After all, she'd been flying for two days before this, across an entire ocean. The Raptors had arrived on fresh wings.

Despair began to overtake Allie. Everything seemed to slow

around her—the screaming people in the boats, the spray of dragonfire burning lines across the shoreline, the rise and fall of Bellacrux's wings. Over all the noise, she could hear her own heartbeat.

Then she blinked, and everything sped forward, a whirlwind of motion and sound and hot, angry flames.

"D'Mara," she said. *We have to at least take out D'Mara. Maybe that would scare the others off.*

Cut off the head, agreed Bellacrux, *and the body dies. Hold on tight. VERY tight.*

Allie did, relaying the order to Sirin. The girls held on with all their strength as Bellacrux performed a spectacular move, flipping herself head over tail and then rolling so that she was now facing their pursers. Allie hadn't even known the enormous dragon was capable of such acrobatics.

Neither, it seemed, had D'Mara. Her expression was pure shock as she suddenly found herself face-to-face with the former Lennix Grand. Valkea was forced to throw her wings wide, like parachutes opening to slow her, or she'd smash right into Bellacrux. They hovered just over the water, their wings whipping up frenzied, white-capped waves.

D'Mara recovered quickly, throwing a firestik that narrowly missed Bellacrux's throat. Instead, it pierced her shoulder. Allie scrambled to pull it out, hissing when it threw sparks that burned her hands. But she yanked it loose and turned it around, aiming right back at D'Mara.

This was it. If she threw now and aimed true, she could impale the woman through her very heart.

But Allie's hand shook.

Now, said Bellacrux. *Take her out!*

But Allie hesitated a moment too long, and the chance was missed. Valkea's head lifted, blocking her shot. Allie dropped the firestik, disgusted with herself for not taking the shot, horrified that she almost had.

I'm sorry, Bell. I . . . I guess I'm not a killer.

She felt Bellacrux sigh even as the Green replied, *I should not have asked it of you, my Lock.*

Tamra on Kardessa and Mirra on Trixtan flanked them, closing off escape to the left or right. Two more Raptors moved above and behind Bellacrux.

They were trapped.

They'd been in this position before, after their mad escape from the fortress, but Bellacrux had been fresh then. Now she seemed barely capable of staying airborne.

Their fight, Allie realized, was over.

She reached back and felt Sirin take her hand.

Bellacrux . . . She couldn't think of anything more to say. She could only send the emotions welling up in her—gratitude, love, sorrow, fear.

In return, she felt her Lock's soothing mental embrace. Even in the face of destruction, Bellacrux radiated calm.

You have fought nobly, Allinson Moran. It has been my honor to be at your side.

Oh, Bell. I love you.

She braced herself, squeezing Sirin's hand tightly. D'Mara raised her hand, the other Raptors waiting for her signal.

"Finish it, Valkea," D'Mara said. "After all, it's not every day you get to destroy a Lennix Grand."

She dropped her hand, and six dragons unleashed their fire all at once.

Allie didn't scream. Even though her eyes closed and her heart stopped beating and she squeezed Sirin's hand so tight the girl's bones crunched, she didn't scream.

But she also didn't feel the flames scorching her flesh.

Instead, she felt a rush of wind and heard a furious, defiant roar that left her head ringing.

Allie opened her eyes.

And gasped.

Lysander!

The Silver dragon had appeared out of nowhere, and now covered them with his own body, his shining wings and tail and claws forming a living shield of flameproof scales. The Raptors' flame rolled off him harmlessly.

"Joss!" Allie screamed.

If her brother had been atop Lysander when the flames hit—

Then she saw them: a pair of familiar, wonderful, blindingly bright yellow shoes dangling under Lysander's wing.

Joss was tucked safely under his Lock's fireproof membrane wing, and he grinned and waved when Allie's gaze met his.

"Allie!"

"JOSS!"

Allie ached to throw her arms around him and never let go again, but there was no time. Lysander pulled away, hurling himself at Valkea and scattering the other Raptors with a mighty thrash of his tail. Joss climbed up and took his seat atop his Lock, waving at Allie and Sirin.

Below him, Lysander unleashed a torrent of fire—and unlike the red flames all other dragons made, his were blue-white, almost blinding to look at.

"Look!" Sirin shouted. "Lysander's got his fire!"

Allie cheered and waved back at her brother, reeling from the sudden joy that flooded her. A moment ago, she'd been bracing for death—and now, Joss was back. Lysander was back. And there was no mistaking the small green blur flying directly at them.

"Sammi!" Sirin cried. She opened her arms and the hatchling flung herself into them.

They weren't the only surprises—a lightning-fast Blue harried the Raptors who'd been attacking the humans, using his superior speed to strike and then dart away again, too quick to catch.

"Declan?" Allie stared. Last she knew, Declan had deserted his family and vanished.

"Long story!" Joss called as Lysander hurtled past them, intercepting Trixtan before he could bite down on Bellacrux's tail.

In the chaos, no one saw Decimus streaking toward them until it was too late, racing over the skin of the sea. Edward roared and raised a firestik in each hand, while Decimus sent a blast of fire swirling toward Bellacrux's unprotected belly.

But then both were thoroughly doused by an enormous wave that seemed to come rushing out of nowhere. A moment later, Allie saw a sleek head rise from the water, hissing and churning up the sea with a lashing, coiled body.

"Thorval!"

The Blue dragon had left his lake at last.

Thorval bugled in greeting before turning back to Decimus.

The Blue couldn't fly, but blood and bone, he could *swim*. And he still had his fire, which he now used to chase Decimus and Edward across the bay.

Allie caught a glimpse of D'Mara's face—stunned, furious, bewildered. But she was the Lennix leader for a reason, and already she had regrouped and gotten control of her flight. Raptors flew to join her, arranging themselves in a circling formation that left them less exposed to Declan and Ramon's sizzling-fast attacks and Lysander's blue fire.

Bellacrux winged away, toward the cluster of tall buildings that seemed to be the hub of the city. Lysander and Ramon followed, and Thorval dipped in and out of the waves. They would do some regrouping of their own. The three dragons landed on the shore, in a shady park filled with humans. Thorval lingered in the water, keeping a close eye on the Raptors, who still circled in the sky above the water.

At the sight of the dragons, the people in the park withdrew, gasping and pointing strange little metal objects at them. Allie wondered if they were weapons—then remembered Sirin explaining the devices back in Oxford.

As if to confirm her very thought, one of the nearest people— a teenage boy in a puffy coat and floppy hat—yelled out, "Dragon dudes! Over here! Say *cheese*!"

They should be running for their lives, she sent to Bellacrux, *and instead they're . . . taking pictures?!*

Humans, returned Bellacrux, as if that explained everything.

Other people now rushed in and ordered everyone to stay back. These men and women wore uniforms and carried objects that reminded Allie of firestix. *Guns*, she realized. She'd heard

Sirin talk about them before. These must be soldiers of some sort. They watched the dragons warily and held the crowd back. Declan raised his hands, to show they were unarmed, but Ramon growled in warning. Everyone backed up farther at the sight of his gleaming fangs and spreading wings.

Meanwhile, Joss had jumped down from Lysander and ran to them. Allie rushed to meet him, colliding in a tangle of limbs and tears and happy laughter.

"You're alive!" Allie yelled.

Joss laughed. "I'm still surprised about that too! Did you get the Heart?"

"If we had, do you think we'd be fighting for our lives right now?"

"We have to find it."

"Obviously!" Even with four more dragons—and that was counting Sammi—they were still hopelessly outnumbered, and now they'd lost the element of surprise.

"Any ideas, Sirin?" Allie turned around. "Sirin?"

Sirin had jumped down, but instead of joining them, she'd walked to the edge of the sidewalk that circled the park. On the other side of an iron railing, waves lapped the shore.

Sammi was squirming in Sirin's arms, licking the girl's face, but Sirin didn't even seem aware of the little dragon. Instead she was staring at the water, her eyes wide and unfocused.

"Sirin?" Allie repeated.

Sammi whined, trying to get the girl's attention, but Sirin didn't even move.

"What's wrong with her?" Joss asked. "Is she hurt?"

Sammi jumped down and ran in frantic circles around his Lock. Alarmed, Allie grabbed Sirin's shoulder and shook her.

The girl started, then blinked rapidly, as if clearing her head. "Allie?"

"You zoned out," Allie said. "Are you okay?"

"I . . ." Again Sirin's eyes wandered to the water and filled with fog. "The Heart . . ."

"What about it?"

"I think I know . . ."

Without another word, Sirin suddenly climbed onto the railing, balanced there a moment—then jumped into the sea.

38

Leap of Faith

Sirin barely felt the shock of the cold water closing over her head. She felt like she was in a dream. Not even Sammi's frantic messages could stop her from plunging deeper into the sea.

Sirin, Sirin, Sirin, Sirin! Come back!

It's all right, she returned faintly. *I . . . I have to keep going.*

Why?

It was a good question, but one for which Sirin had no answer.

She could feel Sammi's panic and confusion, but it was like background noise, a TV running in another room. Easy to ignore.

Harder to ignore was the *feeling* at the tip of her nose, like an itch she couldn't scratch away.

This way! it said, without using words. *Deeper! Farther!*

Sirin swam. She kicked her legs and angled for the bottom of the sea, feeling completely certain which way she should go. The water around her was murky and brown and a bit oily.

Then hands grabbed her. Pulled her to the surface. Held her there as she coughed and gasped.

"Sirin!" Joss said. He had one of her arms, and Allie had the other. They were stronger swimmers than her. Sirin remembered that they'd grown up by the sea.

"What were you *thinking*?" demanded Allie.

"I don't know, except that . . ." A wave splashed Sirin's face and she spat out salty water. "It's hard to explain. But I just have this *feeling*. Please, let me go. I think I can find the Skyspinner's Heart."

"But how do you *know*?"

"I don't. But it came over me all at once. This feeling, like an itch, or a whisper. It's almost like I've been here before, and some part of me knows the way to go even though the rest of me doesn't."

"This feeling," said Allie, "you're sure it's not just, I don't know . . . hunger? Indigestion?"

Sirin shook her head. "I don't know what it is. But I trust it."

"Sirin . . ." Allie looked up, to where the Raptors were still circling in the distance.

Sirin shut her eyes, trying to focus on the strange pull inside her. "There's a cave, I think. Under the water. It's there, right there. It will take us to the Skyspinner. Please, you have to trust me. We have to jump."

"I trust her," said Joss. "Besides, it's not like we have anything else to go on."

Still Allie hesitated.

"Allie." Sirin gripped the girl's arm tightly. "Please."

"Fine," said Allie. "But we're coming with you."

Sirin smiled, hope blooming. "I wouldn't want it any other way."

They dived together, swimming side by side. Sirin led the way, following the tug inside her as if it were a string. The waves were not too strong here, but the dark water made it difficult to see. She swam and swam, until her lungs began to burn and her limbs ached. Doubt made her slow down, and she realized just how stupid this was, swimming into darkness, following nothing but a vague instinct. It reminded her of the time she'd gone hiking with her mum, and had gone wandering off on her own. She'd followed a faint path through the trees for an hour, thinking it was the trail, only to end up totally lost. It hadn't been a trail at all, but her imagination making it seem like the right way. Was that all this was? A wild-goose chase down a false trail?

She began to feel shame, throwing herself into the sea without a moment's thought, and now dragging Joss and Allie down with her.

Just as she started to give up, her eyes going upward to the surface, something brushed her leg. Sirin screamed, bubbles streaming from her mouth. But then she saw a familiar blue eye glinting in the murky water.

Thorval.

Sirin grabbed hold of the Blue dragon and saw Allie and Joss do the same. With her hand around his scales, she was pulled along at four times the pace she'd been swimming. Thorval twisted through the water as if he'd been born in it, and Sirin supposed he might have.

Then Joss tugged Sirin's coat and pointed.

There!

A smudge of darkness in the gloom.

An underwater cave! But as they got closer, Sirin saw it wasn't an ordinary cave. This one was shaped out of stone . . . stone that looked very much like an enormous dragon's skull. The opening was framed by jagged teeth, a gaping maw big enough to swallow them whole.

Her skin pricked as Thorval sped through the open mouth and lifted out of the water, into a pitch-black tunnel almost entirely flooded with water. Between the water and the ceiling of the tunnel was a layer of air—stale, tepid air that stank of fish and garbage—but Sirin breathed it in as if it were a fresh mountain breeze. Thorval opened his mouth and let a thin stream of fire curl over his tongue, providing enough light to illuminate the rough dirt walls and ceiling of the cave. Only now that Sirin could see, she realized it was more tunnel than cave, for it stretched ahead, dark and lined with stone.

"You were right," Allie gasped. "Sirin, how did you know this would be here?"

Sirin shrugged, feeling light-headed. The tug inside her was still there, urging her to go deeper down the tunnel. The goose bumps on her arms weren't just from the cold water.

"This is *her*," said Thorval, flames licking his teeth as he spoke. "The Skyspinner."

"I can't believe it," said Allie. "She would have turned to stone when she died, like any dragon, and then rested here for *two thousand* years."

"So . . . we're in her throat," Sirin said, her eyes growing very wide.

"Gross," said Joss. Then he added, "*Cool.*"

The walls around them must have been the Skyspinner's long neck once. Sirin shivered at the thought. The dragon queen must have been *enormous.*

"Great Scott!" said the Blue, in Nessie's high-pitched voice. "It really is the old queen! And all this time, Thorval, I thought you'd gone bonkers!"

"Bonkers!" Thorval replied to his other self, sounding offended. "Bah! I am *not* bonkers."

Allie coughed.

The tug inside Sirin was stronger than ever, as if a frantic butterfly were trapped inside her ribs, trying to push her forward.

"We have to keep going," Sirin whispered. "It's close. It's so close. This is it. We're almost there."

"I can go no farther, younglings," said Thorval. "As it is, my chest is wedged rather uncomfortably in the old queen's jaws. But I can give you light to guide you."

"Best dunk yourselves under, you lot," added Nessie.

They did, and Sirin looked up to see the dragon breathing fire down the length of the tunnel. In the red light that filtered through the water, she saw Allie and Joss staring wide-eyed, their hair floating around their heads.

When Thorval was done, they popped up again, and Sirin gasped.

"Talonfari!" Allie said. The word for the dragons' form of writing, just like the ones they'd seen in the library of Tashiva Lhaa. Jagged runes were engraved all down the tunnel walls and ceiling. They'd caught and held Thorval's fire, and now glowed dimly red, providing enough light to see by.

"What does it say?" Sirin asked the dragon.

"They are the words of an ancient lament," said Thorval. "Someone must have come here, after the Skyspinner died, and carved them into her stone remains."

"A dragon?" Allie raised her eyebrows. "I thought you were the only one left behind, Thorval."

"Not a dragon," Thorval replied. "These runes are too small and neatly carved. It was a human who left them here."

"Can you translate it?" asked Sirin.

He peered at them a moment more, before shaking his great head. "I cannot. The words are too full of sorrow, too full of suffering. If I spoke them aloud, I should sink to the bottom of the sea with the weight of them in my heart, and not rise for a century."

"Ach," said Nessie, rolling his eyes. "Not again!"

Sirin gasped suddenly, as she felt a flurry of alarm ripple through her. It took her a moment to realize it was coming from Sammi, who was still swooping and diving in the sky.

What's wrong? she asked her Lock.

Tooth and claw and wing! Sammi replied in a frenzy. *I must tear and scratch!*

Sirin turned to the others. "The Raptors are attacking again!"

Allie nodded. "I just heard from Bellacrux. She says she and Lysander will hold them at bay as long as they can."

"I will return and give them my aid," said Thorval. "I have dreamed of wreaking vengeance on Raptor flesh for two millennia."

"Look out for Sammi too," Sirin begged him. "She's not half as big and strong as she thinks she is."

Sammi gave her a mental hiss for that.

"I will," said Thorval. "But hurry. We will not hold them off for long."

"Toodles for now!" piped Nessie, sounding more than ready to be gone from the eerie tunnel.

With that, the Blue dragon withdrew, his head sliding through the water and back out of the Skyspinner's gaping stone jaws.

And the three kids were left alone.

"Right," said Sirin. "Onward, then."

Beneath the glow of the fiery runes, they swam deeper through the black water, down the stone throat of the fallen queen of the dragons.

39

A Tale Writ in Stone

The tunnel—Sirin couldn't let herself think of it as a *throat* or she'd definitely lose her nerve—rose gradually until at last they were wading instead of swimming, then walking on damp stone. Hundreds more runes glowed in the darkness, even beneath their feet. Their breaths and footsteps echoed, mingling with the drip of water.

"This is the strangest place I've ever been," whispered Joss.

"I think it's the strangest place any of us will *ever* be," said Sirin.

Finally, they came to an enormous cavern. It had to be the Skyspinner's torso, though it looked to Sirin more like an actual cave, except for the curved ridges running down the walls—*ribs*, she realized with a shudder. Stalactites hung from the ceiling like sharp icicles, and stalagmites rose around the edges of the chamber to meet them. Drips echoed from every corner, and the whole place was lit by glowing talonfari runes.

"Look," breathed Allie. She pointed to particularly gnarled mass of stone, where stalactites and stalagmites had met to form narrow columns. In the center of these, as if wreathed in stone vines, sat a different sort of rock. This one was smooth and dark, not like the warm brown tones of the stone around it. It was about the size of Sirin's head, smaller than she'd have expected it to be, given the size of the dragon it had once belonged to. "That's it," said Sirin. "It has to be."

That thing, she thought, had once been a pumping *heart*.

Joss approached it first, raising a hand, but not quite touching it. It was so black that it seemed to suck in the light from the runes around it.

"It's broken," he said. "See?"

Sirin leaned over to see it was true. The rock had cracks running over it, and one small place where a piece had been chipped away.

"We came all this way," said Allie, her voice tight. "We gambled our lives and our Locks' lives on this rock. And it's *broken*."

"Maybe it will still work," said Sirin.

Allie rapped it with her knuckles. Sirin and Joss recoiled, gasping.

But nothing happened.

"Bellacrux," Allie whispered, and then her eyes went foggy, which told Sirin the girl was communicating with her Lock, asking for advice.

She and Joss watched Allie hopefully. After a moment, Allie blinked and turned to them. "She wants me to look at the runes. She said maybe there are instructions or something."

So they waited another minute while Allie paced around the chamber, looking at the walls and ceiling, where mysterious ancient hands had carved the stone.

While she waited, Sirin reached for her Lock. *Sammi?*

Sirin. Did you find it?

Maybe.

Find it. Hurry. Sammi sounded exhausted. The battle with the Raptors had to be pushing all their Locks to the limit.

As if in confirmation, Joss looked at Sirin and said, "Lysander can't hold up much longer. They got him with firestix where D'Mara took his scales. He's hurt, Sirin."

Sirin balled her hands into fists. *Be careful*, she sent to Sammi. *I'll be back as soon as I can.*

Her Lock couldn't even manage a reply, but she caught a brief, blurry glimpse of what she was seeing: burning skies, Raptors everywhere.

Finally, Allie returned to them. "Bellacrux couldn't make out much. She had to focus on fighting. But what she did read she said looked like the same lament Thorval saw. But she also saw something else. A name."

"A name?" echoed Joss.

"Sirina."

"Hey," said Joss, "that sounds sort of like Sirin."

"Sirina was apparently the one who carved all these runes," said Allie. "She was the Skyspinner's Lock."

A strange feeling ran through Sirin—like the prick of static electricity she'd sometimes got on playground slides. "The Skyspinner had a human Lock."

"Who mourned her after she died," said Allie. "She's the one who broke the heart."

"Sirina shattered it?" Sirin looked at the dark stone with its cracked surface.

"She was angry, but the runes don't say why. Only that she thought the Heart's power shouldn't ever be used again. She took one piece of it and . . . There." Allie pointed to the set of runes nearest to the darkened stone of the Heart. "This bit says the Skyspinner's Heart would forever be close to Sirina's. That her daughters would bear it through all of time, and long after the rest of the world had forgotten dragons, they would remember."

They would remember.

The words echoed through Sirin as if her heart were a struck gong.

They would remember.

Another voice came rushing behind the words, startled out of the recesses of Sirin's memory. It wasn't Allie's voice, or Sammi's.

It was the voice that, until two days ago, she'd been trying so hard to forget.

A long, long time ago, her mother had said to her, *so long ago that most people have forgotten, humans and dragons lived in harmony together.*

"And here," said Allie, pointing to another line of glowing runes, "Sirina says that just as she and the Skyspinner broke the bond between humanity and dragonkind, one day, her descendant will help restore it."

"Whoa," said Joss. "Imagine having the Lock of the Skyspinner for an ancestor!"

Sirin felt cold and hot at the same time. Her scalp prickled. Her mouth was dry and her thoughts whirled like leaves. Her hand moved to her collarbone and the hard pendant beneath her shirt.

I like to think, her mother had said, *it belonged to one of our ancestors caught up in a dragon battle, and that they survived to tell the tale.*

Sirin lifted her eyes to the burning runes all around her, bearing their tale of loss and grief and fragile hope through the centuries. Joss and Allie were still talking, but she barely heard them. Sound was muffled behind the thumping of Sirin's own heart, and she felt as if she were floating as she moved toward the black stone embedded in the cavern's rocky grip.

The dragonstone was in her hand, her fingers curled over it, its silver band cutting into her palm. A bit of prying with her nail, and it popped free of its setting. She saw, for the first time, that the back of it wasn't smooth like the front. Instead, it was jagged and rough, as if it had been broken off a larger whole.

"Sirin?" called Joss. "What are you doing?"

She couldn't have answered even if she'd known what to say. Her throat was in a knot.

Eyes wide, breath suspended, Sirin held out the dragonstone. Her eyes followed its familiar contours, the blue-green colors on it shifting as always, as if it were alive.

"Sirin!" Allie said. She and Joss were standing behind her now. "Is that . . ."

"No," said Joss. "It can't be. No way."

Sirin swallowed hard.

Then she placed the dragonstone into the small gouge at the center of the Skyspinner's Heart.

It fit perfectly.

All at once the stone began to glow. Veins of blue light spread outward from the dragonstone, and the three kids jumped back. With a sound like splintering stone, the cracks sealed themselves. The chips smoothed over. And Sirin's dragonstone, which she'd worn over her own heart for as long as she could remember, which was her last tangible connection to her mother, melded into the stone until she could no longer even tell where it had been.

Instead, she beheld before her the blue-green shine of the Skyspinner's Heart, whole again, glowing faintly, pulsing with hidden power.

"Nicely done, mudbrains," said a caustic voice behind them, followed by the slow clapping of hands. "I love it when others do the hard work for me."

40

Up and Up and Up

Tamra," Allie sighed. "And I suppose that's Mirra lurking behind you."

"I am not *lurking*," Mirra said sullenly, but she stepped out of the shadows, standing even with her twin.

The girls were dripping wet, having just surfaced from the flooded tunnel of the Skyspinner's throat. They looked terrible, the signs of battle evident in their singed hair and torn clothes. Allie felt a savage stab of satisfaction; Bellacrux, Lysander, Thorval, and even little Sammi must have been giving the Raptors as good as they got.

"Ma was right," said Mirra. "They did lead us straight to the Heart, like dummies. Ugh, this place is *gross*."

"All of you step aside," said Tamra. She'd brought a firestik with her, and now she raised it like a spear. "We'll be taking that shiny rock."

"Taking it right back to your mother, I suppose," said Allie, grinding her teeth. "And Valkea."

"What's D'Mara doing with Valkea anyway?" said Joss. "I thought she was your Lock, Tamra."

Tamra's face hardened, and Mirra snickered. "Not anymore.

Ma Locked with her. They broke their old bonds to do it. Tamra's been puking her guts out for the last two days because of it."

"*Shut up*," Tamra hissed, driving her elbow into Mirra's ribs.

"Ow!" Her twin glared at her.

"I don't even care," said Tamra. "Valkea was a lousy Lock anyway. I bet it was all her idea. Good riddance, I say. Now *move*, or you can eat fire." She brandished the firestik, forcing them to step away.

Allie clenched her fists as Tamra approached the Heart. Mirra stuck close to her twin, while keeping a watchful eye on the Morans and Sirin.

"It's not much to look at, is it?" said Tamra. She shrugged, then used the firestik to begin hacking at the rock around the Heart.

"Be careful!" cried Sirin. "It's fragile!"

Ignoring her, Tamra dug and chipped away until at last the stone was free. Then she picked it up, hefting it in one palm. "It's lighter than it looks," she said musingly. "And so *small*. This Skyspinner must have been a real jerk, with a heart as small as this."

"You saw the Skyspinner," said Allie. "Tamra, you *saw* her in that scroll. Remember? She died to protect to this world. You can't do this."

"Nobody tells me what I can't do," Tamra growled.

"Including your mum?" asked Sirin softly.

Tamra shot them a sour look, but Allie saw her hand tighten on her firestik.

"She stole your Lock," Allie said. "She betrayed you in the

worst way anyone *could*. She's just using you, Tamra. And you'll *still* give her power over two worlds?"

"Maybe *I'll* use it," said Tamra. "Maybe I'll get revenge on *all* of you."

Mirra frowned. "Tamra. Don't be stupid. We're taking it to Ma."

Tamra shrugged, as if she didn't care one way or another, and tossed the Heart, catching it again. Beside Allie, Sirin flinched, her hands twitching like she wanted to grab it from Tamra.

"What about you, Mirra?" Joss said. "It's not like you're exactly D'Mara's favorite. Do you really think she deserves control of all the dragons?"

"He's got a point," said Tamra, smirking. "I mean, it's not like you and Ma are best of friends."

Mirra's face darkened. She stared hard at the floor, a storm brewing in her eyes. Allie felt a stirring of hope. Tamra might be a lost cause, but Mirra had always seemed gentler, more pliant. A little more like Declan, and now he was fighting on *their* side. Maybe it was just Tamra's influence that had made Mirra act so horribly in the past. If she was willing to switch sides, Allie might even forgive her for trying to feed her to Bellacrux.

"You're right," Mirra whispered at last. "You're all right. I'm not the favorite. I might as well be Tamra's shadow. It's always been Tamra, clever Tamra, who seemed in charge." Then at last she looked up, at her twin. Her eyes blazed with fury. "Which is why everything will change when *I* am the one who gives Ma the Skyspinner's Heart!"

Before anyone could react, Mirra snatched the Heart out of Tamra's hand and ran.

"You—" Tamra stared in shock at her empty palm, then at the

receding form of her sister. Instead of running toward the tunnel, which was now blocked by Sirin and the Morans, Mirra ran deeper into the cavern.

"Get her!" yelled Allie.

They all took off running, Tamra in the lead. Her legs were longer and she soon outpaced them.

The walls of the chamber began to change the farther back they ran. Instead of round walls, they saw sharp angles, unnatural corners. These were, Allie realized, the foundations of buildings. The city had dug deep roots into the ground, right into the stone remains of the ancient dragon. And between these foundations ran a great many tunnels and tubes. Soon they were forced to proceed in single file, down the square tunnel Mirra had taken.

"I think we're in some kind of drain system," said Sirin. They were running through shallow water, the *slap-slap* of their shoes echoing around them. A few seconds later, the tunnel branched three ways.

"Great!" said Joss. "Where'd they go?"

They stopped to listen, but sound in this place was warped and confusing, and they couldn't tell where the echoes of the twins' steps were coming from.

"Split up?" suggested Sirin.

"No," said Allie. "We might never find each other again in this maze."

She chose the left tunnel at random.

They ran onward, the tunnel air starting to stink around them. Allie didn't want to think about what they might be running through. Soon, she started to panic, realizing they'd never find their way back now. They'd taken turn after turn, and it was nearly pitch-black. Ten minutes passed. Twenty. Allie's legs were turning to lead. Through her link with Bellacrux, she knew her dragon was even more exhausted. The fight against the Raptors was taking everything the old Green had—and she didn't have much more to give.

They needed to recover the Skyspinner's Heart and end this battle. *Fast.*

"Sirin?" Her own voice sounded high and alarmed in her ears.

"There's a big drain here," said Sirin, knocking on slatted metal above their heads. "If we can open it, maybe it'll lead to the outside. We'll have to catch them in the air now."

They pushed together, and the grate clattered aside onto a hard floor. The opening was just wide enough for them to crawl through.

"Some kind of basement," said Sirin, looking around. The room was dark and large, and mechanical shapes loomed around them.

Joss found stairs, which they raced up, their wet shoes squeaking and leaving a trail of puddles. Up and up and up they ran, the staircase crooking round and round—until they burst out into a shining, magnificent room with stone murals on the walls and ceiling.

"Wait, I've seen this in movies," said Sirin, blinking at a sign on the wall. "It's the Empire State Building!"

"What does that mean?" asked Joss.

"It means we should *run!*" Sirin pushed them both toward the next staircase just as a uniformed man appeared from a doorway, shouting at them.

"You kids, stop right there! We're closed!" he called. "The city's under attack! HEY! STOP!"

They didn't stop. They just ran faster, up and up and up.

In minutes, Allie was panting, her legs aching. But she ran on. The man was chasing after them, roaring at them to come down, but she could hear that he was getting winded too.

Up and up and *up*.

Ten minutes later, they were no longer running but gasping as they heaved their legs up stair after stair.

"Should have . . . taken . . . the lift," groaned Sirin.

"What's . . . an elevator?" asked Joss.

Fifteen minutes later, they were leaning against the walls. Sirin was crawling on her hands and knees.

"Almost . . . *there*," she gasped, pointing to a sign that said OBSERVATION DECK.

Allie moaned and forced herself up another step.

Finally, they came to a door that opened to a balcony, its railings far too high to climb and tipped in spikes. Allie stared at the view beyond. The city gleamed all around them, aglow with lights. Darkness had fallen since they'd been in the cavern, but with all the gleaming windows and signs, it seemed nearly as bright as daytime.

"What now?" said Joss.

Allie grinned, took a moment to catch her breath, then said, "Dingbat. Now we *fly*."

41

The Skyspinner's Heart

Allie ran a few steps, jumped into the air—and caught hold of Bellacrux's claw as the dragon swooped down to meet her.

Did you get it? her Lock asked.

Yes, but then we lost it. And hello to you too.

Bellacrux growled, then wheeled to make another pass at the building. The uniformed man had reached the balcony, his chest heaving and sweat running down his face. When he saw the great dragon soaring directly at him, he screamed and flattened himself against a glass window.

Bellacrux picked up Sirin, and a moment later, Lysander arrived to pluck Joss from the balcony. Then they winged away, Sammi darting in to lick Sirin's cheek.

Allie saw scorch marks all over her dragon, and there was a tear in Bellacrux's left wing.

Are you all right, Bell?

Of course I am. It takes more than a few mewling Raptors to take down Bellacrux the Grand!

The Green's reply was proud, but Allie could feel the strain in her wingbeats. Bellacrux was beyond exhausted.

Mirra has the Heart, she sent. *We have to find her.*

I saw her, on Trixtan, moments ago!

The twins must have found their way to the surface first.

Bellacrux lifted higher into the air, scanning every direction. They soared above the city, the grid of streets below glowing with cars and buses. It seemed even busier than in the daytime. The towers gleamed with yellow windows and signs flashed every color along the shops. Above, she heard a sudden roar like a dragon's snarl and looked up to see a trio of winged machines speed overhead.

"Fighter jets!" said Sirin. "They're fast, but they'll never catch the Raptors as long as they stay low among the buildings."

Sure enough, Allie spotted shadows racing over the streets— Raptors on the hunt.

We took the battle to land soon after you dived, when the human things called fighter jets appeared, said Bellacrux. *We're harder to catch here, both by the humans and the Raptors. And D'Mara's flight has been forced to separate to hunt for us.*

We have to find Trixtan and Mirra before they find D'Mara.

Agreed.

It didn't take long. All they had to do was follow the trail of smoke left by dragonfire. Several buildings were ablaze, and sirens wailed to the sky, sounding like wounded dragons. Allie saw a flash of green scales in the light of a flashing sign, and pointed.

"That's her!"

Bellacrux and Lysander dived in silent unison. Allie could now make out Mirra's face, shifting from blue to red to green as Trixtan soared across the bright signs. Her gaze was intent on a certain point; Allie followed it to see D'Mara waiting on Valkea, above a wide-open area filled with masses of people and lit by hundreds of flashing lights. Valkea bellowed a roar that shook the windows, followed by a wide spray of dragonfire. She was calling the other Raptors to her. A wave of screams rose from the crowds below. People ran in all directions, but a great many stood and took pictures. Others cheered.

Earth humans were, Allie had decided, completely bonkers.

"Times Square," said Sirin behind her. "Oh, Allie, we've *got* to stop her!"

Bellacrux put on a last burst of speed, and Allie knew her Lock was drawing on her final reserves of strength. She tried to will her own remaining energy into her dragon.

But before they could reach Mirra, another dragon darted between them and looped upside down.

Kardessa and Tamra!

Tamra snatched the Heart out of her sister's hands, and then Kardessa righted herself and they flew high, high into the air.

Bellacrux spread her wings, changing course with an audible groan of effort. More Raptors appeared, answering Valkea's summons. They gathered in the air, circling and hovering. Bellacrux, Lysander, and Sammi stopped across the square, just out of range of their fire.

Between them, her hand holding the Heart high, was Tamra. Kardessa's wings flashed like gold as she treaded the air, facing Valkea.

"You will Lock with *me*!" Tamra screamed at the new Lennix Grand. "With *me*, do you hear? I hold the Heart! I command *all* of you!"

"Stop being a fool!" D'Mara yelled, hefting a firestik. "Give it to me, girl! Or I'll shoot you down myself!"

"Shut up!" Tamra called back. "Shut up, shut up, *shut up*! I'm in charge now! Valkea, come to me!"

But the Red remained as she was, her eyes glowering at Tamra.

"Why isn't it working?" Allie asked. "Tamra has the Heart."

Sirin whispered over her shoulder, "She doesn't know."

"Doesn't know what?"

"What it takes to call on the Skyspinner's power."

Allie twisted around to look at the girl. "What do you mean?"

Sirin's eyes held a strange, solemn expression. "After you left Loch Ness, Thorval told me the secret to using the Heart. He said it only works if you bond with it through blood. She should prick her thumb or something to activate its magic."

"I don't think Tamra knows that."

"Maybe D'Mara doesn't either."

Allie felt a little better at that, but D'Mara's next words crushed her hope.

"You can't even use it," D'Mara called to Tamra. "But *I* can. I know how. So this is your last chance, Tamra. *Give it to me!*"

Tamra squared her jaw, then shook her head. "I know what's mine. If you want this rock, first give me back my—"

Without a word, D'Mara hurled her firestik at her own daughter.

Tamra seemed too startled to dodge, but Kardessa threw herself sideways with a panicked roar—and collided with Bellacrux.

Everything happened so quickly after that.

Allie saw the Heart fly out of Tamra's grasp. It fell toward the ground, flashing as it spun.

And in the other direction went Sirin, knocked from her seat by the impact.

The Heart! said Bellacrux.

Time stopped. Allie saw them both as if they were suspended in midair: To her left, the Heart, the key to controlling all dragons, the answer to every problem they'd ever had. To her right, Sirin, her friend, the girl who'd followed them into dragonfire and danger without hesitation.

Which one? Bellacrux asked her.

They could only save one.

The other would break on the ground below.

There had been a time, just days ago, when Allie had thought if she were strong enough, she could save both the world and the ones she loved. But the universe would not be tricked. She'd have to choose.

But Allie didn't even have to think twice.

Go, she said, and Bellacrux knew what she meant.

The Green dived, wings pinned to her side, her tail straight as an arrow behind her. Kardessa spun away overhead and crashed into a building, her screams mingling with Tamra's. Joss was yelling somewhere above. Dragonfire brightened the night. Human screams, dragons roars, sirens wailing . . .

But Allie was entirely, wholly focused. She felt one with Bellacrux as her Lock dived down, down, down . . .

And Allie's hand closed on Sirin's arm.

At once, Bellacrux opened her wings, lifting out of her dive, and Allie pulled Sirin onto the dragon's back.

She looked down just in time to see the Skyspinner's Heart shatter on the sidewalk, surrounded by dozens of wide-eyed humans who were already starting to pick up the pieces and pocket them. There would be no reuniting it again.

But Allie had made her choice, and she regretted nothing.

"You let it go," Sirin gasped. "You could have stopped all of this."

"Yes," said Allie. "But we are sisters, and that's worth more than any old rock, however magical it is."

Sirin stared at her as a slow smile spread across her face.

42

Farrelara, Me Soll

The Raptors fled after that.

Allie saw them vanish one by one into bright bursts of light, portals opening and closing like winking eyes in the night. Many were wounded, and now that their prize had been shattered, they would no doubt retreat for a while, to regroup and lay new schemes. She heard D'Mara's howl of rage cut short the moment Valkea vanished.

Let's get out of here, she sent to Bellacrux.

Agreed, my Lock.

With Lysander, Ramon, and Sammi, the Green flew toward a large patch of darkness spread like a blanket over the center of the city.

"I think that's Central Park," said Sirin.

I will land there, said Bellacrux. *I must rest, Allie.*

Of course.

Passing over fields and gardens and fountains, Bellacrux finally touched down in a small clearing surrounded by forest. It was a quiet spot, shielded all around by trees. The other dragons landed beside her, and the riders all jumped down.

"I should go back," said Declan. "Lysander, could you see us through a portal? Ramon is fast, hopefully fast enough to reach

Fortress Lennix before my family does. I promised I would get Carli out of there."

"We'll take you," said Joss. "Sirin, Allie, wait here for us. It'll only take a few minutes."

The girls nodded.

"Declan, Ramon," said Allie. "Thank you. We couldn't have lasted that fight without you two."

The Blue dragon dipped his head in return, and Declan bowed a little.

"It is only a beginning to the atonement I must make for my family's deeds," he said. "If you ever need me again, find me back in our world, in the western desert. I will continue to do my best to keep the Raptors from destroying the remaining clans. And hopefully figuring out a way to get rid of *this*." He patted Ramon's stomach, where the edge of the Raptor tattoo was visible. The Blue nodded in agreement.

Declan shook hands with Allie and Sirin, then climbed onto Ramon. Lysander and Joss followed them into the sky and vanished with a flash of light.

Sirin lay down on the grass and spread her arms and legs wide. "I could sleep for a week," she said. "What do we do next, Allie?"

Allie didn't answer. She'd stepped in something wet and was studying the sole of her shoe curiously.

"What . . ." Her eyes went to the dark pool on the ground, then followed a trail of the liquid over the grass.

Blood?

It ended under Bellacrux.

Allie rushed to her dragon's side, her hand trailing over her scales. *Bell?*

Hm. The dragon's eyes were shut. She was breathing raggedly.

You're hurt. Let me see.

One of Bellacrux's eyes opened slowly and fixed on her. *No.*

But Allie pushed against the dragon's side until she relented, and she shifted just enough to reveal a broken firestik jutting from her chest. Ugly scorch marks blackened the skin and scales around it. It had to have been the firestik D'Mara had thrown at Tamra. The weapon had instead found Bellacrux.

"*Bellacrux*," Allie breathed, unable to tear her eyes from the wound. "We . . . we can go back to the Dragonlands and get more athelantis. Or . . . or there must be something in this world that can help you. They have so many other incredible things—"

Allie. My Lock. Stop.

But we need to take care of this!

It's too late. It was too late the moment it struck me.

What do you mean? Allie stared at the jutting lance, and it hit her—it had pierced Bellacrux's heart.

Bellacrux sighed a long, rattling breath and shuddered. She shifted, hiding the wound from view again.

Tears filled Allie's eyes. She threw her arms around Bellacrux's neck.

"No," she sobbed. "No, no, no, there has to be a way!" *You can't leave me, Bell. You can't do this to me. I only just found you.*

I am glad that you found me. Thank you, Allinson Moran, for giving me one last great adventure.

We can't survive without you!

Of course you can. You are Allie the Fierce. If there were Grands among humans, my Lock, you would be one.

Allie smiled through her tears, knowing it would be the nicest compliment anyone would ever pay her. She clung to Bellacrux, pressing her forehead to the dragon's.

Noble Bellacrux, she sent, *Grandest of Dragons, most wise and most brave. Being your Lock will have been the greatest honor of my life.*

Farrelara, me soll, sent Bellacrux.

Allie held on to the Green through the next few minutes, not looking up even when she heard Lysander land on the grass and Joss slide off. He asked what was wrong, and Sirin told him in a hushed whisper. They knelt behind Allie and put their hands on her back and said nothing.

Finally, Allie felt it—a wrenching in her chest, as if her heart were being extracted by sharp claws. A warm breath rolled over her, the dragon's last.

"F-f-farrelara," Allie whispered through her tears. "My soul's friend."

She sobbed, hugging Bellacrux tightly, as the Green's brow hardened beneath hers. Lifting her head, Allie watched stone spread over her Lock, from the center of her forehead, down her jaw and neck, the broad length of her back. In moments, she was entirely turned to stone, as if she'd been a statue all along instead of a living, breathing dragon, her wings folded as if she were sleeping. She had curled up like a cat, head resting on the grass.

Peaceful.

Allie wept.

43

This Is Not the End

Thorval's caverns, deep beneath Loch Ness, echoed with drips and ripples of water, but in the past week, Sirin had come to find the sound relaxing. She'd slept in every day and awoken to piles of fish brought enthusiastically by Sammi. The little Green had come to love swimming so much, Sirin half wondered if she might actually be a Blue. At least now they had a small camp stove and pan to fry the fish on, and a store of crisps, soda, and apples to round out the meal. Sirin's last run to town had been a productive one. She and Joss had brought back enough food and supplies to last a month, carried in big waterproof duffel bags, since it was a long, *long* dive through the chilly loch to reach this place. They had no idea how long they'd be hiding out. It depended mostly on how quickly Allie would recover.

The girl was still quiet and withdrawn, no longer crying as much but moving around the caverns like a ghost. The grieving sickness was running its terrible course. She said she was all right but needed time. So that's what they gave her. It was what they all needed.

Lysander wasn't pleased about being stuck underground, with no sky to soar in, and he spent the days sighing and sleeping and staring dolefully at nothing. At least the cave wasn't nearly as dark and miserable as Sirin had feared; it was more like the caves of the Blue islands. Over the centuries, Thorval had worn the floor down to a smooth shine, and the walls were carved with motifs of dragons in flight. He'd even dug out alcoves and filled them with oil-rich seaweed that burned for hours, providing soft orange light that flickered over the stone. Most surprising, however, had been Thorval's—or rather Nessie's—"collection." He had gathered hundreds of souvenirs, from snow globes and key chains to T-shirts and plush animals, and every single one sported a version of his own scaly self. It was probably the world's biggest collection of Loch Ness Monster memorabilia, set up like some kind of shrine. And Nessie guarded them jealously. No one was allowed to touch so much as a bobblehead. But in a way, it made the caves even cozier.

Part of Sirin's trips to the world above were for supplies, but she also was watching for news of more dragon attacks. This was not the end of their trouble. The Raptors would return. It was only a matter of time. And Earth had no idea how to stop them. Planes were too unwieldy and flew too high. Drones were too flimsy and ill-equipped. Dragons were a threat no one was prepared to defend against.

But Sirin, Joss, and Allie knew how to fight them. As the saying went, you had to fight fire with fire. Only as Sirin now put it: You had to fight dragons with dragons.

But right now, they were in no condition to fight anyone. They had a wingless, half-mad Blue, a Green hatchling whose bark still exceeded her bite, and a gleaming Silver who was just half the size of most Raptors. Lysander was still growing, but not at the phenomenal pace he'd been going at the first few weeks of his life.

The humans weren't in much better shape. But once Allie was on her feet again, they'd have to do something. Make a plan. Seek out Declan and Carli.

These were all tomorrow's troubles. For now, Sirin needed to make breakfast.

Sammi curled around her as she cooked, and soon the delicious smell of bacon and eggs filled the cavern. Sirin cooked a few fish too and tossed the rest to the dragons. Joss wandered over, rubbing sleep from his eyes, his hair mussed and wild.

"I got scissors," said Sirin. "Time you had a haircut. You look like a caveman."

"I *am* a caveman," Joss pointed out, gesturing at their current lodgings. "And a very nice cave it is too," he added quickly, when Thorval's head lifted out of the pool at the far end of the cavern. The Blue narrowed his eyes, then chuffed, twin mists curling from his nostrils.

Lysander thumped his tail, demanding more fish. Sammi leaped to oblige, diving into the pool and out the tunnels to the lake.

Keep out of sight, warned Sirin.

Always, sighed Sammi.

No, just for now. Soon, I promise, things will be different.

Because dragons had returned to Earth, and soon, more would follow. It was the only way—the Dragonlands were dying. To survive, the clans had to return from their exile. The Raptors still stood in their way, stronger than ever with their forged Silver scales, and they would have to be dealt with once and for all.

Sirin, Joss, and Allie would be ready when they returned.

The people of Earth would have to be ready too.

The news of dragons had spread over the globe. People had been able to deny what had happened in Oxford—the footage was blurry, and most everyone had cried, "Prank!" But after New York, no one could deny it. The secret was out. When Sirin had gone shopping, she'd seen the same words flashing on every television screen, on every channel, on every newspaper and magazine and cell phone and computer. She'd heard them whispered between shoppers, shouted by children in the park, even sung by a musician with a guitar on the street corner:

Here, there be dragons.

ABOUT THE AUTHOR

Jessica Khoury is the author of multiple books for teens and young readers, including the Corpus trilogy, *Last of Her Name*, and *The Mystwick School of Musicraft*. In addition to writing, she is an artistic mapmaker and spends far too much time scribbling tiny mountains and trees for fictional worlds. She lives in Greenville, South Carolina, with her husband, daughter, and sassy husky, Katara. Find her online at jessicakhoury.com.

READY TO TAKE FLIGHT?

You have two battle options:

1. Play the tabletop version (instructions below)
2. Play the digital version: scholastic.com/riseofthedragons

Tabletop instructions

(for two players)

YOUR GOAL

Score 50 points by capturing the most valuable eggs!

1. DEAL

Shuffle all nine cards and deal three cards to each player. (The players can look at their cards.)

Place the remaining three cards in the middle with the outer cards faceup and the center card facedown. The egg on the center card is known as the "Mystery Egg."

Player A

Player B